Just in Time

Kathryn Shay

ISBN: 1939501245
ISBN 13: 9781939501240

Praise for Kathryn Shay's novels

"Kathryn Shay writes some of the cleanest prose around, and it's my belief she'd make the Yellow Pages sound interesting if the phone company put her on staff. And Ms. Shay knows her way around a steamy love scene."

The Romance Reader

"Shay does an admirable job with a difficult subject, writing...with sensitivity and realism and without shying away from any of the hard issues."

Shelley Mosley Booklist

"What a great book. Controversial subjects handled in a sensitive and yet honest way–characters that just walked off the page, real and warm. The story just kept coming. A heart toucher, about problems with no easy solutions. Wonderful! Don't miss!"

A Reader

JUST IN TIME

By KATHRYN SHAY

Cover art by Patricia Ryan

CHAPTER 1

Present Day

THE AIR IN Dr. Jess Cromwell's office stirred and the temperature in the room spiked. Sparks shot out from nowhere as the entire space crackled. And then, in front of him, on the old braided rug, little lights began to take shape. It was like molecules coming together. Right before his eyes, a human form materialized.

Jess blinked, thinking he must be going mad. But no, he *saw* this. Really saw it. Uh-oh. Not it. Them. After the first body, a second and third formed; three women had appeared, literally, in his Vista Institute office! The scene could have come out of a *Star Trek episode* where the transporter beamed people from one place to another. For an instant, the three of them stood stiffly, then one toppled to the ground, then the second, then the third.

"Oh, good Lord," he said as he rushed to them. Mirage or no mirage, he couldn't stand by and watch three people faint and do nothing.

Disentangling the women from each other—they were solid forms all right—he stretched them out flat on the floor. They were breathing, so he took their pulses first. Fast, really fast, but steady. There was no way to loosen their clothing; he could see no zippers or Velcro on their dull, gray tunics made of some light material, with trousers to match. He'd whipped out his cell phone to call the ambulance when one of them roused. She was the tallest, most muscular and toned. When her eyes opened, they were a startling, pure green. She blinked, like a cat watching a human.

"Greetings," she said in a sleep-slurred voice.

Man, he *was* losing it. The woman had recited an alien's line straight out of some science fiction movie.

When she sat up, she moaned, squinted and massaged her temples. "You are Dr. Jess Cromwell." It wasn't a question.

"Am I?"

Frowning, she scanned the room then nodded. "This is the desired location. I recognize it from the computeller screen."

Just last week, *Science Today,* a magazine in which Jess had published several articles on his research, had run a photo shoot of him, and they'd included pictures of him in his office. The feature had been in print and online. Because he'd been getting quasi-threatening emails, his cop brother, Luke, had had a fit about the publicity.

At his hesitation, she asked, "Are these not the correct coordinates? In the year 2014?"

"Coordinates? 2014?"

Again, she nodded, just as the second woman shifted on the rug. This one came awake fast and bolted to a sitting position. When she opened her eyes, she glanced at her companions. "We made it, Dorian."

"We did, Alisha."

"I ache all over."

This *Alisha* frowned. "As do I. Ignore it." She faced Jess. "Cromwell, right?"

He shook his head. "I'm hallucinating. Helen said I would if I didn't stop working so hard."

"Helen is the spousal unit," Alisha offered.

The bigger one, Dorian, looked past her friend with a worried expression. "Celeste is still unconscious."

Alisha came to her feet shakily and swayed. Jess reached out just in time to catch her. Once again, she *felt* real enough. "Steady there."

Frowning, she stared at his hand on her arm as if she wasn't accustomed to being touched. Then she bent over her friend who was still out cold. "I wondered if she could make the jump, if she had enough stamina." Sticking her hand into some sort of sack she carried—all three had similar black pouches looped around their necks—Alisha drew out what looked like a small tablet, but thicker. The device blinked and buzzed as she ran it above the prone woman's body. "Vital signs normal. Brain activity erratic."

Dorian nodded. "They always are on her."

"No, the central Multimed examined her before we left so I'd have a baseline. These readings are different."

"I hope she's not too ill from temporal displacement. The jump would affect her the most."

Jess said, "I can call nine-one-one."

Alisha cocked her head. "Emergency medical care that arrives on wheels. Primitive life-saving efforts."

"Excuse me?"

"We don't need that." Alisha turned to her cohort. "Help me get Celeste to the sitting conformer." Though their movements were stiff, the two women picked up the unconscious one and carried her to the sofa as if she weighed nothing.

Dorian touched the cushion of the old leather couch that had once graced his family room and he sometimes slept on if he worked all night. "The furniture is hard. I forgot it would be." They placed the unconscious woman—Celeste–on the sofa. "Uncomfortable."

As if to underscore her words, Celeste shifted and moaned, like Dorian had.

Jess took a long look at them. If he was losing his marbles, he was going out smiling. The three of them were knockouts. Very fit. Thick manes of hair, short but beautiful. Nice eyes, nice features…nice everything. Again, Jess shook his head, blinked twice, but the women didn't go away. For God's sake, what was happening here? "Where did you come from? And how did you materialize in my office?"

Alisha stood beside Dorian. "Perhaps you should sit down for this."

He watched her for a minute, then went to his industrial-steel desk, pulled out the chair and sat.

"Okay, hit me with it."

"Why would we do him physical harm?" Dorian asked Alisha. "We're here to protect him."

This had something to do with the threats? Or was Luke jerking his chain? Jess might have believed that, except the women had formed out of nowhere, right before his eyes. Even his excellent cop brother couldn't pull off that little trick. No one could and that included assassins. So he was probably safe.

Trying to stay calm, he asked, "How did you get here?"

"We traveled through a portal"—Alisha pulled out another thick tablet look-alike—"with this device. We're from the future, Dr. Cromwell."

He laughed. "Sure you are." Blank looks. "You're joking, aren't you?"

"This isn't some version of your twenty-first century humor. I assure you, we came from 2514."

"Okay, I'll bite. Why?"

Dorian straightened her shoulders. "Because, Dr. Cromwell, your research to stop carbon emissions which pollute the air may prevent the world's end. However, at some point in the next two of what you call months, someone is going to kill you. We've come to prevent your death from occurring."

• • •

BECAUSE OF THE hammerjack pounding in her head, her sore musculature and the dizziness, Dorian breathed in deeply. She was weakened from the jump, which they'd anticipated would happen, but she wasn't used to even a modicum of corporeal frailty. As head of the Institute for Physical Stamina, her life task was to keep the members of society at the apex of fitness.

Summoning her strength, she stepped closer to the man seated next to his work space. He looked different in real life than on the chips, where they'd viewed his image. He was smaller than she'd pictured and he had interesting lines fanning out from his eyes, though his age was close to hers. Men of this time period lost their hair and his was gone, which was truly odd to witness. And—she sniffed—his smell was unlike the males she'd joined with.

"Dr. Cromwell, I'm Dorian Masters. I assure you we're telling the truth. It's why we teleportaled here, into your work space. We wanted you to see us arrive so that we could convince you who we are and when we come from." She held up her personal computeller. "There's data on this machine that will prove our veracity—you will indeed be killed in a relatively short period of time."

The man paled.

"He's upset. And afraid."

All three glanced across the room, where Celeste had roused and spoken. Her face was pale, her blue eyes bloodshot and she pressed her palm into her stomach. Dorian hoped she didn't vomit.

Closing the distance between them, Alisha scanned Celeste with the first handheld device. "Brain's still irregular, but physically, she's fine."

"I wouldn't exactly say that." When Celeste stood, she winced and wobbled a bit. After closing her eyes to regain her balance, she walked over to Cromwell. Her body was curvier than the others. "Hello, Dr. Cromwell."

"You've got your stories straight, at least."

"Stories?" Celeste asked.

"He doesn't believe us." Dorian didn't blame him.

After a brief hesitation, Celeste picked up Cromwell's hand. She shivered. As a sensitive, she could feel and sometimes take on people's emotions. "He doesn't know what to believe. He's uneasy and frightened. We must show him the proof we carry."

Alisha was already setting up her computeller. She placed it on the surface of the work space. "Enlarge screen."

Dr. Cromwell was wide-eyed as the screen expanded to twenty-by-twenty. He said, "Holy shit."

"Crude expletive combined with a religious term, which makes no sense," Alisha commented. Then she ordered, "Reveal the fate of the inhabitants in 2514."

Buzz. Whir. Click. Then the machine announced, "The world will end seventy-five years from the specified date."

Cromwell's skin was now ashen. "And you know this how?"

"Computeller, explain time travel to Dr. Jess Cromwell."

"Society has the ability to project into the future, as well as backtrack into the past. Projection was approved for scientific purposes in the twenty-fourth century, but only by the Guardians and under strict regulations."

"Who are the Guardians?" Jess asked.

"World leaders."

"What did you find out when you went forward?"

The computer continued, "In our most recent experiments, we discovered some catastrophic facts. As of seventy-five yearlings after the date we traveled from, we hit a wall. No projection was possible beyond that."

"Why?" Jess asked.

"Because, as was said, the world ends. Travelers were able to transport to the future right up until then. However, the events of the previous decade are cloudy. Test jumpers arrived but could not move beyond the portal. They could see only outlines, hear spoken language, no more than that. But in 2589, the researchers could not find even a portal that opens. The conclusion is the future society simply ceases to exist."

Stunned silence from the doctor.

Alisha's brows furrowed. "I helped determine this, Dr. Cromwell. I'm head of the Institute for Archeology which, for obvious reasons, works closely with the Institute of Temporal Studies on backtracking. I can assure you that our generation was the last."

"Humankind dies off?" Jess asked. "Completely?"

Dorian nodded.

Alisha continued, "This explains why we've decided to come back in time and alter certain events in hopes of preventing annihilation."

"And exactly what do I do to prevent this?"

"It will be best to show you." To the computer she ordered, "Activate program on Dr. Jess Cromwell."

"All data?" the computeller asked.

"Affirmative."

The computeller clicked for several seconds. "Information available."

They had hoped Cromwell's scientific curiosity would make him amenable, and it seemed to. He rolled his chair closer to the computeller, his frown showing more of his eye lines. Absently, Dorian touched her cheek. She was glad for the advancements in aging that scientists of her time period had made, then chided herself for being vain when their mission was so serious.

"Jess Lucas Cromwell, born seventeen, oh-seven, 1970. Donors, Allison Leigh and Lucas Cromwell. Ritualized cohabitation on twelve, oh-four, 1965. First offspring, a brother, Lucas Cromwell, four yearlings before Jess. Donors' life work: female was a teacher of science and male a NASA specialist. Offspring's life work: first born, criminal justice and second, research scientist."

The computeller proceeded to track Jess Cromwell's life in text and videos. His schooling, his friends, his relationship with Helen Harmon, their ritualized cohabitation, his education.

Throughout it all, Cromwell's frown grew more intense, and he started to sweat, something else Dorian had never experienced because of their temperature-controlled air. It was fascinating to watch tiny beads of water appear on his brow. "Anyone could know this about me from the Internet," he finally said.

They were aware of the Internet and, now that they were in this time period, would use the network to create backgrounds for themselves once they got settled.

Celeste frowned. "He may not be ready to witness the rest."

"We have no choice." As usual, Alisha spoke without emotion. "Time's running out, pardon the pun. Proceed," she instructed the computeller.

"Jess Cromwell is murdered in 2014."

"How?" Jess asked, his voice gruff.

"Vehicular accident. People of the time period call it a hit-and-run. That is when the perpetrator leaves the scene of a crime."

"Damn. That sucks."

Alisha shook her head. "Don't look at me. I have no idea what that idiom means." As an archeologist, she'd come along to acclimate Celeste and Dorian to this society. She was expected to know idioms and slang, but some terminology escaped her.

"Poor Helen." The man wiped his face with a white cloth taken from his pocket. "Christ. I'm starting to buy into this."

Alisha gave a slight nod. "We'll show you more to fully convince you."

The computeller played videos of newsprint articles about Cromwell's death. But there were omissions in the timeline because many of the chips from 2014 had become corroded. Consequently, they didn't know the exact date of his demise. "I still can't believe it." He looked up at them. "How can I?"

"He needs more motivation," Alisha said. "Let's try this." She forwarded ahead to events after his death.

Cromwell's face reddened. "What the fuck?"

Fuck. A derogatory term for joining.

He glared at the screen. "I don't have a daughter." His pleasant, now-confused features hardened. "If this is some kind of joke, then it's cruel, given how much Helen and I wanted a child and couldn't have one."

"You'll have one, Dr. Cromwell." Celeste's voice was soothing. "By these calculations, your mate will conceive in her womb soon."

"Now I *know* I'm having delusions."

"Listen further."

There was a snippet of a ceremony.

"Helen married somebody else?" His tone indicated umbrage, another thing Dorian didn't understand. "How long after I'm gone?"

"Five yearlings...years."

"I guess that would be okay." He sighed. "Look, this isn't proof. These videos could all be fabricated. It's too unbelievable."

"You died, Dr. Cromwell." Alisha's voice was curt. "And we believe the person who engineered your demise did so in order to preclude the completion of your research on the safe extraction of natural gas from the earth. Your findings led to a myriad of other developments in the eradication of carbon emissions from the environment."

"Look, lady, if I died, somebody else would take up my research. As much as I'd like to think I'm indispensable, fracking is increasing our energy supplies, with a lot of big money behind it."

"You're incorrect. As I said, your research was special in its containment of methane emissions in a way no one else would discover. But the work you did was stopped by your death, and before someone else could pick up the threads or recreate it, a horrible environmental accident occurred and there was widespread contamination of the ground and water. Thousands of people were sickened or killed. All research on natural-gas extraction was halted, and soon after, the oil companies lobbied the governments of most countries and convinced them this area of energy drilling was too dangerous."

"I'm so close to a breakthrough. Didn't people care about what I left unfinished?"

"They were brainwashed, greedy and believed what was most beneficial for them. The dangers of climate change would just start to be taken seriously, and special interest groups would convince the population it was a hoax. That, and your fairly insane electoral process to choose leaders were corrupted so badly, the underminers were successful."

"Dr. Cromwell," Celeste said softly, "someone murdered you over your research."

"My brother was right, then."

"Your male sibling?" Dorian asked. "He's in agreement with us?"

"Luke's been telling me I'm in danger. I've been getting warnings."

"Yes, through an archaic communicative method called email. To date, you've received four. Soon they will stop." Dorian took pity on him. "It makes sense to conclude the sender has some connection with petroleum."

"An employee of an oil company is warning me of this threat to my life?"

"The sender writes to you as watchingoutforyou@xmail.com. He or she obviously knows someone intends to terminate you because of your research. Perhaps the sender is the one who must kill you if you don't heed the warning." Alisha hesitated. "This was his last bullet."

"Excuse me?"

"I may have gotten the idiom wrong. His last...shot at stopping you?"

Sighing heavily, Cromwell leaned back in his chair.

Celeste crossed to him and knelt down. Again, she touched his hand. Again, she trembled. "We're prepared to show you what the time where we come from holds, Dr. Cromwell."

He cocked his head. "Is that why you want to save my life?"

"Yes, we believe that if you do *not* complete your research, the pollution of the future will spiral out of control, and mankind will be doomed."

"My research prevents that from happening?" he asked again. He needed assurance.

"It's the basis for other research, yes, that prevents future destruction."

A slow smile spread across his face. "Man, I'd like to believe that."

"Then let us convince you."

Again he was thoughtful. "Wait a minute. Are you sure you can change the course of the future?"

"Ninety-nine point one percent sure," Alisha quoted.

"Then what the hell? This is one great dream…a daughter, my research changing the course of history."

"It will be if you don't die," Alisha said soberly. "If you do, that dream turns into a nightmare for all of humanity."

CHAPTER 2

HIS FRUSTRATION LEVEL going through the goddamn roof, Luke Cromwell stared hard at his brilliant brother. He felt that way often with Jess, and had from the time they were young. "You're kidding, right?"

Jess fidgeted. Now, when he was nervous, he worried the wedding band on his left hand. When they were kids, he'd scratched his head. "What's the problem? You've been after me to do something about those emails, and I am."

"Hiring a bodyguard without consulting your brother, who's a Lieutenant in the Special Investigations Unit of the NYPD, is ridiculous. Why the hell would you do something like this without my help or at least my advice?"

His brother's face flushed. "I didn't. Vista Institute did. They fund my research, so I told them about the emails—after you got on me about them so much."

Luke remembered the conversation…

You have a beautiful wife. Be a shame to leave her alone. Wise up, will you little brother? Let me track down these warnings or whatever they are.

His chin raised, Jess continued, "They've worked with her company before."

The comment made his blood pressure spike. "Her? Your bodyguard's female? You're going to spend all your waking hours with another woman? Oh, I'll bet Helen will be overjoyed when she learns of the threats *and* of that little fact."

Jess gave a goofy smile that Luke didn't understand. "Helen will be fine once..." He didn't finish, just crooked a shoulder. "She'll worry less now that I have protection."

"I was thinking of jealousy. The green-eyed monster."

"Helen, jealous? Come on Luke, we've been together since high school. Why would I ever stray?"

Precisely because *you've been together since then.* But Luke didn't voice that opinion. He knew he was overprotective of Jess, and also that his own failed marriage—thanks in part to that monster he'd mentioned—had made him cynical. Plus, Jess and Helen were closer than any couple he knew. Not being able to have kids had created a deep bond between them. "Let's table that. What's the new bodyguard's training, background and skill level?"

"I don't know. I didn't ask. I told you, Vista took care of all this."

"Then, I'll find out. All I need is her name and date of birth to run a background check."

"No, Luke, I don't want you to interfere. The company's concerned enough about me and my research that they've provided me protection. They've checked out her credentials. I don't want you to go any further with her."

Stung, he steepled his fingers. "Fine. You don't trust my judgment, the hell with it."

"I trust your judgment. But the situation is under control. Let it go."

"Sure." He pushed his chair away from the desk. "So, when do I get to meet her?"

"She's outside. In the reception area."

"Now?"

"Yeah, she started today. She got into town two days ago." Jess stood and walked to the door. Before he opened it, he looked over his shoulder and said, "Be nice."

Not on your life. "Always."

Briefly, Jess stepped into the hall, then came back with his bodyguard. Jesus, this was worse than Luke had anticipated. The woman was super attractive. Not his type, though, because she was a little too tall and muscular—he liked his women petite and curvy—but she had a face that could stop traffic. Her hair wasn't his preference, either—too short—but it shone under the overhead lights. Nice eyes…

"Dorian Masters, meet my brother, Luke Cromwell."

She strode into the room stiffly, as if she was uncomfortable. Wearing a stark black suit with a crisp white shirt, she spoke first. "Lieutenant Cromwell." She stuck out her hand, he took it, and she gripped his so tightly it would hurt a lesser man. "My pleasure is to meet you."

"Yeah, you, too." He drew back his hand. "Have a seat."

Glancing around the office, she dropped down onto the chair across from Jess's. She winced a bit when she sat and rubbed her fingers on the wooden arm. Her smile didn't reach her eyes when she spoke to him. "Jess has told me a great deal about you."

"Funny, he told me nothing about you."

"Why is that humorous?"

Odd. "Just an expression." Alerted by the strange comment, he studied her. "So, tell me your background. If you don't mind, I'd like to know who's watching over my little bro."

A question in her eyes at his statement. "I anticipate you're concerned about his welfare. I'll inform you of my history. I was born in Virginia, which is just outside of Washington, D.C."

No shit.

"Shortly after, my family moved to South America as missionaries. I attended a private boarding school there and spoke primarily Spanish. We returned to the United Amer…

the United States of America when I was eighteen so I could receive further education." She gave him the satisfied expression of a child who'd successfully recited her catechism. "When I completed eight yearl...years of education, I formed my own private protective agency, Masterminds, which was hired by the Vista Institute to guard Dr. Cromwell. He's received warnings about his safety."

Masterminds, as in Dorian Masters. Cute. "Warnings, which up until now, he ignored."

Her dark brows knit. "I assure you those threats are real. He's in grave danger."

Luke held up his hands, palms out. "Hey, lady, you're preaching to the choir."

Though Dorian had no idea what that meant, she tried to hide it. Alisha had warned her not to show reaction to phraseology she didn't understand. The idioms of this time period were going to be a problem. Dorian could never learn them all, so she had to ignore what she could.

However, she hadn't anticipated keeping who she was a secret from Dr. Cromwell's family. It had taken hours of re-explanation and review of the history chips, but once they convinced Dr. Cromwell who they were, he'd been adamant about secrecy...

"Helen will freak out if she hears I'm going to be murdered. We only have each other. She lost her parents at a young age, so my family took her in. And if she does get pregnant, I don't want her upset by this. It'll be bad enough when she finds out I kept the threats from her. We can't tell her I'm going to die. We don't have to, if you stop this...plot. We'll just say you're my bodyguard. Maybe later we can fill her in..."

"Dorian, Luke asked you a question."

"Repeat please."

He hesitated. "Why don't you outline for me the way this is going to shake out."

Oh, dear.

"We have a plan for protection all in place, Luke." Jess was cuing her, she realized.

"We do. I'll move into his spare sleeping space until the identity of the email sender and the plot against Jess is uncovered. I'll accompany him to work and to other functions."

"So his protection will be out in the open?"

Jess answered. "No, we're going to say she's Helen's cousin and came here to take a job as my assistant in the lab."

"And live with you?"

"She's from out of town." Under his breath, Jess said, "Way out of town. She doesn't know anybody here."

"What about going out at night?"

"We ought to be able to work the cousin thing in that way—we're showing her around town."

In his peripheral vision, she saw Luke watching her so she stifled the urge to fidget. She was used to dealing with powerful men in her life's work. But she never truly understood them, because other than professional contact, and joining, of course, men and women of the future didn't have interaction. As they apparently did in this time period, she'd learned from the chips.

"No offense, Ms. Masters, but I don't like that I was left out of this decision."

That *decision* had surprised her, too. She assumed they'd at least tell the brother, if not his spouse, and avoid more subterfuge. She'd suggested Jess do that…

"We should inform your sibling."

"No. He'll never believe you. If he didn't see with his own eyes what I saw, he'll doubt you. He's always been the skeptic of the family. It's why he's a good cop. He'll buy the bodyguard idea easier, believe me…"

"Ms. Masters?" the cop said now, bringing her back to the present.

"I'll protect your brother with my life, Lieutenant. I swear on the godheads."

"Excuse me?"

"Oh. The term is from an ancient religion I follow." She might have followed a religion if the universe hadn't lost its faith, along with its air and ability to reproduce.

"Never heard that term." The scowl made his face look older. It was a nice face, though, with interesting angles. And his brown eyes were deep and liquid, swirling with different shades. People of her time had pure colored eyes with no variation. His hair was cut shorter than the men of her time and a rich brown.

"Well," he said with an angry glance at his brother. "I guess I have no choice but to accept you. For the record, Jess, I wish you'd done it all differently."

Smiling, Jess answered. "We'll be fine."

"I assume, now that you agree you're in danger, you'll let me investigate the warnings in an official capacity."

Jess looked to Dorian for confirmation. She nodded.

"Yeah, sure," he said. Then to her, "Now, shall we go home and tell Helen about all this?"

"That's acceptable to me."

Luke stood. "Mind if I come along? I'd like to see Helen's reaction." More quietly he added, "I'm sure there'll be hell to pay, too."

Jess agreed, but Dorian could tell he wasn't happy about his brother accompanying him. Neither was she. Her bodyguard status had annoyed the sibling. And she didn't need Celeste's powers to tell her that Lucas Cromwell, Jr. was going to be a problem.

• • •

ON THE TRIP to Jess's dwelling, Dorian sat in the front seat of the auto vehicle trying to breathe only through her nose. The bumpy ride caused her stomach to pitch, and the stink of the gasoline made her gag. No wonder the world had succumbed to covering entire regions with Domes in the future. The bombardment of poisons emitted daily into the atmosphere from hundreds of thousands of vehicles was horrendous.

"You okay?" Jess asked. "You're white as a ghost."

"The smell and movement is causing me distress."

"I'll bet. You obviously don't have cars."

"No, moving walks get us from place to place, and we use air cycles run on crystals for emergencies when we must travel farther, which doesn't happen often."

"Your description of the future is unbelievable."

She gestured to encompass the vehicle. "So is this. To me." She glanced out the aperture. Despite the smell of the car, what she saw there still amazed her. Daylight. And sun—glorious, warm sun—which had been totally obscured by her time period.

After they'd arrived in Jess's office the previous revolution (a total anachronism because they had no sun) and convinced Jess of who they were, they'd walked down from his office to what he called a hotel. Nighttime out of inside had been surreal; people actually walking around in the air was totally foreign to them, though they were accustomed to darkness. But they'd been weakened by the jump and could not fully take in the situation. He'd gotten them a group of rooms called a suite, where they could rest. Only this dawning (another irrelevant term carried over from earlier times) had they actually seen real grass and trees, and gone out of inside to feel the warm rays of the sun. Celeste had come close to leaking moisture from her eyes, she was so moved by their surroundings.

Finally, Dorian and Jess completed the trip. When they drew up to his residence, her mouth gaped. "I've never seen a dwelling so big." She almost couldn't take in the multiple-level living space for only two people.

"We inherited the place from Helen's parents. It is big, I guess. A lot bigger than the hotel you three are staying at."

They'd secured the…rooms with the currency from the diamonds they'd brought with them. In their time, the gems were on display at the Ancient Galleries but had little value. Today, the opposite was true, as they'd researched. Jess had gone to trade the stones in exchange for the current currency in a region called Manhattan, which had not yet imploded on itself and sunk into the water as it would in the twenty-second century.

Once they stopped and exited the vehicle, they entered into the eating space of the dwelling. *Kitchen,* Dorian corrected herself. And the auto-vehicle space was in a *garage*. She'd been trying to think in their terms, but she was still weak from temporal displacement and her mind was not yet functioning with acuity.

"Honey, I'm home." Jess called out the strange message and placed the auto vehicle's starting device into a container on a shelf; she followed him farther into the room. Immediately, her stomach roiled again. The smell in here was so intense, she became nauseous.

"Are you all right?" Jess asked.

She pinched her nose. "The smell…"

He sniffed. "Mmm, spaghetti sauce. Haven't you had it before?"

"No. We have no *food,* as you know it, in my time."

"What?"

"Natural resources ran out near 2200. Survival depends on water drilled from the earth's core by robotic means, purified and distributed in carefully meted dosages. Nourishment is taken in tablet form, three times a day, with vitamin content and nutrients measured for age, body height and weight and muscle mass."

"Aw, wow. What a shame."

"Why?"

Even his eyes smiled. "Wait until you take a taste of supper and you'll find out."

Her stomach contracted at the thought.

A door slammed, and Luke stepped into the kitchen right behind Dorian. This close, he seemed bigger than he had when he'd been seated behind his work space...desk. He was taller than she'd first determined, and his shoulders were wide under his clothing. She noticed how muscular his chest area was. He was an interesting male specimen. "Hey, guys. Where's Helen?"

"I don't know. School's finished for the day, and her car is here. I'll go upstairs and check." He glanced at Dorian. "You okay?"

"Yes."

"Have a seat at the table."

Dorian went into the dining space off the kitchen, trying to cover her shock at the real wood that was everywhere. She'd never seen wooden floors, box-like things that held utensils, and more wood around the apertures...windows, they were called. She dropped down on a chair, still surprised at its hardness. It made her derriere sore and she missed the conformers.

When Jess left, Luke didn't lower himself to sit. Instead, he leaned against a wood box with a shelf made of what looked like real stone and stuck his hands in his pockets. He wore brown clothing with little white stripes through it, a white shirt and blue neck cloth. The outfit appeared extremely uncomfortable, like the one she was forced to wear. Jess had purchased scratchy, impractical items for her. She much preferred the two-piece gray tunic and trousers people of her time dressed in.

Not particularly wanting to be around him, she gave him a perfunctory smile.

"So," he said, his suspicious tone alerting her to focus. "Tell me why the company chose Masterminds to guard Jess."

"I'm in peak condition, I have an IQ of one hundred and eighty-nine, and expertise in weaponry."

"And you speak oddly."

Knowing their speech patterns might not be in sync with the time, before the jump, they'd discussed with the Guardians how to handle the issue. "As I told you, I was raised in another country, a more primitive culture. I was bilingual but didn't speak English for a long time. My speech patterns aren't like yours."

"Yet you don't have an accent."

"I've perfected English."

Those dark eyes bored into her. "I have to tell you, Ms. Masters, something about you bothers me."

"I'm aware that chauvinism is prominent in society, Lieutenant Cromwell. But you have female police officers, don't you?"

"Hell, yes. Some of our best cops are women."

"Then, you object to me why?"

"Because, lady, you just don't ring true."

Lady? It must be a derogatory term, because Jess had also used it that way when they first arrived.

"Hello." The wire mesh on the huge opening of the wall adjacent to Dorian slid back and in stepped Helen Cromwell. Dorian had seen her in the chips, but still, she had to force herself not to gawk as the woman came inside. She was as petite as a youngling, no more than five feet tall. Her features were so delicate that she appeared...breakable. And light reddish hair reached down her back almost to her hips. How did the woman even *survive* with such fragility about her?

"Hi, beautiful." Luke stepped forward and brushed his lips over her cheek. Dorian knew males and females here had contact outside of joining, but she thought that happened only between mates.

"Hey, handsome." She looked at Dorian, her eyes widening and her smile brighter. "You finally brought a woman to meet us."

"Ah, no, Jess brought her here."

A slight frown.

"There you are." Jess entered the room, and when his gaze rested on Helen, his face transformed, causing Dorian to take in a quick breath. He enveloped his spouse in a kind of embrace Dorian had only felt with a man in joining. He smacked his lips with hers. "Hello, love."

They kept arms around each other's waists. It was fascinating.

"Luke says you brought..." She looked at Dorian. "Oh, I'm sorry, I didn't get your name."

"Dorian Masters." Dorian extended her hand and took Helen's. Her bones were also fragile; Dorian was afraid one would snap with too much pressure, so she squeezed lightly.

"Let's sit, honey. I need to talk to you."

The three of them occupied confor...chairs around the table. Luke stayed where he was.

"There are some things you don't know." Jess held Helen's hand in both of his, the gesture tender. "Some things I haven't told you."

"Really?"

Jess explained briefly about the emails.

When he'd finished, Helen raised her chin, and her face reddened. Dorian knew that to be from emotion. "And you didn't tell me any of this? I wasn't aware we kept secrets, Jess."

"I'm sorry. I felt it was best."

The woman looked to Luke. "You knew about the threats?"

He squirmed like younglings did on the chips. "Um, yeah."

Throwing back her chair, Helen stood. She didn't seem so slight anymore. She crossed to the bowl in the shelf—the sink—and turned a metal mechanism. Even though Dorian had experienced it at the hotel, she was still stunned to see actual running water come out of a spigot and how the extra that didn't go into the glass was squandered.

After Helen had sipped the drink, she faced them. "I'm furious with you both. We'll have to deal with that at some point. Right now, tell me the rest."

Jess was visibly upset, but he explained that Vista Institute had hired him a bodyguard. "They chose Dorian."

A brief arch of an eyebrow. "I see." The woman studied Dorian. "And you're the best they have, Ms. Masters?"

"Yes, Mrs. Cromwell, I am."

"Good." She returned to the table. "Tell me how this will work. I'll do anything to help keep Jess safe."

Sighing, Jess reached out for her hand. Helen drew it back. "You're not getting off this easily, Jess. You either, Luke. But we'll put that aside for now."

Dorian had just finished the outline of how the body guarding would work when someone out of inside came up to the wire mesh on the wall. With something alongside of him.

"Mrs. Cromwell, my mother said—" The speaker stopped. "Oops. Sorry, we didn't know you had company."

This time, Dorian did indeed gawk.

Because, though she'd viewed the chips of this, too, she'd never actually seen a living, breathing youngling…or a real drog.

CHAPTER 3

GRIPPING THE REMOTE device in her hand, Celeste stared at the video box while her insides swirled with emotion. "I can't believe this."

From the sleeping conformer, Alisha made a disgusted sound. "It's called fiction, Celeste. That means it's made up." She held out the printed chip—a book—she was decoding. "Just as this one is."

"Making up stories is an odd custom."

They had no fiction in their time, except for those preserved on the chips and a few actual physical books housed in the Ancient Galleries. Society had lost the penchant for fantasy somewhere in the centuries before them because the reality of survival needed so much of their attention. Celeste also suspected the Guardians felt the wild imaginings of impossible events and behavior were unhealthy for people to dwell on.

"You should stop watching this dreadful video, Celeste. The people of today are violent with each other."

"It's supposed to mirror reality. But it *is* awful. Men actually do harm to women in this time period, Lisha?"

"And each other. They're a volatile society."

Apparently, Alisha was accurate. From the books and newsprint, made from real trees, that Jess had brought over, Celeste learned the people of this time routinely carried weaponry, started war and had no reasonable plan for rehabilitation of miscreants. Even organizations that fought for the rights of horrible-weapon owners were in existence. Celeste had been shocked.

Despite Alisha's admonishment, Celeste continued to watch the screen. "Why did the females of the time let themselves become so physically inferior to males?"

"I'm not sure. Some twenty-fifth-century anthropologists say it had to do with reproduction. Women actually carried children inside their bodies and then expelled them; they were weakened by it."

When the view changed to what was called an advertisement, a youngling appeared. With him was a live animal. Celeste reached out and traced her finger over the boy's image. "Aren't they beautiful? And he has a kata. I wish I could see a real one."

Of course, with the dissolution of the atmosphere, plant and animal life disappeared.

"Younglings are not beautiful. They whine. And they have all kinds of ailments. That one has a viral infection, what was called a cold."

"I think they're beautiful." The program began again. "Oh, my Nord, they show joining on this box?" Swallowing hard, Celeste moved closer to the machine. After a moment, her breath speeded up and her pulse skittered. Megadamn, sometimes she hated being so physically affected by what she saw. Still she was enthralled by the couple. "They don't join like us. They're talking during the act. Laughing. And...touching in a way we don't."

"Seems counterproductive to me and takes a lot of time. Look at what they do with their mouths. It's called kissing."

She touched her lips. "I wonder what it feels like."

Alisha wrinkled her nose. "Messy. Who wants to exchange saliva?" Tossing the book down on the bed, she stood and picked up as many of the ones with hard covers as she could balance on her open palm and started lifting them. "We're going to have to find out how they keep themselves fit here. There's no exertrac or jutzi classes."

"Maybe they have something like them."

"They have some of the elements, like yoga, meditation, kickboxing and stepping, but nothing that integrates them all."

A smile bloomed inside Celeste as she stood and crossed to the glass aperture. A real, cool breeze wafted inside and she closed her eyes to savor it. She knew, as long as she lived, she would never get used to daylight, real air and foliage. And the sun was almost incomprehensible. They'd never seen it other than on the chips.

"When are we going to get to go out of inside like Dorian has?" They'd walked to this dwelling, but none of them had noticed their surroundings on the quick trip because they were so diminished by the jump.

"Today, when Jess and Dorian come back. But the environment isn't clean, and germs can hurt us because we have no immunity. So we have to be careful."

"We've taken the immunity injections." And Alisha had had the Institute of Medicine develop some immunity tablets for them to ingest while they were here.

Celeste sighed. "I can't believe the vibrant colors out there."

"I feel that way, too." Alisha's tone had softened, because in the future, looking out of inside from the Domes revealed a big gray curtain, which occasionally exploded into dust and wind storms. There was no day or night, no seasons, like summer.

"We can go for a walking out there, or run like we do on the exertrac. In the *air*, Lisha."

"It *would be* enjoyable. We'll try it when Dorian returns."

"I hope everything goes well for her."

No answer.

"Alisha, when do we put my part in place?" Though they hadn't told Jess Cromwell, their mission was two-fold. Celeste had a task, too.

"I've got the computeller searching for a time and event when we can introduce you to Dr. Alex Lansing's life. But we both need to remain in New York to help Dorian. When she accomplishes her mission, we'll go to Virginia together and take care of your task."

"I hope it happens soon."

Just then the door to the out of inside opened and in stepped Dorian and Jess. It was odd seeing her in the dress of 2014, even though Celeste didn't like the severe outfit in dark colors Dorian wore now. Celeste glanced down at her own comfortable grey tunic and form-fitting pants. She was going to get some of this century's apparel soon but wanted hers in colors.

"How did it go?" Alisha asked.

"All right," Jess said. "But my wife's mad as hell at me."

Dorian frowned. "Maybe we're right to separate emotion from joining."

"Why did you?" he asked.

Celeste's heart hurt at the thought of it. "We didn't do it on purpose. Relationships evolved that way. When having younglings became problematic, sexual encounters became emotionless."

Jess's brow furrowed. "It was just the opposite with me and Helen. When we found out we couldn't have kids, we became even closer." He hesitated. "Why did having children become a problem in your time?"

Alisha shot her and Dorian a warning look. Celeste understood her caution not to reveal too much. "Low sperm motility and diminishing egg viability." She didn't tell Jess why this happened nor how it was related to Celeste's task.

"Helen has endometriosis. She's had several surgeries, but nothing helped."

Celeste clasped his arm and was bombarded by his sadness over his barrenness. In her time, people were accustomed to the notion. "You'll have a child, Jess. The chips are correct about that."

"It would be a dream come true. More than succeeding with my research."

"What's next?" Alisha asked, changing the subject.

"Dorian's coming to live at my house, as we planned. Helen agrees. We came back here to get her things."

From the unit with drawers—called a dresser for some reason—Dorian picked up a carrying case they'd also purchased yesterday. "My belongings are in here."

Jess shook his head. "She'll wonder why you have so little."

"Women of today need more than a change of clothing and some personal-hygiene equipment?"

He chuckled. "Don't look at me. I always thought the same thing."

"Why shouldn't we look at you?" Celeste asked, puzzled.

"Nord, you're hopeless." Already Alisha was running out of patience with her. Though Alisha hadn't voiced any concerns, Celeste knew her friend still had serious doubts about Celeste accomplishing her task. Which was why Celeste couldn't go off on her own.

Dorian sighed. "I'm to leave you."

"We'll miss you." Contrary to male-female contact, women shared emotions with each other, and Celeste meant what she said.

"You'll be visiting me soon. As my siblings." Dorian frowned.

"Why the grim expression?" Alisha asked.

"Jess's sibling doesn't believe my story. And he doesn't like me."

"He's naturally suspicious." Jess wasn't worried, Celeste could tell. "He'll come around."

Alisha eyed the computeller. "Let's hope so."

Dorian shifted on her feet.

"It's all right to be apprehensive, Dorian." Celeste took her hand. "And a bit fearful. It will keep you alert."

"I know. This is good-bye." She hugged Celeste. "I will see you soon, Celi." Crossing to Alisha, Dorian shook her hand. "You, too."

When they left, Alisha approached the computeller. "Search database for Lucas Cromwell."

"Please clarify. Lucas Jr. or Sr.?"

"Junior."

"Dates are required."

"All data available is requested."

The computeller began to hum.

"We need to know more about him," she explained to Celeste.

"I agree."

"I hope he doesn't blow Dorian's cover."

Celeste sank onto the bed. "I have no idea what that means."

Alisha crossed to the stack of books in the corner and retrieved one. "Here, decode this. It will help you understand their slang." She pointed to the video box. "And turn that thing off. It's counterproductive to our tasks. Knowing you, it'll just stir you up."

Celeste picked up the remote device. But before she pressed Off, she saw the man and woman in the picture lying close to each other on a bed. They looked happy. Comfortable. Satisfied.

The man ran his hand down the female's hair. The gesture was tender and made Celeste touch her own short locks. Yearning did indeed stir inside her.

"Celeste?"

She punched Off and took the book. But as she opened it, she couldn't get the couple on the video box out of her mind.

• • •

LUKE CALLED UP the police department's search engine and typed in *Dorian Masters.* While the computer did its thing, he accessed his personal-data folders and started one on her. Something wasn't right with his brother's new bodyguard. He began to type in what he did know. She was born in Virginia. *Which is outside of Washington.* Jesus.

Description: five nine or ten. Muscular, fit, well built. Dark hair, thick, no waves. Grass-green eyes without a speck of another color. Strong features.

Despite her good looks, she'd go toe to toe with most men, which would be good for his brother.

Speech patterns: crazy! Sometimes they were normal, most times not anywhere close. Why? He didn't buy the *grew up in South America* bullshit.

Miscellaneous: seems unfamiliar with common things. She barely touched her supper and winced when she tasted Helen's spaghetti sauce, which nobody on earth could resist. She did manage to down some plain pasta but picked up and examined a piece of lettuce with her fingers as if it were gold. She coughed when she drank coffee. Refused wine or beer.

Outlook: wary. She studied everybody and everything. The tow-headed neighborhood kid who came to the screen door yesterday seemed to fascinate her. She couldn't take her eyes off him. And, when the dog at the door barked, she'd gone totally white as if he was a grizzly instead of a small pug.

Luke leaned back in his chair and closed his eyes, mentally reviewing his contact with her. He knew in his gut Jess wasn't telling him everything.

When he looked at the computer again, he saw that the search engine had stopped. Wheeling in closer to the desk, he read the entries. Only three. Most people, even if they hadn't done anything to bring them fame, had several hits—name in the paper for winning a golf tournament, traffic tickets, etcetera. Hers included an item on her family, college and one brief mention of winning a marathon.

He clicked into the first site. Frowned. The story was on the death of her father. He read the entry. Most of it jived with what she'd said. She was born in Alexandria, went to live outside of Argentina with her parents and two siblings, Alisha and Celeste. Nothing about her activities. He checked the second. Schooled at Columbia University. When he got into their database, her name was listed. The marathon was in some obscure place he'd never heard of.

Hmm. He typed in Masterminds, the security firm she'd said she owned. Nice, slick website, advertising their services. No other personnel listed. A contact email was given but no phone number. Under a dummy address he'd set up for these purposes, he emailed the company with the ruse of needing protective services.

Then he clicked into the motor-vehicles database. Dorian Masters had a driver's license. He tried social security next. Yes, again.

But no matter how many federal databases he tapped, he couldn't find a street address where she had lived or really anything else concrete on her.

"So," he said into the empty office, "Ms. Dorian Masters, who the hell are you?"

• • •

DRINK IN HAND, Jess stared out the window of his den and sighed heavily. What a nightmare. He was still reeling from three women materializing in his office two days ago, and from being convinced that they were from the future. He'd always believed that time was fluid, and someday, someone would invent a way to navigate it. He just didn't think he would be involved in proving the theory. Nor had he suspected the past could be changed. He hoped to God they were right about that crucial detail. If they were wrong, he had only a little time left to live. He'd kept the notion at bay, but now, in the darkened den, the idea chilled him so much he shivered. He and Luke used to play the game, "If you were going to die tomorrow, what would you do today?"

How did Jess *really* want to spend his few remaining weeks if the women weren't successful in stopping his accident? He certainly wanted to be home more.

Even if Helen was mad as hell at him.

She'd blown up after everyone had left…

"How could you keep this from me?"

"As I said, I thought it was for the best."

"*I* thought we were partners, shared everything."

"We do."

Just an arch of an auburn brow.

"I'm sorry. I was wrong."

"That's not enough."

"What will be?"

"I don't know, Jess. How do you win back someone's trust?"

That sobered him and kept him from falling asleep long after she did. Because she was pissed, yeah, but because he was still keeping things from her. And from Luke, whom he'd always told everything. But how could he burden the people he loved most in the world with the knowledge he was supposed to die?

"What are you doing down here?" Helen's voice came from behind him. He turned and could barely make out her silhouette in the darkness.

"I can't sleep."

"Because you're worried about the threats?" Now her voice was raw.

"Partly."

He heard the door close and the lock click. She came toward him. He could see her better now. She wore a pink slip of a thing, the kind she loved to sleep in. Suddenly, he remembered that she would marry somebody else after he died, and the fact drove his blood pressure up. Would that man take the gown off her? Would that man…?

"Why else are you here?"

Swallowing back the bile that rose in his throat at the untenable thought of another man touching his wife, he managed to say, "Our fight. And the fact that you don't trust me now. Shouldn't really."

She shook her head, sending skeins of hair everywhere. "You're always such a puppy when we fight."

"I hate it."

"I know. But things have to be said, Jess."

He sipped his drink and leaned against the window jamb. "Still…I'm a wreck."

After a slight hesitation, she stepped even closer until she was standing in front of him. "I know something that will help." Taking the glass from his hand and setting it on the table, she looped her arms around his neck and pressed her body to him.

"You're mad," he said, already nuzzling her.

"So?" She kissed him long and thoroughly.

He got hard in seconds. Kissed her back, more passionately than maybe ever before. "I want you now," was all he could say as he slipped the straps off her shoulders.

"Yes."

They undressed each other and made it to the couch, him on top.

Urgently, she grasped his nape. "Make it good, Jess."

As he drew her arms up, he remembered the shining face of a baby girl. Holy shit! Was this when conception was going to happen?

He stopped thinking when Helen reached between them and grasped his penis, lifted her hips and took him inside her.

CHAPTER 4

LUKE WATCHED THE statuesque woman seated across from him. Given what he'd found out yesterday, he was more suspicious than ever. She looked normal enough today in the same dark suit, but this time the jacket was spruced up with a more feminine, pink blouse. He said to her, "I need information on the emails and on anything else you both think is important."

Dorian handed him papers. Her nails were clipped and she wore no jewelry, not even a watch. "Here they are."

Luke's eyes narrowed on his brother. "You told me you deleted them."

"I did. Dorian recovered them."

"How?"

"I have skill in computers."

"Did you have outside help?"

"I can't say."

"You're going to have to say, if I'm to go through official channels."

"I'm capable of conducting this investigation on my own. You can recuse yourself."

"Recuse?"

Her green eyes widened. "Recuse means to absent yourself from a case because you have a personal stake in it."

"I know what recuse means. It usually applies to judges."

"Isn't it correct in this instance?"

Jess sat back and smiled. "She's got you there, brother."

"This isn't funny, Jess. And it's not a pissing contest between Ms. Masters and me. We're trying to save your sorry ass."

"There are sparks flying between you and her, and you've only known her a couple of days. It's amusing."

She said, "If I've offended you, Lieutenant, it's been unintentional. I've given you all the information we have. Either you or I can follow this…lead."

"Fine. I apologize. Maybe I am too involved, because we're talking about Jess. But I'm not turning this investigation over to anyone."

"Then I'll assist."

"Give me a few days to check out the emails."

From inside a bag she pulled out more papers. "I've begun to investigate the local oil companies. These are the personnel files for the workers for a group located in Manhattan named Petron. I haven't had a chance to review them in all the excitement of…moving."

"How the hell did you get something like *this?*"

She just arched a brow.

Jess said, "I hate to break this up, but I have work to do, and Dorian has to come with me."

"I'll be in touch by the end of the day." Luke stood. "Will you be at the office?"

"Yep. Me and my trusty assistant." He smiled affectionately at Dorian.

As they left, Luke wondered if Jess was already attracted to Dorian. He had a bad feeling about that, too.

• • •

ON THE DRIVE to the office, Dorian sat beside Jess in Helen's Prius, one of the time period's attempts to produce pollutionless vehicles. Jess thought the ride might make her less motion sick in this model. Suddenly, something darted in front of them and Dorian yelped. "What was that?"

Jess laughed. "A squirrel."

"A squirrel? Oh, a squirla."

"A what?"

"We don't have animals, Jess. Just reproductions. In a museum called Zoolawn where we can view them. They move and roar or chirp, but they're animated. I guess the names were corrupted after animals became extinct."

"That's sad."

A lot of things were sad in the future. She rubbed her arm. Her skin felt scratchy. Probably because of the foreign material—cotton—covering it and because she hadn't partaken of the shower ritual common today. These people actually stood in water to cleanse themselves. Besides the incredible waste of such precious commodity, that kind of primitive hygiene was so…incomplete. Their Repurification Chamber, which rid their bodies, hair and clothing of dirt, was much more efficient. They'd brought along a small handheld one to use for quick cleanups, but she'd have to succumb to the shower eventually.

"You okay?" Jess asked as they drove.

"Yes. I was thinking about all you have here that we don't. And I'm sad about leaving Alisha and Celeste. We have contact almost every revolution in our time."

"You sure you don't want to tell me what's going on with them when you all go to Virginia?"

"The people who sent us made us vow not to reveal our tasks to anyone. We had no choice but to let you know, and your family, if necessary, but this next task must be done covertly."

Dorian hoped Celeste would be able to find a way into Dr. Alex Lansing's life. Dorian had had it fairly easy with Jess. Except for his brother's suspicions.

She pictured Luke Cromwell—his shoulders, which stretched a shirt the color of the sky, hair a little mussed and a nick from shaving—the barbaric way men removed facial hair in this time.

Looking at him made her feel strange. It…stirred her, particularly his scent. Whenever she got a whiff of it, she felt her body tighten. If she was in her time, she would have asked for him on the SexLine. She imagined he was skilled at reciprocal release, and even now, she felt a shiver go through her at the thought of joining with him.

Sighing, she considered the lack of a SexLine in this time period. It was quick, easy and efficient; she wondered how people managed without it. When they reached the office, she accompanied Jess inside and searched the place to insure his safety. Then she sat on one of the rigid couches. She missed the conformers, too. "Jess, may I ask you a personal question?"

He smiled as he crossed to his desk. "Shoot."

She frowned.

"It means, go ahead."

"I was wondering about people like your brother. He has no mate, correct?"

"He did. They got divorced when she cheated on him."

"Cheated?"

"She took another sexual partner."

"And your society values monogamy?"

"Yeah, we do. Yours doesn't?"

"No. Our sexual practice is to register in the geographical community database called the SexLine. When we have the need for release, we program our identity into the computeller, and it connects us with a male or female, depending on our preference, who has the same need at the same time to arrange a session. Of course, if we want to choose a specific person, we can. But typically, anyone will do."

He'd tipped his chair back to listen and almost fell over when she finished. "Honest to God?"

"Clarify, please."

"That's really the custom in your time?"

"It's very efficient."

"I think it's awful."

"Why?"

"Because sex between people who love each other is wonderful."

"SexLine joining is satisfying and meets our needs."

"Emotionally?"

"There are no emotions involved with joining. I'm told same-sex joining is different for females, but I've never experienced it."

"So, you accept same-sex couples in your society?"

Why would he ask that? "Of course."

"I'm glad."

"Oh, Jess, you don't now, in this time period?"

"Not wholly, but we're making progress."

She shook her head. This had not come up on the chips. She'd been mistaken to think that society was always open-minded about all sexuality.

"So, what do you want to know about Luke?"

"Your brother and those without mates? How do they find partners to share this physical and emotional involvement?"

"It's called dating." He explained the process to her.

"Dating sounds inefficient and random. I imagine your people experience a lot of sexual frustration."

"Yes, Dorian, they do."

"Thanks for explaining."

He looked at the computer. "I have to get to work. What will you do?"

She pulled out her computeller. "I'm going to try to find who's sending your emails."

"So you didn't just come to protect me?"

"That's my primary job. But the office is secure, so I can do both."

"Knock your socks off," he said, then caught her look. "Never mind."

Dorian opened the computeller and saw that Alisha had tried to contact her. Stepping out into the corridor so as not to bother Jess while he worked, she pushed the communication button. Alisha's recorded message came on video and audio.

"I'm keeping you apprised of our plans. We've been doing research on Dr. Lansing and his younglings. And his work. He's nearing some kind of breakthrough, just like Jess Cromwell."

Celeste appeared behind her. "I'm trying new things." She gave Dorian a conspiratorial look and angled her head at Alisha, as if she was going to say something she knew would irritate her friend. Though she was a sensitive, she had an admirable ability to jest. "Now I'm going to take a bath where you immerse yourself in real water for a length of time."

Dorian's colleagues looked cute in their new clothes. Celeste wore a pink blouse, which complimented the sweet blush on her face, and white pants. Alisha had chosen denim trousers and a red shirt. They all looked so different out of their tunics. A lot of things were strange here...food, clothing, methods of hygiene. Thinking of Luke Cromwell, she added sex to the list. Then she pushed him out of her mind and listened to Alisha's report.

• • •

CELESTE GRINNED BROADLY as she stepped into the bathtub for the first time. Both she and Alisha had used the shower since they'd been here, and though it cleansed them well enough, she was excited about being surrounded by water.

She sank into the warm tub, which was called a Jacuzzi and had jets shooting out the liquid that was so precious in her time. "Ahhh." Her muscles immediately relaxed, and her pulse slowed. Picking up the bubbles—soap residue that had poofed when she added water—she playfully blew on them, and they scattered. Celeste giggled like the younglings on the video box called a television.

"What's all that?" Alisha entered the bathing space and sat down on the closed lid of the toilet, which was an archaic ancestor to the waste receptacles in their time.

"It's called bubble bath, a gift provided by the host. Isn't it wonderful?"

"Looks scratchy to me. Like the chunks of cleanser in the shower."

"No. It's soothing. I *love* water."

"You *love* too much about this time."

Celeste sighed. "Just because I became nauseous after eating that thing called a burrito, doesn't mean we shouldn't try their sustenance."

"I told you to stick to the supplements we brought. There are enough for a long time for all of us."

She wrinkled her nose. "They have no taste."

"And what you ingested will clog your arteries, raise your blood pressure and make you fat."

"But it was delicious."

Alisha raised her eyes to the ceiling. "Oh, Nord, keep her away from the sweets."

"Sweets?"

"Never mind. You'll find out soon enough." She held up the computeller. "I've been perusing the data on Dr. Lansing."

Despite the soothing water, Celeste's heartbeat escalated. "What did you find out?"

"He requires youngling care. They call it babysitting."

"His younglings are not babies. Three is the cut-off point for that term. The Lansings are five, eleven and seventeen."

"It's just another term these people misuse. Anyway, Dr. Lansing has a keeper of his house during the day and a young adult after school for the younglings."

"I wish I could take care of them."

"That's what I thought. I'm pondering whether there's a way for you to obtain one of these jobs." She smiled. "Since you can practically read people's minds, it shouldn't be too hard to infiltrate your way into their lives."

Celeste blew on more suds.

"But as I said before, we must concentrate on Jess's safety now."

Knowing that Alisha was right, Celeste changed the subject. "How is Dorian faring, do you think? She's always so matter-of-fact."

"She's well, except for her concerns about Lucas Cromwell."

"He's appealing to look at, isn't he?"

"Why would you say that? He has excess body fat, his skin is wrinkled, and he is arrogant."

"I don't know. I just think he is. Alex Lansing is handsome, too. His hair is lighter than any people of our time, and the younglings' even more so." She touched her own dark locks.

Alisha chuckled at something.

"What?" Celeste asked.

"Alex Lansing resembles a performer in one of those video boxes you love. I've studied the time period's speculative fiction, and one of the most interesting was called *Star Trek*. The story takes place in the future, and their predictions were accurate on many issues."

"Like what?"

Alisha took a bead on her. "Never mind. It will just give you ideas."

She raised her chin. "Perhaps I'll call it up on my computeller. I bet I'll *love* that video."

"For all our sakes, I hope Alex Lansing's not something else you just *love*." Alisha stood. "Don't stay in there too long."

"Just a few more minutes."

After Alisha left, Celeste slid down and put her head under the water, enjoying the sensation of submersion. She visualized the chips containing the likeness of Alex Lansing. She couldn't wait to meet him. Meanwhile, she'd have to settle for watching this *Star Trek* show.

CHAPTER 5

"MY LOVE IS yours," Dorian told Alisha and Celeste just before she disconnected on one of their daily calls. She hated speaking with her friends and not seeing them, but they couldn't risk someone other than Jess catching sight of the computeller. So Alisha had contacted her with their newly purchased—though barbaric—cell phones.

From the corner of her eye, she saw Luke Cromwell stroll down the hallway to his brother's kitchen. This was why she used the device common to today: the man always seemed to be showing up without warning and...he hovered. He poured some coffee and leaned against the counter, unabashedly watching her. His arrogant posture made him attractive, something Dorian didn't understand.

"What does *my love is yours* mean?" he asked, his gaze intent.

"Eavesdropping, Lieutenant?"

"Yep."

"I was speaking with my sisters. Saying I care for them."

"Another oddity in your syntax."

"My don—parents taught us the phrase. They wanted something special among the four of us."

"Where do they live?"

"They are deceased. My sisters live in New York now. But, as I told you before, we came from Virginia."

"Which is right outside of Washington." He said the words sarcastically, and again Dorian didn't know why. So she nodded at her notes on the low table in front of the seating conformer—a couch. "Are you ready to talk about the emails?"

"Yeah. Where's Jess?"

"He's on a walking with Helen." She smiled. "He's enjoying a day off."

"My brother?"

"He said he wished to spend more time with his spouse."

"This death threat's got him scared."

"As it should." She studied Luke. Today he was dressed in a tight-fitting, white shirt that outlined every one of his impressive muscles, low-riding pants called jeans (which was also a name) and shoes called sneakers, perhaps because they made no noise when someone walked in them and could come up behind another person without being heard. "Are you not working today, either?"

"Sort of. It's my regular day off, but I'm going to the office after lunch."

"I see. You're a holicworker like Jess."

Silence. Then, a piercing, brown gaze that made her shift on her feet. "Are you for real?"

"I don't understand."

"Neither do I." He came in closer and towered over her. His scent surrounded her. It was almost overpowering. "The word is workaholic. Everybody knows that word, yet you misused it. You misuse words and terms a lot, like Jess is *out on a walking*."

Dorian had watched some videos of women and their interactions with men in this time period. Mimicking them, she tilted her chin. Exasperation and boredom seemed to put the male species off. "This is tiring, Lieutenant. I've already explained why my speech is unusual. And frankly, I find you tedious." She smiled. "I know I got that word right."

His eyes widened, glistening in the light coming in from the window. His breath had sped up, and suddenly he seemed even more male. Which sparked something inside her. The men of her time never affected her like this, never seemed as virile as this one did right now.

Or as dangerous.

Though she wanted to move in and press her body to his, to touch him all over, she turned away to pick up her notes. "Shall we confer?"

Grabbing her arm, he whirled her to face him and gripped her biceps. His hands were strong, and a quick rush of desire surged through her. To counteract it, and to show this male he couldn't push her around, she brought both arms up, broke his hold, jutted out her hand, and splayed his jugular.

Luke's reaction was split-second. He thrust her away, circled her and got her in a headlock.

Dorian wrapped her foot around his leg and took him down. He landed on the ground on his back, grabbed *her* ankle so she toppled onto him.

They were breathing hard, their legs intimately entwined, their chests pressed against each other's. "You're good," he said with an admiring chuckle as he smiled at her. The gesture was...gorgeous.

Battling back a grin, she nodded. "So are you." Then she pinned his arms to the ground but guessed he let her. "Don't put your hands on me again, Lieutenant, unless you're invited to."

Again some mirth, and what was that? An indentation in his cheek? "You thinking about asking me to touch you, darlin'?"

Dorian's body went liquid. She felt *his* harden as they stared at each other, flushed, eyes locked. Suddenly, the air seemed to crackle as much as when they'd backtracked.

"Am I interrupting?"

Dorian glanced up to see Jess had come into the living room. Quickly, she climbed off Luke and stood. He rolled to his feet and they simultaneously stepped away from each other. Dorian remembered a time when she, Celeste and Alisha had been a decade and a half old and had gotten into the history chips Rhea, Celeste's donor, kept in her dwelling. They'd found reading material called *BoyPlay*. Young and old men were posed naked, and the sight had absorbed them. When Rhea came in, she tried to explain why the people of the past liked such odd gazing material; the three of them had been embarrassed by their reactions to it. Like she was now.

The expression on Jess's face was one of amusement. "What's going on?"

Luke's fists curled and uncurled at his sides. His face reddened and his muscles pulsed. "We had a disagreement."

"And fought physically over it?"

"Not exactly."

Dorian shot Jess a warning glance, trying to signal him that they'd talk about this later. "It's not important."

Hesitating, Jess gave her a long stare. "Okay, I'm ready to look at your report. Helen and I are going to a movie marathon today, and it starts in two hours."

Luke eyed him suspiciously. "Jess, is anything going on that I don't know about? You never take this kind of time off."

"Just stopping to smell the roses."

Whatever the hellor that meant, Dorian thought.

Luke seemed to know because he crossed to the table, dropped down and opened his folder. Jess and Dorian did the same. But she was too close to Luke to concentrate, so she moved farther down the rigid couch.

"I've gone through the reports on Petron workers. There are some disgruntled employees who were recently demoted or passed over for better jobs. A few of them might be in a position to know some R&D things. I'm checking them out further."

"Research and Development. Well, that's progress," Jess said.

Grateful he'd clued her into the acronym, another proclivity of their time that had not survived and seemed silly to her.

Luke added, "And there are some environmentalist types who might be trying to scare Jess."

"Or be genuinely worried about the earth." For obvious reasons, Dorian didn't like his dismissal of people who *did* believe global warming was a threat. Her society knew well exactly how dangerous the condition was.

He ignored her tone. "My money is on the CEO"—he took a bead on Dorian—"Chief Executive Officer in case you missed out on the term in South America. He'd be in a position to stop Jess."

Obviously, she wasn't keeping her lack of knowledge to herself and vowed to be more careful. Perhaps Alisha could give her more chips to study.

Luke continued, "I think we should look into who might have knowledge of the brass's plans and is therefore writing the emails to warn Jess." He thought for a minute. "Unless the warnings are a ruse to stop Jess's research in and of themselves."

They discussed how to get more information on the CEO. Dorian's access to the computeller could retrieve the information easily, but how would she explain what she discovered to Luke? Maybe she'd just do it anyway and pretend she didn't know what they were looking for. Megadamn! If they could only tell Luke Cromwell the truth.

"What would happen if we approached this CEO and told him we believed someone at Petron is trying to warn Jess of a threat from within the company?" Dorian asked. "They could hardly put a plan in place if we brought it into the open."

"Not necessarily." Luke's expression was stern now. "We might give him more leeway to do it. He could say afterward that we knew there were threats and someone succeeded in killing Jess." His brow furrowed. "Let me see what I can find out on my own."

Just as they wrapped up the meeting, Helen entered the kitchen. She, too, was wearing faded jeans and a pale yellow shirt. Again, Dorian noted her fragility.

"You guys done?" Helen asked.

"Uh-huh." Jess stood and grabbed her around the waist. "Ready for the film fest, baby?"

Baby? Oh, good Nord, another term of endearment?

"Yes." She smiled at Dorian. "You?"

"Of course. I'll sit a ways back so you can have some privacy." She pictured the current cinemas she'd researched on the computeller. In truth, she was anxious to experience one firsthand.

"That's not necessary." Helen smiled at Luke. "Wanna come?"

"This is your day off, isn't it?" Jess asked.

Helen socked Luke's shoulder. "You could keep Dorian company."

Shooting her a look full of keen interest, Luke's expression was smug. "You know, that might be fun."

Megadamn, Dorian thought once again. This was all she needed. How was she supposed to focus on her task with this attractive male specimen always around her, close to her, even *touching* her?

• • •

LUKE CLIMBED THE steps of the theater, focusing on Dorian Masters, who sat four rows behind his brother and sister-in-law. She was scanning the interior as if she'd never seen the inside of a movie theater. Hell, those thoughts just kept popping into his head. He couldn't shake the feeling that her reactions were due to more than growing up in a foreign country. Almost everything she did underscored his suspicions. But he couldn't wrap his brain around where she might have come from. And now that brain was muddled by the damned-good memory of having her sprawled over him just an hour ago.

Waving to his brother, who'd wanted the four of them to sit together, but Dorian had refused, Luke reached her row and dropped down beside her.

Her body tensed. "Do you have to sit so close?"

Odd again. "It'd look funny if I was seats away. This is how people sit at the movies. Why don't you know that?"

Ignoring the query, she scanned the almost-empty theater. "There are few people here to notice."

"Jess would think we aren't getting along." His tone was dry.

"Why ever would he think that?" Her gaze strayed to the big bucket of buttered popcorn he held, and her green eyes glistened even in the dim light. "Are you going to eat all of the food?"

"At least. I get a free refill." He winked at her. "If you're good, I'll share it with you."

Briefly, she mimicked the gesture with her eye, as if she was trying it out. Then she focused on the popcorn. "There's almost six hundred fat grams in the entire bucket."

"How do you know that?"

"I calculated its approximate size."

"So, you don't eat snack food?"

"Of course not."

His gaze turned lazy and drifted down her body. At his suggestion, she'd changed into something more casual—beige, cropped-off pants, which hugged her ass, and a short-sleeved shirt with a sweater to match. The red looked good on her. Too good. "Must be why you don't have an ounce of fat on you."

"One of the reasons."

"Jess says you use his treadmill."

"Yes, I must maintain top physical condition. I am careful about what I eat since I can't use the exer…since I can't leave Jess to exercise out…doors."

"That isn't what you were going to say."

"It was."

"You don't lie convincingly."

"I don't lie."

He scowled. "If you want to run outside, I can spell you."

Her brow furrowed. "Spell?"

"Relieve you from watching Jess." His gaze sharpened. "Dorian, doll, something is just not right with you, and I'm gonna find out what it is."

"I am not a plaything."

Oh, man. "Figure of speech, again."

The theater darkened and they both quieted. Luke was almost sorry to have the repartee end. He snacked on his popcorn during the previews. When he caught her glimpsing at the bucket, he leaned in close. She smelled like soap and shampoo, and once again, his body reacted. He'd put on a sports shirt and flipped the tails over his middle. "One handful won't hurt you. There's probably only ten fat grams in it."

"Wise butt."

His mind went berserk on that one, even as he burst out laughing.

Tentatively she took a handful. Gingerly, she brought the buttery kernels to her mouth. When she tasted it, she closed her eyes. "Oh." Then, "Ah," then "Mmm."

Jesus, did she have to do that? His mind, which she had been screwing up under normal circumstances, spun a great fantasy that involved Dorian Masters, him, a bed and a hell of a lot of sounds like that.

When his head cleared, one thing sifted out of the rest. She'd never had popcorn. He knew it as much as he knew his own name. Who the hell had never had popcorn?

The first feature film began. Helen had chosen to see a *Mission Impossible* marathon. She had a thing for Tom Cruise and was a thriller fan. Ironically, his brother preferred romantic comedies. When the opening scene flashed on, Dorian shifted, her eyes focused intently on the screen. By the time they were ten minutes into the film, she was sitting on the edge of her seat.

Her hand clapped over her mouth at one of the high-speed chases.

She gasped when Cruise fell out of a window.

But when a love scene unfolded, Dorian's jaw literally dropped. Her eyes widened. Her breath sped up. And through the knit of her shirts, he could see her nipples harden. Fuck! She was aroused. And acting like a kid who'd never seen sex on the big screen.

Or never done it herself. Which, given her dynamite good looks, was about as likely as if she'd come from Mars.

Maybe less likely.

• • •

DORIAN PONDERED THE events in the movie long after it ended. The vehicular chase scenes were exciting, the guns horrible and foreign to her because the sole "weapons" in the future were stunners and only select people could obtain those. In the twenty-third century, they'd banned all types of weaponry that could kill others.

The witty dialogue between men and women reminded her of her conversation before the movie with Luke. But the joining scenes affected her the most. She stood when the lights went on, her hands clammy just thinking about what the man and woman did together.

"How'd you like the film?" Luke asked, watching her in that annoying way of his. He'd moved out into the aisle.

"I found it was interesting."

"You've never seen a *Mission Impossible* movie?"

"I'm not much of a cinema aficionado."

"What'd you like best in it?"

"Um…"

Thank the godheads, Jess waved to her from below. She nodded back. "We need to meet up with Jess and Helen." She slid into the wide aisle in front of him. He grasped her arms and held her in front of him. His touch was firm but gentle, and she could have shaken him off as she had in Jess's home, but heat emanated from him. And she remembered what it felt like to be flush against him. All right, so she liked his touch.

Hellor, it had been a long time since her last joining. Though she couldn't remember the name of the man, she did recall the assignation had been mutually enjoyable. A quick flash of her and Luke Cromwell doing what the people on screen had just done immobilized her.

"Hey, guys?" Jess yelled up, his brow furrowed.

His comment brought Dorian back to reality and she started down the stairs. She stumbled and had to grasp on to the railing.

"Did you like the movie?" Helen asked her.

"Yes."

"She's never seen a *Mission Impossible* film." Luke spoke from behind her. So only Dorian could hear, he mumbled, "Or any one."

"Not everybody's into cops and robbers," Jess said easily. "I hope it was okay for you, sitting through all of them. We like marathons."

"I enjoyed myself."

"She stole some of my popcorn. I'm not sure she ever had that, either."

Helen began, "Why wouldn't she—" but Jess cut her off by tugging her down the steps.

Outside the theater, they waited for the rush of people to pass, then Helen walked down the street with Luke, and Dorian hung back with Jess. When they were far enough back from the other couple, Jess whispered, "You all right?"

"Yes." She pitched her voice lower. "I have a thousand questions."

"I'm sure you do. Let's grab some dinner, and maybe later, we can catch some time alone."

"All right."

"What do you feel like eating?"

She placed a hand on her stomach. "My supplements. This food is not good for me. Or for you."

He laughed. "Chinese. You might tolerate that."

The theater was in downtown Brooklyn, and soon they came to a crossing of the roads. As they waited for the traffic to stop, she noted the many vehicles out at this hour but with few people in them. Why weren't they at least filled with passengers?

The light turned to red—which meant the vehicles must stop—and all four of them stepped off the curb.

From the north, Dorian caught sight of a yellow automobile called a taxi speeding toward them. Her eyes widened and her heart raced. Instead of stopping, the vehicle picked up speed.

"Luke, the vehicle," she yelled as she yanked Jess onto the sidewalk, the momentum carrying her back into a utility pole. Just before she hit the steel structure, she got a glimpse of Luke grabbing Helen and hauling her to safety, too.

As the taxi whizzed past them, Dorian banged her head against the pole and slumped down to the ground.

• • •

DORIAN LAY STRETCHED out on Jess's couch an hour after the renegade taxi had barreled toward them. She'd lost consciousness for a little while after she'd banged her head on the steel pole. Though she was achy, she was awake now. Everyone was grim-faced. To calm them, she said, "I'm all right."

On the loveseat, Helen hovered next to Jess, and Luke sat on the edge of a chair.

"You seem better than you did an hour ago," Helen commented. "Even the bruise looks like it's healing."

The discoloration and swelling would be completely gone by tomorrow if she could manage to be alone and use the Multisalve she'd brought from her time. Its healing powers were myriad.

"I told you there was no need for the medics."

Luke sighed. "What do you think happened, Dorian?"

She couldn't read his expression. "It may have been connected to the threats Jess's been getting."

"Duh? Of course it was."

"That's impossible." This from Jess. Now that she was more aware, Dorian noted his ashen face and how he was furiously twisting his marital band.

"Why, honey?" Helen hadn't let go of Jess's hand since they'd returned to this dwelling.

"Because if the cab had hit us, you would have been killed and not just me."

Suddenly, Dorian was fearful of the truth coming out, which didn't make sense, since she'd requested that these two people be told.

Jess's expression was wild-eyed. "It was only supposed to be me, right Dorian?"

"Ah..."

"That thing said just *me.*" His voice rose a notch. "And not until later in the summer."

Luke assumed his cop glare. "What the hell are you two talking about?"

Shaking his head, Jess looked at his brother. "Her computer thing. It said I was supposed to die before the end of the summer. That's why she's here."

"I don't understand." Helen clutched his arm. "Jess, you're talking crazy."

Luke eyed Dorian. "What's going on? This whole bodyguard thing hasn't added up from the beginning. Helen's right. Now you're talking gibberish. I want the truth. Who the hell are you, Dorian?"

"I'm who I say I am."

"Jess?"

"She is. It's just that she's not from here. Not from now. Oh, fuck it," Jess said running a hand over his scalp. "I thought keeping this from you would be best, but it isn't working out that way." He shot an apologetic glance to Helen, then faced Luke. "Dorian's from the future."

CHAPTER 6

ALISHA WALKED INTO the hotel room after running out of inside. Though she was jaded about the current society, having researched it for decades, the ability to go out in real air and run, work up a sweat, was mind-boggling. But she had bigger things to deal with. "Something's happened," Alisha said without greeting.

Celeste, seated at a table, looked up from the book she was decoding. "Hello to you, too."

"The cat's out of the bag."

"Once again, I have no idea what that means."

Alisha held up her new cell phone. "It means Jess told Helen and Luke Cromwell who Dorian is, more to the point, *when* we came from."

Celeste set down the book. "It was Jess's decision *not* to tell them. What changed his mind?"

"There was an incident." She described how Jess was almost hit by a taxi. "Dorian called as soon as she could to tell us."

"Oh, Nord, Lisha, was that...was that when he was originally killed?"

"I don't know because of the corrosion of the chips. He could have been killed earlier than the end of the summer, for all we know. But Helen would have died this time, too. Luke dragged her back. The computeller says she had a child, and we know for certain that hasn't happened yet."

"Seems coincidental to me." Celi's brow furrowed. "Maybe our very presence here has changed history."

"Or maybe it's related to one of those time paradoxes we discovered at the Institute. If we weren't here, both of them would have died yesterday. So it's like we were supposed to come and stop that, too. Nothing else happened, though."

"What do you mean?"

"Well…" Alisha wasn't sure how much to share with Celeste. But she missed having Rhea and her other institute workers to examine ideas with. Again, she thought back to their meeting with Rhea, which had haunted Alisha…

"Returning to 2514 poses problems," Rhea told the group when they received their assignment. "You need to know this before we reveal your specific tasks. If you don't want to participate after you hear this, the exact content of them will be kept from you."

"Why wouldn't we want to if society needs us?" Celeste asked.

Her eyes on her offspring, Rhea said, "There is a ninety-eight point six percent probability that if you do change the past, we won't be able to return you to the present. If things are different in our time period, which we're *hoping* will happen, we might not even exist as we are now, or our technology may be different. Time travel may not have ever been perfected." Rhea sighed heavily when she finished with the bleak news.

Celeste smiled gently at her. "It's all right to feel bad that you may never see me again." She stood and went to her donor, squeezing her hand. "My love will always be yours, Rhea, no matter what happens."

"You don't have to go, Celi." She scanned the group. "None of you do."

"If the positions were reversed, would you?"

Rhea only nodded...

Now, Alisha decided to share her real feelings. "I guess I've been hoping that if we do change the future and the Domes go away, we'd overcome the odds and the Guardians would somehow know that three of us had backtracked to this time period. Maybe we *could* return to our own time."

"Oh, Lisha, I'm sorry you had this hope. The probability is so small, I accepted right away that we'd never return."

"I know, I think Dorian did too."

Celeste rubbed her fingers on her temples. "Thinking about all that gives me a pain in the head."

"We both need some sleep. We're going over to the Cromwell house at dawning to see if we can help. I wanted to make the trip by taxi tonight, but Dorian said it was too late. Let's get some sleep." Without waiting for a response, Alisha grabbed her sleeping clothes and went into the bathroom, not feeling well herself. Her stomach was reacting to what could be a very complicated development.

• • •

THE NEXT DAY, Alisha sat at a real wood table in the eating space at the Crowell's dwelling. She sipped her tea—one of the few kinds of sustenance in this time period that she liked-and thought about the events of the morning. She and Celeste had arrived at eight a.m. and found the Cromwells with Dorian in this very room. Poor Jess seemed disoriented and his spouse Helen distraught. Dorian showed severe signs of fatigue. And Lucas Cromwell was nowhere in sight. Dorian had told her he'd stormed out of the house after a night of unproductive discussion and intermittent sleep. After they'd been introduced, she and Celeste had spoken with the Helen and Jess for over an hour, then they retired to their bedroom. Dorian had said she'd try to rest, too.

But after only fifteen minutes, she heard Dorian climb the steps from the lower level and come into the room.

Scanning her, Alisha frowned. "You appear even more tired than you did before you went to lie down."

"I couldn't sleep."

Seven hours of uninterrupted slumber was essential to health and Alisha worried about Dorian missing it. In the future, none of them experienced sleeplessness.

"You should go running with me like we planned."

"Probably not. Is Luke back?"

"No."

"Then I couldn't go anyway. I have to guard Jess."

Alisha shook her head. "It isn't logical that his brother still doesn't believe you, even after I confirmed everything."

"Hearing the person you love most dies in the near future would muddle anyone's mind. He said he had to clear his head and went out for a drive."

"I still think he could have handled this better."

Alisha nodded to the basement entrance. The Cromwells had purchased the huge house yearlings ago, for a much lower cost than its selling price today. There was an entire bottom floor equipped with three separate rooms and a common area. Helen and Jess had offered all three women use of the lower spaces now that there were no secrets. "Is Celeste all right? Does she need anything?"

"I looked in on her. She's not feeling well."

"Her stomach has been upset from consuming their sustenance, and with all the emotion swirling around in the air today, she became ill with it." Alisha shook her head. "I'm glad I'm not a sensitive."

Dorian leaned against the counter. "Why don't you go running alone? I'll lie down on the sitting conformer and close my eyes."

"All right." Alisha stood. Hesitating, she stepped closer and embraced Dorian. Alisha wasn't a hugger but she felt sorry for her friend. "Try to get some rest."

Running out of inside brightened Alisha's mood, though once again the sunshine made her eyes hurt. The powerful rays beaming right down on her with little obfuscation by the ozone layer forced her to put on the shaded glasses. She didn't like them because they impeded her vision. And because she couldn't see well and was preoccupied, she collided with someone when she reached the paved path in front of Jess's just as he did. "Oh."

The man grabbed for her shoulders. "Easy there." He had a deep voice and firm grip.

Alisha slid her glasses to the top of her head. "I seek your forgiveness. I didn't see you."

Now that she did, she took in details. He was about four inches taller than she was, broad shouldered, and slim hipped. His face was…interesting. Not as classic as Alex Lansing's or as rugged as Luke Cromwell's, but…nice looking and kind. And his hair had…curls, another anomaly of her time.

Then her gaze dropped lower. "What's that around your neck?" she blurted out.

His hand went to the white ring inside a black shirt.

"This? It's a collar." When she frowned, he added, "I'm a minister. Helen and Jess's minister. Helen called and asked me to come over. She said it was urgent."

Alisha took a moment to recall what she knew about clerics of the time. Spiritual leaders. Heads of congregations. Confessors.

Confessors. Unholy godheads, they couldn't divulge anything to this man!

She said, "My name is Alisha. And I'll go back in with you."

• • •

DORIAN STARED ACROSS the table where she now sat with Jess and Helen. They were unable to rest and had come out to the eating space thirty minutes ago for tea. But when Jess served her some, Helen began weeping and he sat down and slid his arm around her. Celeste had gotten misty-eyed sometimes, but Dorian had never seen women leak tears openly like this. It fascinated her, made her wonder if she could do it.

"Shh, sweetheart, it's okay. I told you over and over, I'm going to be all right. Dorian came here to save my life."

Burying her head in his shoulder, she murmured, "I still can't believe you're supposed to die."

Dorian tried to keep her voice even, but the events of the last twenty-four hours had upset even her. "I'm here to preclude his death, Helen."

The woman raised bruised eyes to her. "What if you can't?"

"It's all hard to comprehend, I know. But as I said, we have evidence to prove we can change the future."

"And you want to? You'll make everything different." Helen sniffed as she asked the question.

"Yes, we want to because by our calculations, society as we know it ends in 2589. I already explained this to you." Several times. To her and Luke.

"I can't take it in. Neither can Luke, which is why he left."

Apprehensive, Dorian glanced up when she heard the front door open. "Maybe that's him."

Instead, a man wearing a black shirt, a white neck-circle and gray pants stepped inside. With him was Alisha, her expression even more dour than usual.

Jess stood and held out his hand. "Hello, David."

David, the pastor. In the time Dorian had been here, they'd told her about him, but she hadn't met him.

The men shook hands, another odd custom, which surely transmitted germs. "Jess." David moved to Helen and touched her shoulder. "Helen, what's wrong?"

Alisha stepped forward. "Jess, Helen, I have to insist you keep what we've told you to yourselves. Please ask this person to leave."

David spun around and faced her. "There is no way on God's earth I will leave this house until I find out why my friends and parishioners called me." He sat down at the table and grasped Helen's hands. "Do you want to talk to me alone, Helen? Without these people to intimidate you?"

"No, it's nothing like that." Her grip on David tightened. "It's just..."

When she didn't finish, David glanced at Jess.

"Dr. Cromwell," Alisha warned. "Please, don't say anymore."

Jess looked to Dorian with pleading eyes. Dorian said, "Alisha, we've shocked Helen and Luke, too. From what Jess has told me, this man's job is to help with problems. Maybe he can make everybody feel better. Helen's been leaking tears since she came out here."

"Pregnancy makes women of this time period emotional." Alisha made the statement matter-of-factly.

Helen's head snapped up. "What did you say?"

Silence in the room.

Dorian cleared her throat. "We think maybe you're pregnant, Helen."

Horror suffused Helen's face. "Pregnant? I don't get pregnant. I can't. We tried for years." Now she started to sob. "How could you say this so carelessly? Do you have any idea what it's like to not be able to have a child?"

"Yes," Dorian said gravely, "we do."

"You *could* be pregnant now, honey." Jess leaned in close. "Or you will be soon. I saw it on their computer thing. We have a daughter in the future."

Helen wept even more.

The minister just watched them all, taking in the scene. But he didn't say anything, and Dorian admired his restraint.

"This is too much for her to digest," Jess said angrily.

"I know." Dorian gave a little shrug. "I seek your forgiveness."

Finally, the minister spoke. "What's going on? Please, tell me. As a minister, I'm good in crisis situations. And if it's a matter of confidentiality, I'm bound by my position not to reveal anything."

Alisha said, "No," just as Dorian spoke, "All right." She faced her colleague. "What can it hurt?"

"Only about a million things."

Jess straightened. "I'm deciding this. David, these women came from the future to save their world. As crazy as it may seem, because I don't finish my research on fracking safety measures and methane emissions, there are huge ramifications for the coming generations. And I don't finish it because I'm going to be killed by the end of the summer."

Dorian watched the minister's brow furrow. He waited a long time before he spoke. "Hmm," he said, calmly. "What are we going to do about that?"

From the doorway, Dorian heard, "They've got it all figured out."

She turned to see Luke Cromwell had come in from the sunny day, but with thunderclouds on his face.

• • •

"YOU CAME BACK."

Luke was surprised at Dorian's pleased tone. *He* still wanted to strangle her and her buddy there. He wondered where the other one was. Hell, she could have beamed back to wherever the fuck she came from. "Of course I did. I just needed to cool off."

Her expression was confounded, and now he knew why. Yet it was so hard to believe…

Jess said, "I'm glad you're here. We need to work together on saving my life."

"I still can't internalize what you've told us." Luke ran a hand through his hair. "They could be feeding you a bunch of bullshit, Jessie."

"Your crude reference is not appropriate here." Alisha faced down Luke. "We're telling you the truth and your brother's life is at stake."

"Why would we lie about this, Luke?" Dorian asked.

"Who the hell knows? To sabotage Jess's research maybe." He sighed. "But on the unlikely chance that this is true, I'm ready to be convinced."

David sighed. "I believe it's possible."

"Without proof?"

"Yes. But what I meant was I believe it's possible to travel in time. Maybe even change the past. They could be who—from when—they say they are."

Dropping down on a chair, Luke watched Alisha pull out a computer that resembled a BlackBerry.

"Brace yourself for this, Helen," Jess said gently.

The computer screen grew. That was the only word to describe what happened. Luke knew he was agape, but, what the hell?

Alisha talked to the machine. "Call up chips on the theories of time travel."

"Greetings," the woman who appeared on screen said. "My name is Rhea Hart and I'm one of the ten Guardians of the world in 2514. If you're viewing this, Celeste, Dorian and Alisha have arrived in 2014 and are trying to convince you of their mission."

"She looks like the other one, Celeste," Luke said. "Same hair and eye color. Same build."

"She was Celeste's donor." Dorian's tone was matter-of-fact.

"Her what?"

"We'll explain all that later."

Dorian asked, "Should we call Celi to participate in our explanation?"

"All this turmoil has affected her greatly." Alisha shook her head. "Let her sleep."

Rhea continued, "I'm going to give you some theories of time travel that were the basis for our experiments. I'll explain the first with an illustration."

On a flat-topped surface, she laid out several twelve-inch-long threads. They were thick and comingled with each other. "The Institute's research theorizes that time is a continuum, existing all at once." She gestured to the threads. "The first third of these is the past, the middle the present and the rest the future." She marked off each third with her hand. "Given this theory, it's believed that travel among all three dimensions is possible."

No one spoke.

"There are two distinct theories on traveling to the past. The most accepted one, and the one we've based our calculations on, is that it's possible to backtrack into the past"—again she placed her finger on the last third of the threads and drew an imaginary arc in the air to the first—"and change only one thread." She plucked out a silvery strand as an example. "The future will be altered for this particular aspect of society." She gestured to what was left on the table. "These threads remain the same."

"That makes sense." This from David, the pastor.

"So if we go back to change one thing in the past, the future will be altered but not the entire future. Other threads, as I said, would remain intact."

Again, silence

"But, of course, there's the opposite theory of time travel—that the threads of time are weaved too tightly and no change can be brought about."

Luke raised a brow. "If that's true, you can do nothing if Jess is really in trouble."

Alisha froze the chip. "The computeller predicts a ninety-nine point one percent probability that the past can be changed." Her tone was hopeful. When Luke nodded, she started the video.

The explanation began again. "There's a final point that needs to be made. Some researchers contend there are paradoxes in time travel. One purports that if a person of the future goes back to change the past, and succeeds, he or she was meant to make the changes all along. That's called the fatalist theory."

Alisha stopped the chip again. "Any questions?" she asked.

"Uh, yeah! But keep going." Luke's tone remained skeptical.

The recording began once more. "The computeller pinpoints the location of a portal. Picture it as a small break in the threads of time. This was part of the Institute's discovery yearlings ago. Once again, video chips and some of the speculative fiction of your century show openings like this in time."

The presentation ended and a collective silence settled over the room.

Alisha spoke again. "There's more." To the computer, she said, "Call up data used to show what happened originally."

"Affirmative."

The machine spun into a remarkable tale. Luke was prepared not to believe. But holy hell, if this was a hoax, it was pretty damn good. He gasped at one of the pictures. It was of him, holding…Lord, holding Jess and Helen's daughter, Jessica. A beautiful baby in a tiny pink dress. Then it hit him. Jess was not in the picture with Helen and him.

Jess was dead?

He glanced at his brother, and his hardened policeman's heart stuttered in his chest. He and Helen were both crying openly as they stared at the screen. Helen reached out and touched the face of the child she thought she'd never have.

Was it possible to believe in miracles?

Shaking off the sentiment, he focused on Dorian. He couldn't risk Jess's death under any circumstances. He'd work with the devil to prevent it. Besides, this explanation put together some pieces of the puzzle that was Dorian Masters. "It makes sense now. Your distaste of our food. Your misuse of words and unfamiliarity of little things."

"Believe me, *hotshot?*"

She'd learned another new word.

David said, "Can I ask something?"

Alisha nodded.

"What happened with religion in the future?"

"History chips show that in the twenty-second century, people began building the Domes before the pollution they knew was coming became untenable. Just as they finished, a cyber war broke out among a myriad of countries, and chemical weapons were released into the air and spread throughout the world. Sixty-nine percent of the population was destroyed. The Domes saved civilization, but all people were confined inside. Later that century, a fertility factor threatened the population. Though endangerment of our very existence caused the world to unite by 2300, it also erased hope. And faith."

"Your language?" Luke asked. "You use the word Nord."

"A negation of your concept Lord."

"The godheads?"

"Reducing your god to a figurehead."

"Hellor?" Luke asked. Dorian had slipped and used it in front of him.

The women looked at each other. Alisha shrugged. "I have no idea."

"That is so sad." David's expression made even Alisha squirm. "All of it was lost?"

"I seek your forgiveness, yes."

He was thoughtful. "So, you say if you keep Jess alive, the future will change?"

"Not necessarily. There's another factor we must address in conjunction with this one."

"The other one's working on it—Celeste, right?" Luke asked.

"Yes. She has a different mission."

"Does it have to do with the fertility problem you mentioned?"

Alisha's face grew stern. "We're not discussing this. Suffice it to say, we've narrowed down the end of the human race to two causes. One is climate change. There's another, and yes, it has to do with fertility. But that's all I'll say." She glared at Dorian. "All any of us will say."

"You expect me to just accept part of the story and not get all the information?" Luke's anger increased.

Dorian seemed uneasy.

Alisha didn't. She said, "In fact, we're going to have to insist."

CHAPTER 7

SITTING IN THE huge sleeping room, awash with green-and-blue walls and accents, the sleeping bed plump and fluffy, Celeste stared at the likeness of Alex Lansing on the computeller. He was very appealing. His hair was the color of wheat fields she'd seen in the Ancient Galleries. His eyes were as blue as the water bodies in this era, which she'd viewed in preparation for coming here and hoped one day to visit in person. But it was the younglings that mostly affected her. She'd encountered some real live ones when she walked out of inside, but she wasn't able to examine them. The Lansing younglings were all fair-haired, blue-eyed and beautiful.

She thought back to the *Star Trek* chips she'd watched after Alisha remarked on the resemblance of Alex Lansing to James T. Kirk. Dr. Lansing was taller and with lighter eyes, but the resemblance was remarkable. And they had the same...magnetism. She'd enjoyed watching the predictions in the show that had come true—the unification of the world, though it didn't seem theirs came out of desperation. Equality of men and women. Friendship among men. Alien species. Often Celeste had wondered if other worlds did exist. Earth's society was never able to pursue contact with extraterrestrials because people were too busy securing their own survival.

She looked up. Someone was at the door. A gentle knock followed the precognition. "Come inside," she called, setting the device on the night table.

Helen entered. Red-rimmed eyes testified to water leakage—tears, she must remember to call them. Even from across the sleeping space, Celeste could feel the woman's acute pain. Her posture, petite to begin with, seemed shrunken under the weight of what she carried—a serving tray with containers, which she set down on the high thing called a dresser. "Hello, Helen. Did you want to talk to me?"

Crossing her arms over her chest, Helen shook back all that hair. Would Celeste's grow that long? In her time, everyone kept theirs short, but here, people seemed more concerned about appearances, and long locks were considered appealing.

Helen said, "Maybe. Mostly, I wanted to get away from the powwow going on up there." She angled her head toward the stairs.

Native Americans had come to the Cromwell's home? Celeste's expression must have betrayed her confusion because Helen continued, "Jess, David and Luke are in heated discussions with Dorian and Alisha, and I couldn't take it anymore."

"David?"

"My pastor. That's um, a person who heads our church."

"We have no church in our time."

"I feel bad for you. No God, no religion is almost impossible to take in. Everything about your situation is."

For a moment, Celeste studied her. "You're exhausted. Sit down." She indicated a place next to her.

Helen sank onto the chair without wincing at its hardness. "I am tired. And upset."

"I can feel it." She wanted to help this woman. "Give me your hand."

"Why?"

"I can alleviate some of your fatigue and anxiety."

"How?"

"I take it on myself."

"I don't understand."

"I'm a sensitive, which means I not only feel people's emotions, but in certain circumstances, I can drain them of some of it. I can also block the transfer if I want, but I'd like to help you."

"Amazing. But no. You're already pale. You've had to rest all day."

Celeste put her palm on her stomach. "I've been eating your sustenance. I believe I've overindulged. But I feel much better now."

"I came in here to see if *I* could help *you*. I brought some tea." She gestured to the tray.

Celeste struggled to place *tea*. A beverage. Made from leaves. "Would I like it?"

"Hmm. With some honey. It calms an upset stomach, and the soul, I think. Truthfully, I could use a cup." She rose without waiting for a response, poured some liquid and something else, must be this honey, into cups and brought one to Celeste.

She sipped and her eyes widened. "It's wonderful. Sweet." A frown. "Are you sure this is good for me?"

"Yes."

After Helen ingested some of the tea, her state of anxiety decreased.

"So, they've told you everything, Helen?"

She nodded. "I still can't believe Jess lied to me."

"He thought it best."

"It wasn't."

"I seek your forgiveness." Helen looked puzzled. "Oh. Your wording is *I'm sorry*. He didn't think you should know he was going to be harmed."

"Killed."

"That's the term you use."

"Do you honestly think he would die without your intervention, Celeste?"

"Of course. That's why we traveled to your time."

"I'm glad his research would—will—change the world, but all of what you say sounds like fantasy."

Celeste drank more of the lovely brew. "There's good news, Helen. We can stop it."

"You can't be sure."

"The computeller predicts a ninety-nine point one percent probability that we can."

"God, I hope so. But what if we're in the nine tenths of a percent? Somebody has to be."

"Then our world will end. And your life will change irrevocably."

Helen shook herself. "No, I'm going to believe Jess will live."

"As do I."

"They said you've come to do something else, too. That you're not even sure it's Jess's work that causes changes in the future."

She glanced at the computeller where Alex Lansing's face beamed out at them. "I'm unable to discuss that with you."

"That's what the others said."

Contrary to the men of this time, Helen seemed able to accept their reluctance to reveal the next task. Gesturing to the computeller, she said, "That thing's amazing."

Celeste tried to nudge the machine away so Helen couldn't view the screen. In doing so, she disrupted her teacup and splashed the liquid down the front of her shirt. "Oh, my."

"Tea stains," Helen quipped, stood abruptly and hurried into the bathing room. She returned with a cloth. Before Celeste realized her intent, Helen had removed the cup from her hand and began to blot the liquid from Celeste's chest.

It was like being hit with a blast from a sand storm in the future where all the noxious, unstable elements out of inside spun together and shook the Domes. Emotions exploded inside Celeste. Helen felt so deeply, as deeply as other sensitives in Celeste's time. Her fear, pain, anger, and abject sadness filled Celeste's heart. But…there was something else. Something so small she might have missed it. She focused on it and oh, by the godheads!

Helen was talking, but Celeste was not listening. She concentrated on the tiny sound that grew louder and louder. A feeling of pure joy superseded the negative emotions coming at her from Helen.

"Are you taken aback, Celeste?" She held up the cloth. "Was this too intimate for you? Don't women touch each other in your time?"

"It isn't that." She grabbed Helen's hand.

"Oh, no, please, don't take on my pain."

"I'm not. There's something else."

Helen cocked her head in confusion. "What now?"

Celeste said, "Helen, you're carrying a child in your womb."

Literally jumping back, Helen covered her stomach with her hands and burst into water leakage.

"I don't understand." Celeste was bereft. "You thought you were unable to conceive. This should make you happy."

"No, no, I'm not happy. Don't you see? If I'm pregnant already, Jess could be killed any time. I was hoping...if you're right, conception would be further away. Now I know I could lose my husband any minute."

• • •

DORIAN SAT AT the eating table watching Luke and Alisha discuss the situation. They'd been arguing since Helen left to lie down. Jess hadn't said much and Pastor David listened intently to everyone, but Luke was brimming with anger. He'd pounded his fist on the table, kicked a chair when he'd stood, and...Nord, what was wrong with these people?...gone to a cabinet and pulled out a bottle of amber liquid. Alcohol. They drank substances that would make them feel differently! Whenever Luke took a sip, it seemed to make him even angrier.

David spoke. "Luke, they're not going to reveal their other task. Can you table your frustration over it so we can hear more about Jess's situation? Maybe let them make plans for protecting him."

Luke's dark eyes narrowed on Alisha. "She's the stickler. Dorian would tell us."

"I would not." She didn't often lie, she *would* tell them, because she couldn't see the harm except for the contract they'd made with the Guardians. But Alisha would be angry with her.

"You're a lot easier to get along with than she is." This from Luke—begrudgingly.

David said, "That's enough!" Up to now, the mild-mannered minister had been calm and sensible. So everyone quieted at his sharply uttered words. "Jess's safety is paramount here. Not your egos."

"I have no ego." This from Alisha who, despite her declaration, wouldn't know how to take orders from men.

Luke snapped, "Of course you do. I highly doubt people have changed that much in your time."

"We put the welfare of society above our own...preferences. That's how the world united."

David smiled broadly. "Now, that's good news."

Dorian watched Luke. He ran a hand through his hair and took a deep breath. He could benefit from some therapeutic massage and pulse-point calming. She knew how to do both and, for a moment, longed to ease his anxiety.

He surprised her, though, when he began to calm himself. His hand fisted as if he was trying to contain his emotion. "David's right. I'm being obstinate. I—" He glanced behind Dorian to see his sister-in-law and Celeste. "Helen? Are you all right?"

Helen nodded.

His eyes narrowed on her. "You seem more upset than when you went to take a nap."

Jess rose from his chair and crossed to his mate. "Honey, what is it? Did Celeste upset you? She's a sensitive and—"

"I did upset her."

"I've only know you a few weeks, Celeste, but you wouldn't hurt a fly." At least Jess could control his temper.

"Why would I...? Never mind. We have some news."

"Oh, Nord, not more revelations." This from Alisha. "Megadamn you, Celi."

"Mega what?" This from David.

"Helen touched me, Lisha. That's all."

"Why didn't you take away her fear?"

"She resisted that. But I experienced something else." She placed her hand on Helen's shoulder. "Tell Jess, Helen."

Helen's lips trembled. "I..." She closed her eyes. "I'm pregnant."

Dorian froze. Alisha's mouth dropped open. Celeste's eyes filled with moisture.

Jess hugged Helen, kissed her head and began to cry.

"Oh, this is just great." Luke's tone was frustrated. "You're all going to fall apart now."

Angered, Dorian whirled on Luke. "You have no idea how monumental this is to us. We have never heard anyone utter those words before. Pregnancy within the womb doesn't happen in our time. It's like an urban legend to us."

Luke didn't cower. His body language became more hostile. "Yeah, well, all this announcement means to me is Jess is one step closer to his date with death."

Everybody stilled. And Helen fainted.

• • •

LATER THAT NIGHT, still chagrined at his behavior—these women drove him crazy and brought out an ugly side of him—Luke walked onto the racquetball court with his brother. "I'm sorry I scared Helen into a faint." Stopping to shed his light overshirt, he was again filled with so many emotions he couldn't think straight. Which is why he'd asked Jess to come with him to the gym to let off some steam. He glanced up above, where Dorian sat with Alisha. They'd have no idea what the phrase meant. At least it all made sense now.

"Luke, I know you're upset by what's happened." Jess managed a kind tone and benevolent expression. "But truthfully, I'm so damn psyched about the baby, about Helen finally getting her dream, that I'm not even mad at you."

"You could use some of my anger, Jess. After what you've found out from the Sisters of Doom." The notion struck Luke to the core—he could lose his brother.

Jess chuckled. "Don't let Alisha hear you call them that." He lifted the hem of his long-sleeved shirt and pulled it over his head. "I'm thinking about the future in a different way. That I'm going to have a daughter. Uncle Luke," he laughed.

Trying not to douse his brother's good mood, Luke gave him a more genuine smile than he'd managed lately. "It *is* cool." He picked up his racquet. "Ready?"

"Yeah, though you'll kill me. As usual. I don't even care."

"You're getting better at the game."

Still, Luke took it easy on his first serve, sending the ball below the blue line, but not too hard. Jess got the return shot and hit it into the corner. It bounced back over Luke's head. He ran toward the back of the court, nabbed the ball with the end of his racquet, and it spiraled through the air. Before he turned to see where the shot landed, he got another glimpse of the women. Alisha was working on her computer thingy, but Dorian was leaning over the railing—looking as though she'd never seen a game before. Which she probably hadn't. He'd have to ask her about sports in her time. Jeez, he hoped they still had some. If not, what would men do? What would they talk to each other about?

"My point."

Luke pivoted.

"I got the ball back. While you were checking out the Sisters of Doom." Again, he chuckled on the reiteration of Luke's term.

Luke got back in the game and tried to continue the easy play. But the competitor in him took over, and after winning a set and serving again, he sliced a tough-to-reach shot into the wall, which ricocheted back. Jess dove for it and slid across the floor.

"Ow…" Jess grabbed hold of his leg.

"Jesus." Luke flew to him. "Are you all right?"

"Twisted my ankle."

"Sorry."

"It's not your fault."

Luke didn't understand how noncompetitive his brother was. "We'll have to quit, though."

The door to the court flung open, and in rushed Dorian, carrying some kind of device. "Is he hurt?" She seemed honestly worried.

"Twisted ankle."

She scanned the enclosed space. "I didn't think anyone could get in here. But…" She sent a troubled gaze to Luke. Suddenly, her sass was gone.

"He's okay, Dorian." Luke reached out and touched her. She stared at his hand on her arm as if…as if a man didn't do that so casually in her time. Didn't touch a woman to comfort her. But how could that be? He nodded to the device. "What's that?"

"My weapon."

The thing was metal, sleek and had a trigger-like mechanism. "A gun?"

"No. We call it a peacekeeper. It incapacitates a miscreant."

Fascinated, he asked, "Can I see it?"

Alisha entered the court, precluding her answer. From her bag, she pulled out another device and knelt down next to Jess, who was still stretched out on the floor. She said, "Let me see your injury." She felt his leg, his ankle. "Some tendons are over-stretched. And swelling. She settled the device close to his skin, switched it on and ran it over his lower-leg area. A low hum emitted from it.

"What the fuck?" Jess rarely swore, so Luke took note.

He asked, "What happened?"

"The pain's gone."

"And the swelling," Alisha pronounced.

"What *is* that thing?" Luke wanted to know.

"It's a mini-Multimed."

Luke shook his head.

"It's a medical device from the future," Dorian explained. Among other things, it calms injured muscles and tendons. I don't know exactly how it works. The best minds in the future have collaborated together for centuries to make technological advances like this. There are larger Multimeds at medical centers, but we brought the miniature version."

"Man, you could make a fortune on that in our time."

Alisha pulled Jess up by the hand. "Feel better?"

"Yep." He shook his head. "I could get used to having that around."

Luke caught sight of Dorian. She'd picked up the racquet and swung it back and forth. She'd snagged the ball with her other hand and now squeezed it. Then she looked up at him. "Can I play?"

Just what he needed. "You don't know how."

"I perused your Internet on the drive over to the gymnasium. I have the basics down." She held out her foot. "I even wore these sneaker shoes."

His eyes narrowed on her. "Maybe you're sandbagging me. Maybe you've played in your time."

"I have no desire to build sacks of sand around you."

He burst out laughing.

She didn't look amused. "Oh, it's another idiom." She held up the racquet. "Well?"

Alisha started to say something, but Dorian sent her a pleading look. "I want to, Lisha. Please. It won't hurt anything and you can watch Jess for a few minutes."

"All right. It'll be nice to see you beat the pants off of him."

Dorian just shook her head.

Without even limping, Jess left the court with Alisha, and Luke took up his position; Dorian knew right where to go. She also knew how to serve the ball, return what should have been an ace from him and lunge for the little blue sphere. Finally, she missed.

Her brow furrowed. "I miscalculated the angle of impact on that. I was off three degrees."

Luke rolled his eyes. He glanced up to see Alisha and Jess studying the multi-mini or whatever the hell she called the healing device.

"Want to keep going? They look okay up there."

But Dorian didn't answer. Her eyes had widened and her jaw went slack. First, she ran her hands over her face. Then down her arms. She felt her armpits. But when she started at her thigh—they'd all worn shorts in the warm April night—and slid those fingers over her flank and knee, Luke almost swallowed his tongue. Was she trying to seduce him? "What are you doing?" he asked harshly.

Finally, she looked up. Raising her fingers, she slid them together. "I am leaking water and not from my eyes."

"You're sweating." At her blank look, he said, "Perspiring from the exercise."

"I know what it is," she said, so damn serious he bit back any retort he might have made. "I've run out of inside but haven't experienced more than a dampening of my skin."

"You don't sweat in the future? You said you're in top physical shape. So, you must exercise."

"On the exertrac and in jutzi classes. But our air is controlled and we don't do this sweating thing."

"Don't you play sports?"

"We have no sports in our time. We don't foster competition. It's bad for people." Then she looked up at him, her face alight, and very pretty. "But it feels very good to sweat."

"Maybe there's hope for you yet, doll." And he couldn't help but smile.

CHAPTER 8

THINGS HAD SETTLED down by the Sunday after the news broke about Alisha, Dorian and Celeste's mission. Jess and Helen insisted they attend church services, and Dorian had gone along to watch over Jess. Celeste accompanied them because she wanted to experience a religious ritual.

To insure Jess's safety, David, who was a combat chaplain in Afghanistan, had enlisted the help of two former Marines in his congregation, and stationed them at the doors, greeting members and checking for new faces. He'd told them he'd heard there might be some violence against his church. It rang true because not long ago the building had been hit by some vandalism.

Luke and Alisha had stayed back at Jess's house to work on tracking down the threat that came in the emails from watchingoutforyou@xmail.com. They still didn't know if the sender was trying to stop Jess's research by making vague threats, and meant no harm, or if his intentions were malevolent.

At the other end of the dining-room table, Alisha ran programs on her fancy computeller. Luke had asked a buddy in the Secret Service for help analyzing the threats. The agent had put their request through their threat-assessment computers, and her reply came back just after the others left for church.

"Luke,

The team's computers have analyzed the emails your brother received. There's a high probability that these are benign missives, meant to keep him safe, not to threaten him. Basically, there are two reasons why:

1. The wording is intentionally vague. Most hostile notes threaten directly.
2. The phraseology isn't that of a psycho killer. Our best deduction is that this is from a female and she does not want to do him harm.

Don't forget, babe, you owe me for this. Any trips to DC planned? I'm here. Waiting.

Lissie"

"Holy shit!" he said from where he worked at Jess's desk.

Alisha swiveled around in her chair. "That is the craziest expletive." She shook her head. "Tell me what news you received from your government."

He printed off the email and handed her a copy.

She read it quickly. "This is interesting. I'm honing in on where the emails were sent from, and they do not appear to come from a corporation, which would make the most sense. I've narrowed the sender down to a region outside New York."

"Region?"

"You call it a suburb." Her dark brows knitted. "You would be more likely to find an amateur on the outer limits of a city, but I don't understand why that would indicate a female."

"I—"

She interrupted him. "Lissie is an odd name. And her use of *babe* for you is foreign to me. When said as slang from one person to another, it describes someone who is attractive."

For a moment, he pictured Lissie's toned body, red hair and blue eyes the last time he was in bed with her. "Babe is also a term of endearment."

"We don't have those in our time."

"What do you call a…mate or lover?"

"By his or her first name. I don't fully comprehend identifying him by anything else."

Taking a bead on her, he realized she was attractive. Her hair was light brown and her eyes almost the exact same color. He mocked himself. He'd been too…absorbed in Dorian's gorgeous body and the innate sexuality she emanated to notice the others as women. "It's been a whirlwind of confusion for twelve days. I haven't had time to find out much about your society, except that you live in Domes and have a problem with fertility. And the religion thing."

"I will be glad to explain our social systems and government when we're done here. But perhaps we can find the origin of these emails if we align our brains."

"Excuse me?"

"Work to combine our opinions."

He burst out laughing. He couldn't help it if their misuse of sayings amused him. "Put our heads together, Alisha."

Now her eyes sparked fire and turned almost amber. "Whatever."

He slid his chair over next to hers and said, "Let's see what kind of *region* we're looking at."

• • •

DORIAN SAT BESIDE Jess, who was settled close to Helen. Celeste was at the end of the wooden seat called a pew. The whole church was foreign to Dorian, yet in some ways appealing. She bet Celeste was reveling in the scents of candles, the colorful windows, the strange musicals. Also, the warmth emanating from the attendees, called a congregation, reminded Dorian of the groups of friends she had back in her time.

The man they knew as David—a man of religion, a close friend to Helen and Jess and a very astute thinker—stood up at the pulpit, dressed in a black robe. Interestingly in her time, people called their speaker platforms pulps, which must be a derivative of this term. Off to his right was a woman dressed in a white robe. David had introduced her as his assistant pastor, Lee Ann, before the ceremony began.

"Good morning. Welcome to Community Christian Church." David glanced toward the four of them. "Especially to those of you who've come from far away. Since today is Earth Day, we've organized our service around taking care of the world God has given to us."

Dorian's mouth fell open. Jess leaned over. "He didn't plan this service because of you three. I know because I worked with him on the energy angles before you arrived."

"Amazing."

David continued, "First, I'd like June Ayers to come up and talk about the environmental fair we're having after church."

A young woman with bouncy, reddish hair, wearing a shirt that said, Be Kind to Your Mother, with the sphere that was representative of their planet, strode down the aisle. She told the group about displays in the fellowship hall that detailed what they could do to save energy and prevent pollution. Congregants could peruse each table during the coffee hour—a gathering time where they consumed caffeine—after the service.

Opening statements—they called them prayers—were led by David. Now, that was a concept Dorian could *not* internalize.

Contacting their supreme being through thoughts helped the thinker? How odd.

Next, David sat on the red rug as the younglings approached. Dorian would never get used to seeing them. They were in all shapes and sizes, different in skin, hair and eye color, babbling loudly. Her heart ached for her society's loss of them. And made her more determined to see hers and Celeste's tasks through.

"How many of you know what recycling is?" David asked as the younglings gathered around him.

One raised a hand and blurted out, "The blue box."

Dorian didn't understand the laughter that followed. No one joked about the climate in her time.

Grinning, David said, "We put stuff in the blue box, but why do we do that?"

A little blond girl stood up. "To make it into something else."

David spoke at length of recycling, letter writing to the city government to stop the carbon emissions that came out of their vehicles and why all that caused the polar ice caps to melt. After he finished, the assistant pastor led the entire group in singing "For the Beauty of the Earth." Its words were meaningful, and Dorian wished like hellor they'd been heeded.

When the service ended, people began to leave the main part—the sanctuary—of the church. Celeste, pale and shaky, dropped back down on the pew. Dorian moved close to her.

"Are you all right?" she asked her friend.

"No." She grabbed Dorian's hand. Celeste's was ice cold and trembling. "They *knew*, Dorian. They *knew* what they were doing to this planet. Why didn't they stop while they could?"

"People like David *were* trying to stop it, Celi. They ran up against corporate greed."

"Ironic. We have no use for individual currency or corporations in our time. What we value is what they're squandering away."

"You, Alisha and I are here to see if we can change that."

"I'm even more committed to our mission now."

"So am I."

They exited the pew and reached the back of the church, where David greeted his congregants. It was then that Dorian noticed the Marines who had been guarding the door. Though they had no armed forces in her time, she understood that their job was to keep people safe, but instead, they had to fight in conflicts other people started. It made her simultaneously admire them and shake her head at this convoluted government.

One of the men walked close beside Jess. Suddenly, Dorian was flooded by fear. How much did David know about him? What if he was planning to harm Jess? Quickly, she sidled herself between the two of them.

The Marine frowned. "What's the matter, lady?"

She raised her chin. Men did not intimidate women of her time. "I've something to discuss with my cousin," she said in response and led Jess and Helen away.

"What's that all about?" Jess asked. "We wanted to go to the coffee hour."

"Precaution. The two Marines have not been vetted." But she would get their names from David before they left and run a search on them.

Meanwhile, she was stickling like gluz to Jess.

• • •

"WE HAVE NEWS," Dorian announced when the four of them arrived at the Cromwells' after church.

Luke noted that her cheeks were rosy and her eyes sparkled like emeralds. She was excited, which did nothing to calm his libido. Ever since they'd wrestled on the floor and he'd watched her play racquetball, he'd been having X-rated thoughts about her.

"We also have information." This from Alisha, who crossed directly to Celeste. "Are you all right, Celi? You seem upset."

"I became agitated in the church, but we can discuss why later. Dorian's found a lead, I think they call it."

Dorian held up her small computer. "I checked the background of two of David's congregants that he, with all good intentions, asked to stand guard at the church doors. Rick Carson is in private security but he began his career in a contract with a local oil company. Petron."

Alisha added, "Which would mean the threats could be coming from them."

"Not necessarily." This from Luke. "First off, thousands of people in New York have worked for Petron because their headquarters is in the city. But more so, my Secret Service friend says otherwise." He filled them in on what Lissie had found. "After reading her notes from the threat assessment team, we're pretty sure the emails came from a woman."

Dorian cocked her head. "Perhaps. But I'm going to do some more shoveling."

"Digging, Dorian," Alisha corrected.

She shrugged. "What do you have?"

Again, Luke gave them the same rundown he'd provided Alisha. "And," he finished "We've narrowed the IP address to a little town in Connecticut."

"One of our regions," Alisha explained. "It's called Dunbar."

"I'm trying to get a fix on exactly where in the town the emails came from by running my information through more police databases. We should have the answer in about an hour."

"I'm going to put out some food," Helen announced. "I invited David over for lunch and I'm starved."

"You're eating for two now, love." Jess grinned. "I can't wait for the doctor's appointment this week."

All three women—Luke was becoming partial to the Sisters of Doom tag—transferred their gaze to Helen's stomach; each of their expressions revealed intense longing. For the first time, Luke felt bad for *them*.

CHAPTER 9

"PASS THE MACARONI salad." This from Helen, who'd already heaped her plate with animal products and green vegetables.

Dorian's senses had become accustomed to the smell of their food, and truthfully—especially after tasting the popped corn at the theater—she wanted to experience more of those exotic flavors and textures.

Luke shot her a grin. It was as if he could read her mind sometimes, which elevated the level of her anxiety. He lifted the bowl Helen passed to him. "Have a taste of the macaroni salad."

"I want to, even though I had difficulty with the pasta my first night here."

"You've had more time to acclimate," Celeste put in. She'd taken a tiny amount of each dish.

"I don't think you two eating all that"—Alisha gestured to the sustenance—"is a good idea."

Surreptitiously, Dorian noted there was no food of this time on Lisha's plate, though she'd taken some tea that had been iced.

Luke caught Dorian's gaze and handed the salad directly to her. "Live a little," he said, and as with almost anything, his tone was challenging.

She watched him. God, those eyes were so appealing. Dark and liquid looking.

Alisha elbowed her, then said, probably to bait him, too, "So, Luke, you wanted to know about the social customs of our time."

"You betcha."

Having arrived just in time for the meal, David nodded. "I do, too. I'm still bummed by the absence of religion."

Alisha scoffed. "I don't see what good it does except to give people false hope."

A benevolent smile came from David. "It's good to know you have God on your side."

"If you believe god exists."

Luke intervened. "I'd like to know about the dating and mating rituals."

Oh, no, Dorian would not discuss *that* with him. Her attraction to him was increasing daily, and talking about men and women joining would exacerbate that.

"Isn't it indelicate to talk about those things with men and women in the same room?" Celeste asked.

Luke scanned the group. "Anyone object?"

Jess, whose arm was draped around Helen's chair, shook his head, the expression in his eyes mischievous. "Not me. Dorian, you told me you don't date when you asked about Luke's situation."

Now Luke winked at her. "You wanted to know about my love life, babe?"

Dorian knew he was trying to upset her. "I used you as an example of how someone copes with his sexual urges without a spouse."

"I do just fine."

David asked, "You don't *date* in your time?"

"No," Alisha said matter-of-factly. "We spend our free time with those of the same sex if we are attracted to the opposite one."

Celeste put in, "And if someone is monosexual, she actually befriends those she joins with. Most people, I hear, are satisfied with that, but I don't understand it."

"So," Dorian added, "We don't *socialize,* as you call it, with men."

"No wonder we can't get along." Luke's sarcasm made everyone laugh. Except Dorian. They'd get along well in bed, she knew.

David was wide-eyed. "Let me get this straight. You don't socialize with prospective spouses or partners. How do you meet someone you might want to marry?"

"There is no marriage in our time."

His fork clattered to the plate. "Seriously?"

Alisha seemed puzzled. "Earnestly. I do not joke."

"None of you do." Luke again. "That's obvious."

"I jest," Celeste put in. "I'm known to have a...what do you call it, Lisha?"

"A sense of humor. Most sensitives do."

Helen smiled at Celeste. Dorian could tell the two women had taken a liking to each other, which was perfectly normal.

"In any case," Luke continued, "what *do* you do for physical companionship."

Enough! Dorian spoke up because she wanted to put the infuriating man in his place. "We have a SexLine. When we are in need of joining, we go on to the computeller, find a person in our geographical area who is also in need and meet in one of the structures created for the contact. Here you call them hotels."

Luke, who'd taken a swig of his beer, spit it out all over his plate. After he mopped up, he stared at her agape. "You sell yourself online and meet at a brothel?"

Alisha's eyes widened. "We do *not* sell ourselves. And I have no idea what a brothel is. We simply...hook up at a convenient spot. Think of it as an extended version of your online dating."

David shook his head at this revelation. "Isn't it…hollow to have sex with someone you don't know?"

"We achieve sexual release." Dorian turned a hot gaze to Luke. "Several times."

He looked as if he might choke again. "A modern man's fantasy."

"Not mine." Jess tugged Helen to him. "I can't imagine it. Helen and I are so close."

"Women are close to women. There's a deep love bond between them. Men feel the same about men. We garner emotional support that way." Celeste looked to Jess. "Much like you and Luke."

"Still," David mused. "That's so foreign to me. I believe sex should be an emotional connection as well as a physical one."

Alisha snorted. "By the godheads, wouldn't that be messy?"

Luke chuckled when he looked at his brother. "I'm not touching that one with a twenty-foot pole."

Rolling her eyes, Helen changed the subject. "So, when you could have children, how were babies born?"

"In my generation, it's rare," Celeste explained. "But in my donor's time, children were conceived in producеries. A man's genetic material was combined with a female's, and the fetus was conceived. The child was nurtured and grew in a large container similar to your incubator. When the fetuses were viable, they stayed at the producerie for a few years, then went to live with their donor until they became adults. But basically, raising younglings was everyone's responsibility."

"Which donor?" David asked.

"A male child lived with a man. A female child lived with her female donor." Celeste smiled. "I love my donor, Rhea. And I miss her."

Always the minister, David laid his hand over Celeste's. "We sort of met her. On the video she sent to convince us that you're telling the truth."

"It pains me to watch it. I'm glad I was sleeping."

Helen, who'd shoveled food into her mouth continuously, pushed her chair away from the table. "No wonder you want to change the future." She put her hand on her stomach. "I'm tired now. I'd like to lie down."

Jess stood, too. "I'll come with you. Luke, would you clean up the meal?"

"Sure. Go rest."

David asked, "Alisha, can we discuss religion—or the lack of it—a bit more?"

"Of course. Let's go for a walking."

Celeste added, "May I accompany you?" She faced Luke. "Unless you want me to assist you. I love putting my hands in water."

"No, Dorian can help."

"I—"

"Come on, see what it's like to socialize with a man. We're not so bad."

"That's debatable. But I will help."

He gave her a sly smile. "You can tell me more about this joining."

She felt her face heat. Because, as he teased her, the feelings of need came back even stronger than before. She swallowed hard, hoping to ease the desire that slammed into her.

• • •

"ISN'T THERE A machine to purify those?" Dorian asked the question because Luke, who had rolled up the sleeves of his light blue shirt and tied a drying cloth around his waist, was about to fill the sink with precious water.

"I like to wash the dishes by hand. It reminds me of my mom and dad. They got to be alone in the kitchen every night this way."

"Are your donors still alive?"

"No. They died within six months of each other a few years ago."

"I'm sure that was sad."

"It was, but Jess and I had a storybook childhood. That's why he's so well-adjusted."

"What about you?"

"The jury's still out."

Instead of asking him to explain the idiom, Dorian stared at the water, which gushed out of the faucet when he turned it on. "You had so much, but you squandered it away."

Immediately, he sobered. Some things you just didn't joke about. "I know. I'm sorry. It must be hard for you to see what we do to the environment."

"It is."

"Maybe you'll change the results?"

"I hope so." She leaned against the counter. "So, you believe me now?"

"There doesn't seem to be any other explanation." He thought of Jess. "And I'd do anything for my brother, even go along with this bizarre idea."

"I feel the same about Lisha and Celi."

"See, sweetheart, we're not so different."

"You're wrong. We fight like katas and drogs."

Once again, he laughed at her. When she seemed to realize her mistake, she smiled.

"I know you saw the dog that first day we came here. Have you ever seen a cat?"

"Only on the street. He was beautiful."

"Have you ever been to a zoo?"

"Only Zoolawn." She explained the concept as she picked up a towel and began to dry a dish, then placed it in the cupboard.

"I'll take you to the real one sometime."

"Perhaps when Jess is safe, we'll all visit."

He thought of something, stopped washing and faced her. "Won't you return to your time after you go to Virginia?"

She froze, then said solemnly, "The chance of that is minimal, Luke. If we succeed in changing the future, we have no idea of who or what will exist. Our plan is only to fix your society so the future's inhabitants will be able to produce younglings and live out of inside."

"And you have to stay here?"

"That's correct."

His heart turned over in his chest. He had no idea what they were sacrificing. "That is so unselfish, Dorian. I'm sorry you have to give up so much to right our wrongs."

"A small price to pay for the salvation of society."

Despite what she said, Luke admired the altruism of the three women. "What will you do here?"

"I have no idea. None of us have planned that far in advance."

"I think you'd make a good cop."

Her face broke out in a big grin. "Earnestly?"

"Uh-huh."

They began to wash and dry again. His parents really knew what they were doing. He was feeling close to her, and now he felt bad for what they had to give up to come back in time. "Once you stay, what will you do about sex with no SexLine?"

She shook her head. He noticed her hair had gotten longer in the weeks they'd been here. "We've all been wondering about that. We've been without release with a man for weeks now." She closed the cupboard. "It's uncomfortable."

"Well," he said half joking. "If you want, I'll stud for you."

She glanced at him. "*Stud* means?"

"To provide sex."

Her gaze was hot. "I don't believe we'd be compatible."

"That, darlin', is a total lie. I've seen the way you look at me."

"And you at me."

Wash...wash...wash. If he stopped, he was afraid he'd lunge for her. The discussion in the living room had gotten him hard, mostly because he'd been thinking about sex with Dorian. And he'd been *without release* for a long time, too. "At least I admit I'm attracted to you."

"I never said I wasn't attracted to you, even though you have excess body fat, hair that turns white and other unpleasant physical features."

"You really know how to sweet talk a guy, Dorian."

"I don't understand that idiom. But back to the issue. I meant that you probably can't fulfill me."

Luke had taken a plate off the counter and had been about to put it in the sink. It slipped from his hands at her insult and crashed to the floor. She startled. Leaving the dish where it fell, he whipped off the towel and propped his hands on his hips. "That sounds like a challenge to me."

"No, just a statement of fact. I've watched the chips. Even in the *Mission Impossible* film, mates only have release once. Maybe twice."

His mouth gaped. "And you have how many orgasms?"

"We don't use that term. But we peak to climax four or five times in one session."

"Jesus, how long does this joining last?"

"About twelve and a half of your minutes."

She had him there. He'd never come that many times and never brought a woman there every two minutes. But hell, she was looking so smug he had to do something to save his honor.

"What do you do in between? Kiss and pet?"

"I don't know the latter term. And we don't kiss." She touched her fingers to her mouth. "It seems unclean and unnecessary. Genital parts stimulation works the best."

For a minute, he was shocked she was so frank about sex. "Don't you feel shy talking about all this with me?"

"No, I discuss matters of this kind all the time with men when we join." She cocked her head as if she didn't understand. "How else would each of you know what to do to please the other?"

"Intuition."

"You must fumble around a lot. Your mating doesn't sound very efficient."

That was it. His ego couldn't take any more. Stepping over the broken dish, he stalked to her with one thing on his mind. When he got close, she backed up, but eventually, the wall stopped her retreat.

When he reached her, she said, "As before, I did not give you permission to touch me. I know in your world men do that all the time without women's consent, but I will not allow it."

He stopped. Thought about that. "Let me show you how we do things in our time."

"No."

"Why? Scared?"

"I am not afraid of you."

"I didn't mean you were afraid of me. You're afraid of what I can make you feel."

"I am not!"

"So what's the harm? Let's call it a scientific experiment. You seem to love those."

She glanced around the kitchen. "We do not mate in any room but sleeping quarters."

"We won't mate. We'll kiss. And pet."

She held his gaze and he saw her pupils were dilated. "All right, Luke. You can touch me."

• • •

HE HADN'T EVEN put his hands on her, yet her heartbeat escalated because of his nearness. She also felt that odd perspiration under her arms, between her breasts and on her palms. Then Luke lifted his hand and brushed his knuckles lightly down her cheek. Her breathing sped up even more. He whispered, "Keep your hands to yourself for a while. Let me just touch you. Your skin is like velvet. Soft. Sensual."

Dorian had no idea what velvet was, but she understood the tone of the comment. He liked touching her. She liked it, too. Without conscious intent, she leaned into him.

"Tell me what you're feeling," he whispered coaxingly.

She wasn't accustomed to conversation during joining. All talk stopped after expressing what you liked in sex. "Aroused."

"Already?" He glanced at his watch. "I must be doing good on time then."

That he'd joke during something so serious shocked her. But she felt a smile lift up the corners of her mouth. She couldn't hide her feelings, didn't want to. "You're doing this adequately." She closed her eyes when his thumb went to her mouth and rubbed. She opened her lips to taste him. His skin was hard there, a bit salty. Unbelievably male. "Hmm."

"More?" he asked.

"Oh, yes."

His hand traveled to her neck and he caressed her there. *Wonderful*, was all she could think. Then it went lower, to cup her breast. "Luke, that feels so good."

"Surely you must have felt this before."

"I have. But never through clothing. The scrape of material against my nipples is infinitely more exciting."

Leaning in close, he drawled, "I'll remember that for when we get to the real thing."

She couldn't form a sassy retort as he kept up the tender abrasion. *Tender*. Nothing in her world was ever tender between men and women.

His hands left her breasts; she groaned a protest. His fingers threaded in her hair and he massaged her scalp. How on earth could that feel so good?

When his lips grazed her forehead, she startled. He brushed them across her closed eyes. "Oh, by the godheads."

She felt him smile against her cheek. "I think our version is *oh, God*." His mouth went lower. Licked around her lips. Suddenly, she wanted those lips on hers. "Luke, my mouth. Do the kissing thing."

"All right. If you insist." He was still teasing, but she was bursting with need.

He pressed his full mouth against hers. Um...she was vaguely disappointed. Not much to this...oh! He brushed his lips back and forth, back and forth. That felt better. Then his tongue probed them. She was meant to open her lips! What the hellor? But she parted for him, and his tongue darted inside. Immediately, she bucked against him. Never had she felt this erotic sensation. And it continued. His lips still pressed to hers, his tongue explored her. He drew away only for a second and said, "Try it. Put your tongue in my mouth."

He resumed the unfamiliar connection and she eagerly took part. His taste was of alcohol and sweetness. He'd eaten something called a cookie. But then his own taste, his own scent came through, and she was lost in the sensation of him.

Suddenly, his mouth grew more insistent. It seemed as though he was trying to consume her. He tasted, bit (oh, wow!) and devoured. For one of the first times in her life, Dorian experienced helplessness.

And she didn't like it.

But she couldn't stop him.

She didn't have to. Too soon he pulled away. She moaned. "Why did you stop?"

He took her hand rather roughly and pressed it against his jeans.

"Oh, you're ready to join."

"Goddamn right I am." He stepped back. "Let me tell you something, Dorian Masters. For a novice, you knocked my socks off with that kiss. And you didn't even touch me."

"I forgot to."

"I'm glad. I wouldn't be standing if you had."

Again, she smiled.

"So," he said, capturing her gaze as he'd captured her mouth. "Did you like this new thing called kissing?"

"Yes. I want to do it again. Right away."

Before he could answer, the door flew open, and Luke stepped back. In rushed Alisha. She barely glanced at the shattered china on the floor. "Luke, Dorian, come quick. The computer has the information we need."

Dorian straightened and tried to calm herself.

"We have the location of the person sending the emails. It's a female named Kara Krueger."

CHAPTER 10

THE REVELATION OF who was sending the emails to Jess had been disturbing Dorian's slumber for two revolutions, and this evening she'd gone out of inside and dropped down on the seat that swung back and forth on the front porch. But it wasn't just the situation with Jess that had given her insomnia. She was also trying to sort out the emotions that Luke Cromwell had engendered in the kitchen on Sunday. She could still hear his heart beating close to hers, feel his mouth pressing down on her lips, how he cupped her breasts with an intimacy she'd never known. She wanted to do it again. She longed to join with him. And despite her protestations to the contrary, she liked him, which was a problem. She didn't want to like men here. The foreign emotion was too confusing.

Luckily, he'd been assigned a case at work that had taken him out of the region, so she wouldn't have to see him for a few revolutions. She'd have time to let her feelings for him diminish and get back to the woman she was when she'd arrived.

An auto vehicle pulled up in front of the house. From the dim light of the lamp stick rooted in the grass, she could see a man—big and muscular—exit the vehicle. It wasn't Luke, returning early, she could tell by the walk and stance of the intruder. Wary, she felt her body tense in case she had to take action. The stunner she'd brought from the future was in the pocket of her robe.

When he came closer, she recognized Rick Carson, the Marine she'd muscled Jess away from at church. She didn't have time to get into the house and avoid him, so this would mean a confrontation. Eying him, she decided she was in top shape and, despite his girth, could probably take him.

Was he the one who would harm Jess? Their documentation showed Jess had been killed in an auto-vehicle accident. Carson couldn't drive straight through Jess's bedroom because of the greenery on the front lawn. Then she remembered the day of the taxi near miss. She also recalled the conversation after Helen found out where they came from. *Who knows, we could have changed the method of murder just by being here. One of those paradoxes in time.*

Slipping her hand into her pocket, she stood and walked to the top of the steps. "Stay right there. What do you want? It's late."

Stopping, he looked up at her from the sidewalk. "I want to know why you're investigating me."

Megadamn. "How do you know I did that?"

"I'm a security expert. It's what I do."

"Specifically, tell me how you found out."

He stared hard at her. "I have warnings built into the Internet that flag when my name is mentioned. It lets me know when someone is checking up on me, too."

"I didn't know those existed." *In your time.*

"As I said, I'm an expert." His voice softened. "Listen, let me come up. I'm not going to hurt you."

She gripped the stunner. "Of course you won't." He didn't seem angered, and she might be able to find something out about his guilt or innocence. Nothing other than working at Petron came up on either the Internet or the computeller after an extensive search. "All right."

He climbed the steps and leaned against the porch railing, crossed his arms over his chest and his feet over one another. It was not a threatening pose. She stood, too, several feet away from him. He asked, "Again, why are you investigating me?"

What to say? "David Ryan is my friend from a long time ago. I wanted to make sure you were who you say you are, since the church is being threatened."

He arched a blond brow. "So David said. I don't believe him or you."

"It doesn't matter what you believe, Mr. Carson."

"Since you probably know the color underwear I have on, I think you can call me Rick."

With his joking, his face softened and she noted he was handsome, too. She gave a weak smile. "Honestly, I'm making sure the church is secure."

"As Jess's cousin?"

"Well..."

"Try again, Dorian. You don't look like Jess's cousin. You're taller, more fit...and different from most of the women I know. Besides, you own a private security firm."

"So, you investigated me, too?"

"Tit for tat."

For some reason, she knew that idiom. "I'd say that makes us evens."

"Evens?"

"Whatever."

He shifted a bit and she thought of asking him to sit but decided against it. "I did a search on you because you did one on me. Just tell me why and I'll forget about this." She didn't respond. "Is David in trouble?" The words held genuine concern.

"David? No."

He nodded. "Then it's Jess you're protecting."

Drawing in a deep breath, she waited to answer. If she confirmed what he knew, Alisha would be furious. "I've said as much as I'm able."

"David wouldn't tell me anything, either. But I know something's going on."

"Can you just let it go? I swear David and your church are not in danger."

As if assessing her statement, he looked her up and down, probably taking in the short robe, beneath which she wore a skimpy gown. He waited a long time, too, before he said, "Okay, if you have dinner with me."

"What? Why?"

"So I can get to know you better. Make sure you're on the up and up. For David's sake."

"I—"

"It's the only way I'll let this go, Dorian."

Hellor, how had this happened? She'd have to accept. Maybe she could turn the situation to her advantage. Though she didn't doubt her findings, talking to him would deal the seals. "All right. When?"

"Thursday night?"

"Agreed. Where shall I meet you?"

"I'll pick you up."

That couldn't possibly mean…"I don't understand."

He looked at her oddly, then added, "I'll drive here and get you."

"Earnestly? Why?" Maybe it was a custom she didn't know.

"Like for a date."

She remembered Luke's description of the ritual. "This isn't a date."

"Whatever," he mimicked her, squeezed her arm and then headed down the stairs.

By the godheads, what had she gotten herself into?"

• • •

IN UPSTATE NEW York, Luke sat in an unmarked car with Jack Marino, a fellow cop, watching a farmhouse. The sedan's windows were down, and the April air was so clean here, it almost hurt to breathe in. "Go ahead, close your eyes, Marino. We could be here all night."

"Good idea. You catch some zees, too, after I wake up."

"Agreed."

Once Jack fell asleep, Luke's mind hurtled to Dorian and the kiss they'd shared in the kitchen a few revolutions ago.

Man, he shouldn't be thinking about her. He *wouldn't.* He'd think about the case he was on. The NYPD had been asked to do legwork for the RICO Task Force and stake out suspected mob-related connections. Was there one between the man staying in that small structure and a consortium of organized criminals? Luke should be trying to figure this out instead of daydreaming like some lovesick kid.

Or he should be working to solve Jess's case. His captain had asked him about his preoccupation, and Luke was worried Al Patchet would sense his mind wasn't on the job. He hated to let the department down, but hell, he needed to be close to his brother now.

And Dorian.

There she was again. Prowling around in his brain. Jesus, he couldn't believe how aroused he'd gotten from a simple kiss. But it hadn't been simple. Not to her, and consequently, not to him. Knowing she'd never been kissed had been a big turn-on for him, and his pride has surfaced, too. Some guy might be able to *bring her to release* four times in twelve-and-a-half minutes, but Luke had given her something she'd never gotten from anyone. Was that why it affected him, too?

There was movement in the front of the house, so he picked up the binoculars. He nudged Marino. "Jack, wake up. Somebody just came out. We need photos." The specially equipped camera Marino operated would take clear shots at night.

Luke stared harder while Jack got the camera ready. "It's not Curran." The drug dealer.

"Who is it?"

"Marco Genetti. Looks like we got our connection."

• • •

SITTING ON DORIAN'S bed, Helen smiled over at the two-piece, silk outfit she'd helped pick out. She'd told them silk was the best, and it had been made by worms. Hellor, before tonight, Dorian didn't even know what a worm was. But the material was soft, and Celeste said the color went well with her skin tone. At the store, the clerk had called it watermelon. Which Dorian had never eaten, so Helen had stopped at the grocery store and bought one. It was so sweet, it made her eyes mist.

"Turn around so I can see the back," Celi told Dorian. The clothing was formfitting, tight at the breasts and nipping in at the waist. "Hmm. The clothing looks superb on you."

"At least the bottom's pants. They're comfortable."

From across the room, seated at a desk, Alisha turned her head. "And practical. If necessary, you can defend yourself."

"From Rick Carson?" Helen scoffed. "He's a pussycat."

"Repeat, please." Now Dorian was confused. "I thought *pussy* was a crude reference to female genital parts."

Helen laughed out loud. "I'm afraid it is. But we also call cats that."

"Why?" Dorian asked, adjusting the belt at her waist.

"I have no idea what the connection is between the two uses of the term."

Alisha took out her computeller. "I'll check."

As Dorian finished dressing—including gold round her neck and hands that Helen had loaned her–she found herself optimistic about this *date* tonight. Perhaps being with another man would get her mind off Luke Cromwell, who had wide shoulders and coarse hair and the greatest hands. After four revolutions of his absence, she'd still been thinking entirely too much about him, about what his mouth felt like on hers, his hand on her breast, how he drew her to him so their bodies were close.

Helen stood and crossed to the bag of things she'd bought when she purchased the fruit. "Sit down at the dressing table. I want to do your hair."

"Do what to it?"

"Style it. Use some spray."

"Is that necessary?" Alisha asked. "Aerosol sprays are harmful to the air."

Helen dropped the can she'd removed from the sack, and it landed with a thud on the floor. "Oh, God, Alisha, I'm sorry. I wasn't thinking."

"That was the problem of your time. No one heeded the warnings you already had."

Gently, Dorian grasped Helen's shoulder. "Don't feel bad. That's why we're here. To change things."

"I keep forgetting. I can't believe I don't think about your mission every minute." She placed a hand on her belly. "It's just that I'm so happy about the baby." She gestured around the room. "And truthfully, it's fun for me to have you here. And Celeste. I never had any sisters."

"I can't imagine," Dorian mused. "Though we're not blood bonded, I'm very close to Lisha and Celi."

Alisha held up the computeller. "I found three meanings. Pussy, as in cat, comes from the German word for puss, which means cat. That explains one. The crude pussy is from *pucelle*, a Medieval French word referring to a virgin, so someone not sexually competent. When applied to men, as in you're a pussy-cat, it comes from pusillanimous, meaning tiny spirit, or weak or cowardly."

Now Helen laughed uproariously. The girlish giggles filled the room. "I never thought I'd have occasion to know all that about the word pussy."

All three of them joined in the mirth. Thankfully. Dorian didn't want Helen to feel bad. She'd come to care about her, too.

• • •

"GOOD JOB, LUKE," Al Patchet said when Luke walked into his office on Wednesday afternoon. "RICO's got almost enough now for the indictment." Al sat behind a scarred oak desk, messy with the endless forms that had to be filled out.

"Do you want me to do more surveillance for them?" Luke asked.

"No, this was the only task they needed our help with. For now, at least."

"Glad to do it. That's what Special Investigations is for."

Al watched him for a minute then nodded to a chair. "Have a seat. I wanna talk to you about something."

Luke dropped down across from him. "Shoot." He smiled inwardly. Dorian would have a field day with that idiom.

"Are you glad to help? Really?" Al asked.

"Why would you question that? Of course I am. Anyway, it's my job."

"I ask because you've been preoccupied at work for the last couple of weeks." He stared at Luke through piercing brown eyes accented by his bald head. "Something going on I should know about?"

Hell, he thought he'd been more circumspect. He didn't mean to fidget, but he was unaccustomed to being questioned. "Going on? What do you mean?"

"Don't bullshit me, Luke. We're friends as well as colleagues."

"All right, yes. There's something in my life that's taking up my attention. It has to do with my brother Jess. But the situation's personal. I can't go into it."

His captain was momentarily silenced. "Why don't you take some time off? You have vacation coming. And if need be, you could always take a leave of absence. I know how close you are to your brother."

Luke had thought about taking leave, of course, but making the actual decision…hell, work was his life.

Other than Jess and Helen.

"I'd hate to lose any standing in the department. It could be a month, maybe more before this is cleared up."

Al laughed. "Luke, you were the youngest man appointed head of SI, and you've already received the Medal of Honor. The brass loves you."

He gave a small smile at the recollection of how he'd barged in on a drug bust gone bad and saved five NYC police officers; he'd been shot in the process.

"Your team respects you," Al went on. "I'm sure we can do without you for a few weeks."

Why the hell not? He'd earned this. "And if it's longer?"

"Go for it. I'll also add that if my brother needed me, I'd do the same."

Well, *that* decision was made. He'd be able to help Jess.

And spend time with Dorian, which made him smile. Suddenly, he couldn't wait to see her.

• • •

THE RESTAURANT RICK chose was elaborate, with black cloths on the tables, dim lighting and soft musicals from a three-piece group he'd called a band. Rick turned out to be a fine date. His muscular build—he was bigger than Luke—short blond hair and gray eyes were attractive, too. She sipped her wine—*just one glass,* Alisha had warned—and enjoyed the ambiance as he told stories of his experiences in the Marines. She listened intently to the firsthand account about this time period's military.

"Seriously, we were stark naked when the colonel came in."

Dorian laughed. Who knew men could be so entertaining?

You did. You're very entertained by Luke Cromwell.

No, she wasn't going to think about Luke tonight. But some primitive female element inside her did wonder what he'd think of her being out with another man. Would he be jealous, an emotion she'd never experienced? He was still away on a mission for the police of New York, so he might not ever know about tonight's excursion.

"Shall we order?" Rick asked, picking up a menu.

"Yes. I'm hungry." Dorian and Alisha had called up the offerings online and picked out healthy food. The idea of being able to have such a variety of sustenance was astounding. She chose the salmon, broccoli and brown rice.

"Are you a health nut?"

"What is that?"

He looked at her askance. "Someone overly conscious about her diet."

"I wouldn't say overly. Everyone should eat right and exercise."

"I agree." He gave her a male perusal. "It's obvious you do, too."

His interest in her body didn't set off any fireworks, as Luke's had. After they gave their orders to the person called a waiter, she smiled over at Rick. "I know you didn't bring me here for just conversation. Ask me what you want."

"Who are you to Jess? David said not to pry about it, but I care about him, too."

"First, tell me about your job at Petron."

He blinked. "That's a *non sequitur*."

She didn't question the term, just said, "Answer it anyway."

"All right. I got a job there when I left the Marines. Eventually, I worked my way up the ladder to head of their security."

"Wasn't that enough for you? Why did you leave and start your own PI firm?" She knew people of this time were ambitious in their employment. In 2514, members of society worked only for the good of the community.

He gave her another odd look. "You're not a spy for the oil company or anything are you?"

Spy as in *someone doing covert observation*. In a way she was. "Of course not."

Nodding, he frowned. "The company is into some shady deals."

"Shady?"

"Yeah, when they lobby for their product in Washington, they threaten those who balk. I didn't want to be part of that."

"I see. Then you are an ethical man."

"Yes." Now the corners of his mouth turned up. It was a nice mouth but… "Are you an ethical woman?"

"I am."

"Then tell me why you checked out my background."

She and Alisha and Jess had agreed on a story that was partly the truth. "Jess is getting some weird email. Possibly threatening. Vista Institute hired me as his bodyguard until the source can be found."

One of which she and Luke would investigate when he returned.

"That's awful. Jess is such a good guy." He cocked his head in a very appealing way. "And you thought I might be a threat…why?"

"Because you worked for Petron."

"You think the oil company is behind the emails?"

"The police don't know. I'm allowing them to find the perpetrator."

"I see. And if what you're doing is to keep Jess safe, I'm all in."

"You're a nice man, Rick." She'd heard a phrase on the video box. "One of the good guys."

"I do my best," he said with a wink, the kind Luke gave her.

Oh, my.

• • •

AT NINE THAT night, Luke took the steps to Jess's house two at a time. He was anxious to tell his brother he was taking vacation time and, okay, anxious to see Dorian. He let himself in and found Jess, Helen, Alisha and David at the kitchen table. "Hi, all. I'm back."

Jess's face lightened, making Luke sure he'd done the right thing by accepting Al's offer. "Hey, buddy. I'm glad you're here. No offense to Dorian, but I feel safer when you're around."

"Good. Then you'll like my news." He scanned the kitchen. "Where is she, anyway?"

"Dorian had a date," Alisha said.

"A date?" The notion stopped him cold. "With who?"

"Rick Carson."

"The guy she suspected in church that day? Why the hell would you let her go out with him?"

David spoke up. "Because I've known Rick for years. He's not involved in Jess's emails, Luke. But he found out Dorian was investigating him and came over the other night and confronted her."

"Confronted?" Luke remembered how she reacted to confrontation. "Did he hurt her?"

"No, of course not." This from Jess. "I'm good friends with Rick, too. I told you we didn't need to investigate him. He was pissed, rightly so, and insisted Dorian go out with him to tell him why she did a search on him."

"She didn't have to go out with him to do that."

David chuckled. "I think he took a fancy to her. Which is nice, because Rick hasn't dated much since his wife died."

Shit, Luke couldn't even hate the guy, if he was a widower and if David liked him. Luke wasn't hurt or anything like that, because he and Dorian didn't really have a relationship. Only one kiss. But still…

He crossed to the fridge and snagged a beer. He could use something stronger but needed his wits about him. Taking a seat at the table, he pretended nonchalance. "So, are we waiting up for her?"

On cue, Helen yawned. "Not anymore. I'm going to sleep."

Standing too, Jess took her hand. "I'm going along with her. Want to stay over, Luke? I'll make up the bed in the den."

"If I stay, I'll do it myself."

"What was your good news?"

"I've taken a leave from my job until this whole thing is... resolved."

"That's great, buddy, really great." Jess's voice was hoarse with emotion.

Rising, Luke kissed Helen's cheek. "Good night, honey."

After they left, David said, "Alisha, I'd like you to show me some things on the computeller device you have. Some religious history. Do you think that would be all right to do now?"

"Yes, of course, if you're staying."

The good pastor gave a mischievous grin. "I am. Now that Luke's back, Dorian might need protection."

"What does that mean?" Alisha asked.

Luke glared at the good reverend, who had a teasing streak. "Nothing. I'll wait up here for her."

"Ah, I understand. There will be—what do you call them, fireworks?—between you and Dorian because you weren't consulted on this." Alisha narrowed her gaze on Luke. "You have to be more levelheaded. Everything we do is for Jess's safety."

"I know. I'm okay with what she's doing."

Having told the bald-faced lie, Luke went outside. They'd all agreed that, though Jess was supposed to be killed by a car, something might change because the Sisters of Doom were here. Consequently, they should take other precautions. Luke had already spoken to a buddy of his, Dick Anderson, who owned a security firm. Luke was thinking of asking him for some general coverage outside of the house until Jess was safe.

After walking the perimeter of the grounds, he was circling back to the front yard when a car pulled up. Stopping abruptly behind a bush, Luke watched as both Carson and Dorian got out of the vehicle. She turned to him when he reached her side and said, "Good night, Rick. I had a wonderful time."

The man watched her then drew her to him. It didn't look as if they kissed—he just hugged her—but it drove Luke's blood pressure up. Carson mumbled something then she headed for the house. When she reached the bottom of the steps, she turned around and waved. Carson got in his car and drove off.

Luke strode toward her. Before she climbed the steps, she searched for her key in a purse he'd never seen her carry. He reached her there. Jesus, what was that clingy thing she had on? Thinking of the hug, he grabbed her arm more roughly than he intended.

She whirled on him, yanking his arm forward and stomping on his foot. "Ouch," he yelled as she elbowed him square in the solar plexus.

Around coughs and choking, he said, "Dorian, it's me, Luke."

Stopping, she stared at him, then shook her head as if to clear her mind. "What the hellor are you doing here at this hour of the night? You scared the life out of me."

Rubbing his stomach, he grumbled, "I guess I don't have to worry about any man attacking you."

"I'm not used to being grabbed. I don't like it." She let him go. "But I didn't mean to hurt you."

Straightening, stepping nearer, he grasped her hips and tugged her close. "This okay?"

She nodded.

"What happened with Carson tonight? Where did you go? What did you do? Did he kiss you?"

Raising her chin in that haughty way that made him hot, she said, "I don't have to explain anything to you."

Placing his thumb on her mouth, he brushed it back and forth. "Shh. Don't be mad. Just tell me that."

He thought she was going to refuse to answer. But then her whole body softened and she leaned toward him. "No, he wanted to kiss me at the car. But I stepped back."

"Why?" he asked. A bit smugly, he'd have to admit. "You let me do it."

In the light from the lamp on the grass, her look was pure, unadulterated sexy. "I didn't want to share that special thing with him."

"You did with me."

"Yes," she whispered, moving in closer. "And I'd like to again."

"Ah, a girl after my own heart." He'd just touched her lips with his when the porch lights went on.

"Dorian?" Alisha called out. "Is that you?"

Luke shook his head. That woman *had* to stop interrupting him just when things were getting good with her friend again.

CHAPTER 11

DUNBAR, CONNECTICUT WAS a sleepy little town that might have been the model for one of the Thomas Kincaid prints Luke's mother had collected. In the balmy spring of late April, windows were open on the suburban houses; dogs barked and kids played in yards while the scent of cooking meat emanated from backyards. It was too nice of a setting for the visit he, Alisha and Dorian had to make. They'd looked up the Kruegers—Kara was married—and the history chips on them were corroded. Still, Luke felt in his gut that this was a solid lead.

Alisha rode shotgun while Celeste took the backseat. Alisha commented, "What *is* that scent? It's making me gag."

"Barbeque."

"I think it smells wonderful," Celeste put in. "Maybe we can stop for some on the way back to New York."

"Celi, you have to be more conscientious about their sustenance."

Celeste mumbled under her breath, and when Luke looked in the rearview mirror, he saw her eyes sparkle with mischief.

Concentrating back on his surroundings, he took a right turn and stopped at a red light. "The town doesn't look like a sinister place where threatening emails might come from."

Both Celeste and Alisha did not respond. He shot a glance at them. They were staring off to the left, where a woman in a bathing suit sprayed a hose at two little children and a puppy.

Squeals of joy wafted through the open windows. Both Alisha and Celeste were smiling. "It's so idyllic, isn't it, Lisha? Why couldn't we have that in our time?"

"Greed, negligence."

Luke got a glimpse of the scene. Would he ever want the perfect family they were longing for? Thoughts of kissing Dorian in the kitchen, then outside the night of her date intruded. Jesus, where did that association come from? Afraid he knew the answer, he said, "Maybe you two can have children if you change the future."

Alisha's head snapped around just as the light switched to green. "What do you mean?"

"You have to stay in our time, right?"

She nodded.

"You could get married, have kids and settle down like those people. It'd be sort of like a perk for the sacrifice you made."

"No, not us." Celeste's voice was sad. "We won't be able to conceive. No matter what happens in our next task, our bodies will always be genetically inferior."

"Celeste, stop! He doesn't need to know the details. Hellor, who knew you and Dorian would turn into mouth blabbers."

Luke didn't react to the misuse. He wished he knew what their next task was. Maybe he'd try to wheedle the information out of Dorian the next time he kissed her. Truthfully, he worried about these three, now that he knew they were babes in the woods here. Damn it, though, he'd gotten overly concerned about them. Especially Dorian.

"There's number thirty-four." Alisha pointed to a small house with yellow siding, surrounded by the proverbial white picket fence. A woman sat on the front porch swing.

Luke pulled the car over to the curb. "Let me do the talking."

"Agreed," they said in unison.

When they exited the vehicle, he noticed they wore the kind of slim, black suits that Dorian sported when she was pretending to be a bodyguard. He hadn't really looked at how they were dressed, but it was the right attire for their cover. Dorian must have advised them.

They traversed the sidewalk, opened the fence gate, which creaked, and climbed a few steps to the porch. The woman stood. She was petite and pretty, with steel-blond hair and wide, blue eyes. Which seemed troubled. "May I help you?"

Luke flashed his star. "I'm Lieutenant Luke Cromwell from the NYPD, and these are FBI agents, Hart and Law. We need to ask you a few questions, ma'am."

The woman paled and grasped the railing. She asked simply, "He already did it? He killed Dr. Cromwell?"

• • •

CELESTE MADE SURE she sat next to Kara Krueger after the woman invited them into her house. Kara had practically tumbled onto a big couch that seemed to swallow her up, even after Luke had said, "No, Dr. Cromwell isn't dead. Yet."

"I'm sorry. I'm not usually so weak." Kara's shaky voice belied the comment. "I've had to be strong."

Touching Kara's hand, Celeste felt her fear. And fatigue. She siphoned off some of it. "Can you tell us what all this is about, Kara?"

"I don't want to get him in trouble." She glanced at the photos on the end table of two little, blond girls, who shared their mother's coloring. "He's the father of my children."

Luke sat forward, his hands clasped. "Mrs. Krueger, we need to know whatever *you* know about the emails Jess Cromwell's gotten." When Kara simply stared at him, he added, "He's my brother, ma'am."

Water leaked from her eyes. "I didn't make the connection. Oh, dear." She covered her face with her hands.

Celeste was forced backward a bit, the emotion in Kara so strong it reached out to her without contact.

Alisha asked, "Mrs. Krueger, are you afraid of your husband?"

"We can protect you physically," Luke added stiffly. "If you're concerned he'll come after you."

"Craig hasn't been home in seven months."

"Will you tell us why?" Luke asked.

"H-he moved out and in with another woman." Her eyes narrowed. "It's good for me to remember he cheated on me. And took all our money."

Cocking her head, Alisha asked, "Surely your government protects you from poverty. There are laws against such things, right?"

"Craig hid money in secret accounts. Bought a boat and a host of other things to grab some of our net worth. Those men at work he was hanging around with? It was because of them that he started acting so horribly. He used to be such a nice man." She wiped her eyes. "How could he do this to his children?"

Luke's face flushed with anger. "There are ways to make him pay child support."

"He does pay the required amount. But it's put into a trust that dictates how we spend it. Very little goes to rent, which is why the girls and I had to move to a smaller home in a different neighborhood. I'm an elementary school teacher and couldn't afford the one we used to live in. Though I don't need more. I never did."

"When did Craig stop being such a nice man, Kara?" Alisha asked.

Kara's hands fisted in her skirt. "When he got involved in corporate research."

The three of them exchanged glances. Luke asked, "For what company?"

"Petron. In college, he got an assistantship to help with a professor's research. He loved it. He decided to become a researcher himself, but none of his projects ever panned out. When this job came along at Petron, he jumped at the chance."

"What kind of work does he do now?"

"It's confidential. From what he let slip, I don't think he focused on one project. I think he kept the company apprised of research done around the globe on forms of alternate energy. They paid him a lot of money." She shook her head. "That would have been okay if he hadn't kept company with the hot-shots. He was bullied as a kid, so the in-crowd paying attention to him changed him."

"How is your husband connected to my brother, Mrs. Krueger?"

Kara swallowed hard and her eyes misted again. Her light complexion became mottled, making her freckles stand out. "One night, I was on the computer and his email mistakenly came to me. It was a fluke as we had separate accounts, though the same server. There were a few messages between him and other executives at the company where he works. She got a far-away look in her eyes. "It's also how I found out he was cheating on me. When I confronted him, he closed down both email accounts and moved out. But he must have snuck in here when I was at work and taken the computer."

"So, you have no proof?" Luke's voice was hoarse. He'd been hoping for more, Celeste knew.

"No. He took the computer that had the emails on it."

"What exactly did they say?" Alisha asked.

"There were three of them. The first said Dr. Cromwell was getting close to perfecting a technique to extract natural gas from the ground safely. How what he was doing was not good for oil companies." She scowled. "Another, from his boss, said this was the kind of thing they expected him to stay on top of. He should be causing a stir about the safety of fracking Dr. Cromwell was researching."

"What was the third?"

"One that threatened Craig's job."

Luke's lips thinned. "But none of those things directly show he wanted to do Jess harm."

"Not *those* things."

Again, Celeste touched Kara's arm and felt a stirring of anger. "Why did you start emailing Jess a month ago?"

"I saw the article on Dr. Cromwell in *Science Today* magazine and thought about the emails. Next to the photo shoot was an article by a Petron executive, highlighting the drawbacks of the research." She hesitated. "It made me remember boxes in the basement of our old house that Craig left behind. They're filled with papers, but when I moved them here, I saw they were work related. I got a bad feeling from the emails, so I went down where I stored them and found folders full of information on Dr. Cromwell."

Luke stilled. "Can we see the folders your husband collected?"

"Ex-husband. Though I heard he isn't with the woman he left me for." She stood. "Come with me. I don't know if you'll view these as threatening, but I know Craig. He was obsessed, and his focus on Dr. Cromwell was unhealthy."

Celeste squeezed her hand. "I'm so sorry you were hurt."

"Thank you. But if I'm right, stopping Dr. Cromwell from being killed will ease my mind."

The basement was dim and Celeste started to cough from the precipitation down here. On one of the shelves, boxes were neatly stacked and labeled. Two were marked *Craig, the asshole.*

Kara gave a shy smile. "Sorry, I was so angry when he left, I couldn't resist. I'm better now."

Luke chuckled, but Celeste didn't understand.

Taking one of the boxes down, Luke set it on a table. Inside were neatly filed folders. The labels read, *Armstrong, wind; Lakefield, solar; Lincoln, clean coal.* One very thick file read *Cromwell, natural gas.*

He opened it. "Wow. There have to be a hundred articles in here." He began leafing through them. "I don't know if this constitutes..." He stopped speaking when he reached a specific photo of Jess in his office, smiling broadly.

On the photo, Krueger had drawn a bright red target.

"See what I mean?" Kara stated.

"Yes." Celeste had been reading up on archery because one of the Lansing younglings took lessons in it.

"What are you going to do?" Kara asked, sounding defeated.

"Take this to the authorities." Which Celeste knew was not true. "If we need you to come in to give a deposition to the police, will you?"

"Oh, I don't know. He's my children's father. And as I said, I'm not as mad as I was when I labeled the boxes. Can't you just work with what you have?"

When they went back upstairs, they took their leave, but Celeste stayed on the porch when Luke and Alisha went down the steps. Again, she touched Kara Krueger's arm. Now anxiety swirled inside the poor woman, so Celeste opened up fully and drew more of it off. She managed to say in a normal voice, "Kara, we'll stop this. You have my assurance."

"You know, I believe you."

"Try not to worry about it."

"Maybe I can stop now that someone with authority knows." Kara's face showed a puzzled expression. "For some reason, I feel better than before you came here."

"I'm glad."

"But Agent Hart, seriously, I don't think I can actually testify against him. The kids and all."

When the three of them were settled in the car, Alisha spoke up. "Can we do anything with this information, Luke? It's really not proof."

Luke said, grimly, "No. If it wasn't for what your computeller reveals, I wouldn't feel so strongly about Jess being in danger. But we know my brother is going to die; we know Krueger is a kook and might be planning a murder. We just have to find the proof."

• • •

DAVID HAD JUST stepped through the church's front door to get some air when he saw a lone runner, jogging down the street. He recognized her when she got closer and waited. "Fancy meeting you here, Alisha."

"Reverend Ryan, hello. I was running out of inside to clear my mind and decided to come see your structure."

His brows knit. Though she was flushed and a thin film of sweat formed on her face, he was surprised. "You ran all the way from the Cromwell house?"

"It's only five point two-five of your miles. I'm energized from it." She scowled, the lines marring a totally wrinkle-less face. "We had an interesting visit yesterday."

"How about if I walk with you while you cool down and you can tell me what happened? It's a beautiful day. After that you can see the church."

Her expression was serious, as it always was. So he said, "You must feel so bad being here after what we did to the future."

They started walking. "I try not to think about that."

"*I* try to reaffirm to my congregation the abundance we have and the importance of conserving our resources."

"We haven't talked about this, but I found the Earth Day celebration you had interesting when Celi told me about it. I understand she became agitated."

"Why?"

"Because you—as a society—knew what could happen to the environment and didn't succeed in preventing the ruination of the air."

A sense of guilt invaded him and he stuck his hands in the pockets of his jeans. "I guess I always knew we might go down the wrong path."

She perused him with an odd expression on her face. "You're dressed differently from other times I've seen you."

"I wear casual clothes when I'm not preaching or visiting the hospital." She kept staring, and something drove him to tease her. "Do you like what you see?"

Her mouth gaped. The sun beat down on her, highlighting her amber eyes. "Are you flirting with me? No, you can't be. Men of religion don't flirt. Or join. Or espouse."

Laughing heartily, he had to settle down before he could answer. "I guess I am flirting. Men of religion *do* flirt, *do* join, and do get married."

"I saw different information on the chips. Though I must confess, the chips were vague about the religion of the time."

"Some religions don't allow their clergy to mate. That must be what your chips revealed."

"Ah." She glanced down, then up again. "So, do you have a mate?"

"No."

"How old are you?"

"Forty-one."

"I don't understand. How do...?"

Her words trailed off when her cell phone rang. "I have to get this...Alisha here." A pause while she listened. "All right, I'll come back."

"Problems?" David asked when he she clicked off.

"Yes. I must go to the Cromwells immediately. Could you transport me?"

"Of course. Maybe I can help."

• • •

DORIAN WAS WAITING for Alisha on the front porch, surprised but pleased to see Reverend David Ryan with her. Maybe he could be of use in dissolving the contention that had sprung up among all of them like a sand blast.

"What's happening?" Alisha asked when she entered the foyer.

Her friend seemed flustered, but Dorian had to dismiss it for now. "Luke and Celeste have come up with a suggestion on how to get proof of Krueger's involvement in a plot against Jess." Dorian tried to keep her face neutral though she was very unhappy.

Alisha shook her head. "Your expression tells me that their plan isn't acceptable to you."

"It isn't. Let's go to the family room and you'll hear why."

They entered the space where Luke, Celeste and Jess sat on the couches. Every day, Dorian thought more and more in terms of their language. "Alisha is here," she told the others. "Pastor Ryan accompanied her."

"Where did you two meet up?" Jess asked.

"Never mind that. What have you proposed?" Alisha glanced at Celeste. "And how are you involved?"

Leaning forward in his chair, Luke stared directly at her. "We've come up with a plan to trap Krueger."

"Not one I agree with," Jess put in.

Luke gave his brother a look of consternation. Since Luke had kissed her, Dorian felt more attuned to his moods, an ability she didn't particularly like. He said, "It's a good plan." He nodded to Alisha when she and David took seats. "I think *you'll* agree, at least. Of all the Sisters of Doom, you're the most rational."

"Sisters of Doom?" the three of them said simultaneously.

"Oh, sorry." His face turned an appealing shade of red. "My pet name for you."

Dorian took immediate umbrage. "Our message is nothing to joke about."

"I agree." Alisha's tone was disgusted.

Celeste laughed. "I think it's humorous."

"The plan?" David asked. He had great skill at redirecting the conversation. "We need something new now that we've checked out Rick Carson and Jake Sterling, who were totally innocent, like I said they would be."

Dorian's gaze flew to Luke's. But he wasn't watching her. "We have to get access to Krueger. It's rumored that he's become quite a ladies' man."

"Meaning he likes many women, right?" Alisha clarified.

"Right. We think the best person to get to him is Celeste. She can practically read minds; she'll know how to manipulate him. And hopefully, disable him. When she does, she can search his computer, his phone, whatever else he might have written emails on that indicates his, or Petron's, plot against Jess."

"Or he might even tell me," Celeste added. "I can be very persuasive."

"It's too dangerous for her!" Dorian protested. "She could take on his negative emotion and get ill."

"I can block emotion when I need to."

Alisha stared ahead. "What would you have to do to get his confidence? His trust?"

"We don't know exactly." Luke leafed through a few papers then held up one. "He frequents a bar called The Mix. I'm sure if we go there, Celeste can attract his attention. Especially with the right clothes."

"No doubt." Dorian spoke up again. This was outrageous. "That's the problem."

"Attracting him is not a problem." Celeste sounded exasperated. "It's part of the solution."

"For the godheads' sake, she might have to join with him to gain his trust!"

"What's wrong with that?" Alisha asked.

David recoiled. "It's unethical."

"It's seedy," Jess put in.

"If it's necessary," Luke said, "We'll go for it."

Dorian rounded on him. "Have you done this? Used your body to sway women in an investigation?"

His damn blue eyes twinkled. "I take the Fifth on that."

"The Fifth what?" Celeste asked.

"Amendment. It means I won't answer. Look, you said sex is different in your time. That you don't necessarily know your partner, get only physical release from it and go on with your business."

"Joining will be different here. With one of us and one of you." Through her anger, Dorian's heartbeat escalated just thinking about what it might be like to be with him.

Luke gave her a meaningful stare.

"What is transpiring between you two? I'm getting odd vibrations from you." Celeste, of course, would be the first to catch on.

"Nothing." Still standing, Dorian crossed her arms over her chest. "I'm agitated at this entire conversation. And angry at you, Lieutenant, for suggesting something so unacceptable."

"It's logical," Alisha said.

"No."

Celeste rose, too, and crossed to Dorian. She tried to touch her, but Dorian stepped back. "Dorian, I don't understand your concern."

"I do." Jess scowled at them. "I can't be part of a plot where one of you pimps yourself to help me."

"I can." The comment came from Helen, who'd come to the doorway of the room, looking stronger than she had in weeks. Her shoulders were straight and her chin raised. She hadn't been present until now. "I'd do it myself, to save your life."

David sighed. "Isn't there any other way?"

"This may not even involve sex." Celeste again. "I may be able to succeed in getting information, without physicality entering into it. But in general, I don't see why joining with Krueger would be an issue, either."

Helen took a seat next to her. "Women of our time react differently from you three to joining. It creates a bond between people."

"I know that," Celeste answered. "But we're immune."

"Are we?" Dorian's voice rose. "I'm not sure anymore."

"Why?" Alisha asked.

Again, Luke watched her like a hawka.

But she avoided the question. "It isn't just that part. Celi is more fragile than I am. If anyone's going to approach Krueger—and join with him if necessary—it should be me."

"Like hell." The words seemed to slip out of Luke.

"What in the godheads' names is going on here?" Alisha matched Dorian's anger. "All those exchanged looks! There's some kind of subtext between you and Luke that I don't understand."

"We're all miscommunicating. But it's a moot point." Celeste scanned them all. "Besides, it's my decision. And though I'm physically weaker than you, Dorian, I'm much stronger in emotional reading, manipulation and getting my way than you are."

They were all silent.

Because everyone knew she was right.

"So," she said when no one else spoke. "When do we start?"

• • •

WITH THE MAY night breezes drifting in through the windows, Celeste lounged on the large sleeping conformer in her quarters with her two friends. She'd engineered this time together because she was better at achieving compromise than either of these two were. Contrary to what it seemed to everyone else, Celeste could be stubborn, and because she was a sensitive, any fight with her was basically unfair.

"So, we're all in our sleeping attire," Alisha commented impatiently. "Why did you bring us here?"

That sleeping attire indicated the differences among them. Alisha had chosen plain, white-cotton shorts and an elbow-length top to match. Dorian picked red bottoms and what they called a skimpy, polka-dotted top, though Celeste didn't understand what the color had to do with dancing. She herself wore a baby pink dress-like thing, with ruffles around the bottom and poofy sleeves. She resembled a princess she'd seen on an animated show on the video box.

"I brought you here for a pajama party," Celeste said sweetly. "Where the female sex of this time period gets together to gossip. Men call them hen parties."

"What good are they?" Alisha whined. "I'm fatigued and need my sleep."

Celeste said, "You'll see." Climbing off the bed, she crossed to the dresser where she'd placed a bottle and glasses; she poured them full of nearly clear liquid.

"What is that?" Alisha asked suspiciously.

"Wine. Helen gave it to me when I told her I'd requested this meeting. She's also the one who explained to me about pajama parties." Celeste served one glass each to the women.

Dorian took a sip. "Wow, that's good."

Alisha set hers aside. "I'm not consuming alcohol. It turns to sugar in your body and makes you less cognizant."

"Please, Lisha, just try it. You have to get more acclimated to this time period."

Alisha shook her head.

So Celeste took her own glass, sat back down and turned to Dorian. "I want to gossip. First and foremost, I want to know why you objected so vehemently to the possibility of my joining with a male of this time period."

"For all the reasons I said. Celi, it would be a lot safer for me to pursue this."

"Your objection is based on more than that, I can tell." This from Alisha, who'd apparently decided to join in the talk, at least. "It has to do with something between you and Lucas Cromwell."

Reaching over, Celeste touched Dorian's shoulder before she could move away. "You're swirling with emotion. Not all of it negative."

Dorian blushed as Luke had earlier.

"Oh! You've joined with him?" Celeste's voice was full of awe.

"No!"

The look Celi gave her was skeptical. "Something happened to stir you up so much."

Picking at the spread on Celeste's bed, Dorian blew out a heavy breath. Then she looked up. "All right. Yes, something happened between Luke and me, but we didn't join."

"Tell us, Dorian." Celeste's tone was gentle.

"He kissed me."

"Against your will?" Even Alisha's eyes widened at the thought of the violence men did to women in this time.

"No. I agreed."

"Why would you do that?" Alisha was genuinely bewildered by the notion.

"I miss joining."

"I do, too." This from Celeste.

Alisha grabbed for the wine, after all. "Me, too. But still... oh! This *is* delicious."

"There's more to what's happened with me and Luke. I... like him. He's good-hearted and tireless in his vow to keep his brother safe."

"I think he's stubborn, hardheaded and driven." Alisha again.

"Hmm." Celi tried out a wink on Dorian. "Sounds like somebody else we know."

Dorian and Celeste giggled and even Alisha smiled at their little dig against her.

In her excitement, Celeste came up to her knees, then sat back on her legs. "So, what was kissing like?"

"It was wonderful. So raw, so elemental. So intimate. He smells wonderful, his body fits to mine, and the way he touched me… Let's just say no man has ever made me feel this way."

"Because you've opened yourself up to it?" Alisha's query was genuine, not a complaint.

"I don't know. I've been attracted to him almost since we arrived here. I don't understand, Lisha. I never experienced anything like this in our time. Why would I now?"

"I'm afraid I don't have an answer for that, Dorian."

Celeste blurted out, "I enjoy looking at Alex Lansing's picture."

"Megadamn." Now Alisha *was* upset. "Let's not forget our mission here."

Dorian raised her chin. "I've done nothing to jeopardize our task."

"Yet. You'll lose your focus if you keep getting the vapors when he's around."

"I do not faint or feel ill when I'm near him. I become aroused."

"Which could take your concentration off our task to fix today's society. While you're preoccupied with Luke, somebody could kill Jess."

Dorian inhaled a sharp breath. "I hadn't thought about that." She scowled. Looked thoughtful. "Then I have to try to neutralize these emotions."

"Before you do," Celi said, "tell us in detail what it felt like to have a man's mouth on yours."

CHAPTER 12

LUKE GLANCED AROUND The Mix as he sat with David Ryan at a small round table for four. They'd been lucky to snag it and only had because they'd gotten here early. The club was swank, all silver and chrome, with an onyx bar. Some loud jazz was piped in over speakers. The tables were close together, and the seats were damned uncomfortable. Luke preferred a neighborhood bar with padded stools and a TV tuned to sports. "I forgot what these places were like."

David chuckled. "Me, too."

"Ministers go to bars like this?"

"Clergy go to bars but not usually pick-up joints, which is what this is. We weren't born with collars around our necks, you know. I sowed a few oats in my time."

Luke rolled his eyes. "Oh, yeah, I'll bet you were a real wild man."

David got an odd look on his face. "You'd be surprised."

Luke didn't pursue what he guessed was something out of David's past. He had his own secrets that he didn't want to broadcast to the world, especially his debacle with his ex-wife. "What if one of your parishioners sees you here?"

"I'd deal with it. I don't worry too much about the future."

"Ironic, isn't it? I'm that way, too." He shrugged, thinking about the computeller thing, which showed exactly what had happened because people of his time period were thoughtless. "Maybe we should have worried more."

"You got that. Can you believe what they told us?"

"It's a shame. And we don't even have the whole story. I wish I knew where they were going next."

David sipped his Scotch. "For personal or professional reasons?"

"What does that mean?"

"I'm a psychologist as well as a minister, Luke. I've watched you and Dorian together. There's a spark between you two."

"Yeah, I guess. It can't go anywhere."

"Why? They have to stay."

"I think—" Luke stopped speaking when three women entered the bar. "They're here." He shook his head and swallowed hard. "For Pete's sake, look at them."

Turning, David practically ate his tongue, too. The Sisters of Doom paraded into the room as though they owned the place. If any guy here wasn't staring, he was blind. Dorian led the way, wearing green silk and sequins and killer heels. Her legs looked a mile long and her curves were unfortunately well-outlined by the dress. "My God, how are we ever gonna protect them?"

David appeared not to hear him. "Look at Alisha. She's so strong but, in that outfit, so feminine. I've never quite seen her like this."

Luke took a bead on the woman. She did look stunning.

"She wore copper to match her eyes." David's voice was hoarse.

Uh-oh. "You got the hots for her, Rev?"

"No. I've made a study at controlling myself."

Again, he glanced at Alisha. "Good luck with that."

Then his gaze snagged on Celeste. "Oh, fuck," Luke swore. "Little black dresses have always been my weakness."

"I think *little* is the operative word. They must have poured her into it."

"The slithery material doesn't help."

"Or the stilettos."

"Watch," Luke said. "They'll go in for the kill right away."

Sure enough, all three sauntered over to Craig Krueger, at the bar, who was hitting on the woman on his left. Ostensibly going for drinks, they lined up behind the three people on the other side of Krueger. After a few minutes of waiting, one woman turned and said something to Dorian. In no time, all three women surrendered their seats to the girls.

"They're policewomen, right?" David asked, watching the show.

"Yeah. Off duty. I treated them to drinks if they'd save seats for me. They look freakin' good, too." And one was really Luke's type. Small, blond, curvy. His gaze strayed to Dorian.

Well, the small and curvy one *had* been his type.

• • •

HER BACK TO Craig Krueger, who reminded her of an actor she'd seen on LifeLine Television for Women, Celeste smiled over at her *Sisters of Doom*. (She really did think Luke's moniker was amusing.) "Easy," she whispered. They were both nervous, and Celeste could feel it emanate from them. They wore some scented water called perfume, as she did, and it was a lovely smell. There was male cologne and alcohol also tingeing the air.

"I'm trying." This from Dorian, who had not scanned the place for Luke and David.

A big man with a smile on his face approached them from behind the bar. He wore a shiny jacket and trousers that matched. A suit, Luke had called it. Alex Lansing wore one in a lot of photos she'd seen of him. "Hey, ladies. Just about every unaccompanied guy in this place wants to buy you a drink."

The bar was a U-shape, with perhaps thirty seats, and many of the occupants were staring at them. Celeste guessed the outfits they'd chosen had worked to attract the opposite sex. (They *did* look pretty in their new dresses. Helen had taken them shopping and had almost as much fun as they had.)

Giving the bar worker a big smile, Dorian ordered. "We'll have a bottle of champagne. Your best. And we'll pay for it." Luke had instructed her on what he called the *classy* things to drink and not to let anyone buy them or they'd be approached.

Frowning, Alisha turned to them both and spoke in a hush. "I know I need to participate. This is just so primitive. People come here to engage in flirting to get sex? Godheads, I wish they had the SexLine."

"Remember why the SexLine developed. Because of our infertility."

Celeste thought about Helen and Jess. "Helen is delighted with her fertility. She went to the doctor who specializes in babies and he told her everything was coming along fine."

"We knew she was doing well," Alisha said, "After you touched her."

"Still, she needed the confirmation." Celeste put her hand on her own stomach. "I wish I could have a child."

Before Alisha could scold her, the bar worker reappeared.

"Here you go, ladies. Only the best." He watched them. "Which you three should have." A loud pop, then the bottle fizzed. As he poured the drinks, he said, "You from out of town? You seem different from the usual crowd."

They mumbled their affirmative responses, and the man finally went away.

Celeste sipped. The taste was tart, and the bubbles tickled her nose. "I like their champagne."

"Wine gave you an ache in the head the other night. No more than one glass of this stuff. I looked up their alcoholic beverages online after our little tasting. We should have red wine because it has some nutritional properties. But Luke directed this false drama and thought champagne would be the best."

This *was* a drama, and Celeste was the main actor. A fission of something went through her. She knew she could do the work but also knew her friends were worried about her. "I'm sure everything will go smoothly." She captured Dorian's hand and squeezed it. Took away a bit of her anxiety. "I'll be fine."

"You're a babe in the woods." This from Lisha.

"I won't even ask." Celeste had studied the idioms for tonight, but *babe in the woods* hadn't been one of them.

As they waited, they sipped their drinks and talked about the chosen topic—clothes—until they heard behind them, "Hello, there, ladies. I'm Luke, and this guy is my buddy David."

• • •

DORIAN LOOKED OVER at Luke. You'd never know he was an officer of the law. Tonight, he wore a light coat the color of a deera. Beneath it, a shiny shirt of the same color. His hair, longer now, was styled in a way she'd never seen it—a sexy tumble of locks—and his smile was one that people wore when they met just before joining. "Hello, Luke."

Leaning in close, he whispered in her ear. "You, look like a million bucks, babe."

She smiled. "I assume that's a compliment."

He chuckled and grazed her arm with his.

David angled himself next to Alisha. "Love your dress, doll. Care to tell me your name?"

As planned, Alisha turned a sexy look on David. By the expression on the minister's face, he was affected by it. "Alisha." She pretended to be thoughtful. "David. What a Biblical name."

The minister smiled. "I'm anything but holy."

They all laughed at the outright lie.

"So, you come here often?" Dorian asked. It was the pickup line she'd learned.

"Not enough, if I've never seen you before." Luke moved in closer. Dorian caught a scent on him he'd never worn before. She had to resist the urge to inhale deeply.

"You're leaving me out, guys." This from Celeste. It was true. Though it was the plan to leave Celeste alone at the bar, Luke was totally focused on Dorian, and David couldn't take his eyes off Alisha.

Luke muttered under his breath, "Want to dance, beautiful?"

"Yes."

"You, sweetheart?" David asked Alisha.

She smiled and took his hand.

They'd taken only a few steps away when Craig Krueger abandoned the woman on the left side of him and swiveled his chair to the right. He'd gotten a glimpse of Celeste. "Must be my lucky night," then, "I'm Craig."

"Hmm," Celeste said sexily. "We'll see what we can do about your good fortune."

• • •

"I'M CELESTE HART."

"Hel-lo, Celeste Hart. I want to know everything about you."

She leaned in so he could see what they called her cleavage. Her breasts were supported in a ridiculous archaic garment that dug into her and squished them together. "As do I. About you." She had to keep herself from wincing. He'd used an excess of scented water and it almost gagged her.

"Ah, I'm an open book."

Someone who was read easily. She gave him a perusing glance. "I'll see about that, too."

Returning it, he asked, "So, what do you do for a living?"

"My life's work is in research."

"What do you research?"

"Fertility." Another sexy smile. "Are you interested in the reproductive organs of men and women?" This flirting thing was easier than she thought it would be.

"Of women. So you're an expert at that?"

"I'm an expert at a lot of things. Tell me what you do."

"I research, too. For a corporation."

Play the femme fatale, Luke had recommended. *Cater to his feelings of masculine superiority.* "Is your subject matter more interesting than mine?"

"Right now, nothing's more interesting than"—he peered down at her chest— "yours."

And so the plan was executed. She had his interest and would capitalize on it. Jess's life depended on her success.

• • •

DORIAN WAS CONFOUNDED by the nature of this thing called dancing. Two people came together on the big square area, held onto each other's arms, then barely moved. She glanced at the others, also out on the floor. No, some people moved more than she and Luke. He whispered in her ear. "Stop staring as if you've never seen people dance."

"I haven't. This ritual stumps me."

He pulled her a little closer. "I'm all for it." He sniffed her hair. "You smell great."

"Helen suggested we buy something called perfume. Though we have unlimited funds, the expense of it was staggering."

"Well worth every penny."

"You smell different, too. This also confuses me. Why do I like it?"

"Because scents set off pheromones that attract people to each other."

"Everyone smells the same in my time. The chips said nothing about the smells being different now."

"Seriously?"

"Earnestly. It must have something to do with the controlled atmosphere of our time."

"That is really sad, Dorian." His voice sounded genuine enough.

"Our future is sad, Luke." Though she was tall, she still had to look up at him. Her gaze landed on that little dent in his cheek again. She liked that, too. "Do you think this plan tonight will work? I have concern for Celeste."

He nodded to the bar. "She's hooked him already. And she knows how to play it. All five of us will leave within the hour, and she'll make arrangements to meet him again." He smiled. "God, she's beautiful."

Dorian stiffened. And couldn't figure out why. She... resented the comment he made about Celeste. Whom she loved dearly.

"You're frowning." His voice sounded amused.

"I don't like what you said about Celi. And I have no idea why."

He laughed out loud. "You're jealous, sweetheart."

"The emotion you felt when Rick Carson hugged me." He started to protest. But she spoke again. "I do feel it, but I don't understand it."

"I can't wait to explain that to you." He kissed her hair. "Later."

• • •

IT WAS NEARLY midnight by the time they returned to Jess's. When Luke pulled up to the house, he took out his phone and dialed the number of his friend Anderson, whom he'd hired to watch the family while the four of them were away. "Hi, Dick."

"Hey, buddy."

"We're here. Alisha and Celeste are coming inside. Can you stay another hour? I have something to work out with Dorian."

"Ha! I know the meaning of that. Go for it. I'm good till one."

After Luke clicked off, he turned to the women in the backseat. They'd already dropped off David at his apartment. But not before a heated discussion on how to trap Craig Krueger into revealing information to Celeste and how to get proof of the plot against Jess. Celeste had told them when she touched Krueger's arm, his vibes were such a mixture of negative emotions she'd been taken aback by them. The argument began over that tidbit. David worried about them. Dorian continued to claim she should have taken this on. And Alisha was good to go. Celeste acted as if the decision was made and no one was going to change her mind, which was probably true.

He angled his body so he could face the three of them in the back of his Bronco. "Dorian, get in front. You two go on inside and get some rest. We can continue debating the wisdom of what we're doing in the morning."

Chin high, Alisha said in a snotty voice, "Whatever you have to work out with Dorian concerns us."

Luke could be stubborn, too. "No, it doesn't. Good night."

"Dorian…" Alisha's voice was strident.

Dorian seemed torn—and tired. She'd had so many new experiences tonight, he felt sorry for her. Before he could retract his offer, she said to them, "Go ahead. I want some time alone with Luke."

Celeste laughed. "That's what concerns Alisha."

Moving up closer in the backseat, Alisha said, "We decided two nights ago, you would stay away from Luke."

"We?" Luke responded. "What the hell?"

Celeste opened the car door. "Come on, Lisha. You're not going to stop this thing between them by telling her what to do."

"She agreed." Still, Alisha slid out behind Celeste.

When they were gone, Luke turned Dorian to face him. "You told them we kissed?"

"Yes. Shouldn't I?"

"I don't know. It was private."

"They guessed something had occurred, Luke, and I wanted to tell them. Women share everything in our society. One time, when I joined with a very virile man on the SexLine, I couldn't wait to tell them what he—"

Luke put his hand to her lips. They were covered with lipstick, which she'd said tasted like fruit. "Hush, I don't want to hear about your meaningless sex with some other guy." Jealousy was in the air tonight, he guessed. "Let's go somewhere we can talk."

"I *did* agree to try not to get closer to you."

"Yeah, well, that's not happening."

He drove to the park down the street and pulled into a deserted lot with a couple of dim streetlamps.

"Luke, Lisha says I'll lose my focus in protecting Jess because I'm thinking about you."

"There are a lot of people watching over him. You, me, Anderson. And we're all adults, professionals. Kissing you—and more—won't harm his safety." Taking a strand of hair, which had been moussed and blow dried so it was puffier than before, he rubbed it between his fingers. "Regarding that, have you thought about my offer?"

She touched her temples. "You make my head spin. What offer?"

"That I stud for you?"

She frowned.

"What's wrong?"

"The kisses we made. They weren't like our joining."

Now they were getting somewhere. "Yeah, why not?"

"I experienced emotions. Conflicting ones."

He ran his thumb across her lips. "Good or bad?"

"They felt good. I'm not sure they were healthy, though. They seem unnatural."

"No, Dorian, what we did *is* what nature meant. Your time lost something very precious."

Her eyes flashed. "We lost it all because of what *you* did in this time period."

Honestly, he said, "I know. I'm sorry. I hope you can change things. We're all trying to be better environmentally since you came."

That was true. They turned faucets off immediately. Did not waste food. Tried to use the cars less.

"I seek your forgiveness, too. I'm all…jittery after what we did tonight."

"*Wound up* is the term we use. So am I."

"Because of our plan?"

"No, because of this."

He leaned over the gearshift. Threaded his fingers through her hair. And lowered his head.

Sparks shot through him. He'd been thinking about kissing her, *joining* with her from the minute she walked into the bar in that should-be-illegal dress. Through the silky material, he cupped her breast and pressed more deeply onto her mouth.

She clutched at him. Opening her lips, as he'd taught her, she explored him. When she nipped his mouth, he bucked toward her. After a few minutes, he had to break the contact. "Dorian, we've got to take this further."

Her green eyes were liquid in the dim light.

So he asked, "What do you want?" He touched the skin over her heart. "Here?"

"I want to be with you. But it's more than Alisha's protest. I'm…afraid." She frowned. "Something I rarely feel."

Because she was being truthful, he decided to return the sentiment. "I'm afraid, too. But I want this to happen between us. We'll figure it out together. I won't hurt you."

However, in the back of his mind, another truth formed. He probably would hurt her. And what's more, she would probably hurt him, too. Right now, though, he didn't care about any of that. He *had* to have her. But not in the backseat of a car. He'd find a time and place for privacy.

Meanwhile, he took her mouth again.

CHAPTER 13

AFTER HOURS OF discussion after last night's escapade, Jess was so tired of the bickering about his safety and the best route to trap Krueger, he had to escape all these people in his house. So he stood and said, "I'm done here. My brain is fried. You guys make the decision." He held his hand out to Helen. "Come on, let's go watch some TV in our room. We haven't done anything normal in weeks."

"We seek your forgiveness, Jess." This from Celeste. "We know this is hardest on you and Helen."

"Don't apologize, please. I'm grateful that you're here. It's just that it's been about a month. A lot of time to know you're..." He glanced at his wife and shut up.

"You're going to die." Helen stood and faced Jess. "Look, I know you're worried about Celeste handling this Krueger guy. But I'm not sure how much more waiting we can take." She grasped Jess's hand and smiled. "Instead of watching TV, let's go sit on our patio."

"No can do," Luke pointed out. "Only if Dorian or I go with you."

"Luke," Jess said, exasperated. "The entire backyard is fenced in. Nothing can happen to us."

"No."

Shaking his head, Jess left the room with Helen. When they reached the sanctuary of their bedroom, he said, "Come on," and opened the sliding doors that led to their private patio.

"No, Jess, you'll be exposed."

"I'll be fine. I'm getting cabin fever. I only go from here to work and then we spend evenings planning and arguing. I wish this was over."

"Me, too, honey. Okay, outside for a few minutes only."

The May sun was hot on their faces. A profusion of geraniums sat in the corner of the patio in a big fat pot. And they could hear the birds chirping in the trees. "It's beautiful out here," Helen said as they dropped onto deck chairs labeled *his* and *hers* and grasped hands again. Jess turned his face up to the heavens "The rays feel great."

"Yeah, it's hard to believe we lose all this." Real sorrow laced Helen's voice. "And sad."

"Hopefully, for our sakes, too, that will all change."

"I admire those women, Jess. They're very brave. And they're sacrificing so much."

Placing a palm on her belly, he changed the subject. "How's my girl?"

Helen giggled like a high schooler. "Great. I can't wait to feel her move."

"Me, too." His eyes misted. "I hope—"

An explosion rent the air.

The tool shed in the backyard burst into flames. Red-and-yellow fire shot out from the roof, and the two little windows shattered. Helen and Jess bolted to their feet. The rest happened in a blur.

Gun blazing, Luke rushed into the bedroom, with Dorian behind him. When his brother saw him coming in from the patio, he said, "Fuck!" and raced to the glass door. He grabbed Helen and dragged her inside just as Dorian lunged for Jess and brought him to the floor.

They were fully inside the bedroom when they heard the shots.

• • •

"I DON'T UNDERSTAND." Helen was shaking like one of the leaves on their precious trees. "What happened?"

Jess held her tight to his chest and gazed out the window. Fire trucks had arrived and Luke had gone out to meet them and brought them around back. Dorian watched as the squad lifted a hose; it shot out real water. She went to the glass doors and cracked one open.

Sickeningly noxious elements wafted inside from smoke, which she'd seen only in the history chips; she shut the door again and tried to keep from gagging.

When she turned around, Jess was behind her. "Dorian, what do you think happened?"

"We need to wait for the department of fire to report."

"This has to be related to me."

"One would think that," she said calmly. "But the chips did not have any indication of literal fire or gunfire. Alisha is reviewing what we have again. This could be coincidental."

"I don't believe in this kind of coincidence. There were shots, for God's sake."

"They sounded like shots, yes."

The Cromwells moved to a sofa off from the others and talked quietly with each other. Dorian continued to stare at the fire. In her time, there were no people to calm fires because fire was not a part of their lives. Everything ran on lecci crystals, which self-charged. Soon, the blaze was doused, but in some ways, it had been beautiful. Then a man in one of those suits Luke wore when he worked entered the backyard. He spoke directly to Luke and they headed into the house while the fighters of fire finished their task.

The man and Luke stepped though the sliding aperture after Dorian opened it, bringing in more of the odious smell of burnt wood.

"Hey guys, this is Captain Max Lyndon. He's one of the arson investigators for the city."

"Nice to meet you." The man was older than Luke, with much gray shot through his hair. "Sorry it's under these circumstances." He glanced at Dorian, then Celeste, and stared at them a bit too long. Men here weren't used to women of their stature and fitness.

"Hello, Captain." Celeste greeted them.

He looked around the room. "Is there some kind of meeting going on here?"

"Oh, no," Jess put in. "These women are Helen's cousins. Along with another in the den."

Lyndon nodded.

"This is my brother, Jess, and his wife, Helen," Luke added. "They were on the patio when the shed exploded."

The man whipped out a pad with precious paper on it, and also a pen. He would write this down? Why didn't he just use a recorder? "I'll need to hear exactly what you witnessed."

Helen turned to Jess, who explained the sequence of events. "Then we heard the shots."

"If they were shots. Sometimes, things in a shed like that explode and they sound like firearms."

"I thought the same thing." Luke spoke somberly.

After the women discussed what they'd seen and heard from the family room, the investigator went back out to confer with the others and examine the shed.

A pall came over the group. Finally, Jess spoke. "I'm sorry we went outside. It was foolish."

"Water under the bridge." Luke sounded tired. Dorian had the strong urge to comfort him. "We can talk more about it later. Just try to be cooperative, Jess."

"I will." He tugged Helen even closer.

Before the firemen left, the investigator confirmed that there'd been no gunshots fired. The noises, which resembled shots, were in reality small explosions from the fire, precipitated by the spontaneous combustion of oily rags in a dusty bucket. Jess had left them there some time ago and had forgotten about them. In turn, miscellaneous materials had caught fire, too.

Alisha came out of the den. The expression on her face indicated to Dorian that she did not have good news. "I've reviewed the data. The summer chips are sketchier than I remembered. There's nothing at all on today. The only evidence is still that Jess is killed in a car accident. Of course, if we changed the future by just coming here, this computeller wouldn't be updated to integrate that."

Helen said "Maybe you already saved Jess somehow."

Still frowning, Alisha drew in a breath. "No, we didn't. I saw something I hadn't picked up on the times I went through these particular chips."

"What?" Luke asked.

"A small notice in a scientific journal. We missed it in the future because we weren't looking at Jess's writings. But a week or so ago, I started checking the chips on all the papers Jess wrote about his research in the summer of 2014. I was making my way through them, but hadn't finished." She swallowed hard. "The last was an update on his work, but it had a...postscript, I think you call it."

"What did it say?" Jess asked hoarsely, but Dorian had guessed already.

"It notes that the writer of the article died before its publication and his research was under scrutiny for flaws."

Luke asked, "When was the journal dated?"

"June one."

Helen shrieked, "Oh, my God, Jess, you're supposed to die in a few weeks."

• • •

WEARING A DRESS the color of emeralds, Celeste swung her foot back and forth as she sipped a drink called club soda. The clear liquid would appear to be alcohol to fool Krueger, without the side effects. She'd asked the bar worker to keep secret from her companion the fact that she wasn't imbibing. As if her thoughts conjured him, Craig Krueger strode into the bar.

"Sorry I'm late. I got tied up at work."

Another silly idiom, though the image was amusing. "On Saturday?"

"The city never sleeps. But I hate to keep a girl like you waiting."

"I don't mind. I like the sights and scents of this place." The space was a nice change from the smell of smoke, which lingered in the air at Jess's, and the tension among everyone. She turned her attention to Krueger. "I hope the work issue isn't a problem."

Dropping down into the seat next to her, he leaned in very close. He'd done more than work. The distinct odor of alcohol exuded from him. "The higher-ups always cause problems."

She batted her eyes as Helen had taught her to do. "I thought you were a higher-up." In this time's culture, women liked men in power. Celeste felt just the opposite. Powerful men had big egos to nurture, and she'd clashed with some in her work at the Institute of Fertility.

"I am, babe. As a matter of fact, I'm taking point on this huge problem we're trying to...erase, I guess you could say." He smiled at his wording.

Celeste experienced a spark of anger. He and his co-conspirators looked at the situation as *erasing* Jess Cromwell, a man she'd come to care about and respect. Megadamn him.

"Now, that sounds interesting." Reaching out, she rubbed her fingers on the lapel of his suit. "I like men in power. Men who do things outside the...let's say...the boundaries of society."

"Then I'm your guy." He called the bar worker over. "I'll have a manhattan. Get the little lady another." He turned back to her. "God, you're beautiful."

"Why, thank you. I find you...attractive, too." Not. There was no character in his face. Not like Luke's, David's, Jess's. Even Alex Lansing's innate personality came out in photos.

During the next hour, Krueger consumed three strong drinks.

After which, his eyes glazed over. "I know it's only eight but how about finishing our evening at my place? It's not far from here." He moved in even closer. "Who knows how the evening will turn out?"

"Hmm. That sounds like fun. I'd love to."

• • •

ALISHA AND LUKE sat in his auto vehicle outside Craig Krueger's apartment building, while Dorian stayed at home with Jess. Everybody was on edge—and scared, after today's incident with the fire. Luke had wanted to call off Celeste's date with Krueger, but she had insisted they forge ahead.

She'd just gone inside the apartment with Krueger. She was wearing a wired microphone—Luke had insisted—so he'd know what was going on. Still, this was dangerous.

"I'm worried about her." Alisha had agreed with the plan because it was the most logical, but her concern matched his.

"She's handling it like a pro." Luke tried to comfort Alisha. He rarely saw her vulnerable. "She got him back here. Now she just has to finish up."

Over the mic, they heard Celeste speak. "Do you have any wine?"

"I, um, guess." His words were slurred.

"I'd like a glass."

"No more for me," Krueger mumbled, "if I'm gonna satisfy you, baby."

"Yuck." Alisha wrinkled her nose. "He offs me."

Despite the gravity of the situation, Luke burst out laughing. "I hope not."

"Did I say it wrong?"

"I think you meant puts you off. *Offing* somebody has a variety of meanings—one is murder and one is bringing someone to climax in sex."

The two began speaking again, precluding a reaction from Alisha.

"Thank you, Craig. Would you mind putting on some music?"

"Sure. Set the mood and all that."

Alisha asked, "This is where she'll dump the drug into his drink, right?"

"Yeah. A fast-acting sedative."

"We don't need those in our time."

"Of course you don't."

Again, the conversation in the apartment began. "Don't you like your wine, Craig?"

"I guess. I'd rather be in bed fucking you."

"What a jerk." Alisha used the contemporary term, which seemed to be appropriate.

"Oh. But *I* need a little more loosening up."

A few minutes of small talk interspersed with silence.

"Okay, do…" Krueger finally said, "Um, Jesus, I don't feel… What the hell…"

Luke and Alisha stilled when they heard a thud. Then Celeste's voice, no longer flirty and fun. "Okay, come on up. Krueger's out of consciousness. We're in Apartment 4467. I'll buzz open the door from here." Then she added, "He's an asshole."

"She got that word right," Luke said as he and Alisha exited the car.

After Celeste buzzed them in, they took the elevator up to the fourth floor and got inside the apartment—all modern glass and chrome—in minutes. Luke strode immediately to Krueger and checked him out. "He's down for a while. I'll get him into bed now so when he wakes up, he'll think we went there last night."

"Good." Alisha scanned the room. "I'll go work on his computer."

When she crossed to the desk, which housed a state-of-the-art system, Celeste said to Luke, "Let's hope Alisha finds evidence of the plot against Jess. Krueger got close to me tonight. He's ambitious, greedy; his sexual longings are dangerous, I think."

"Man, I don't like hearing that," Luke told her. And neither would Dorian.

• • •

"NOTHING?" JESS ASKED incredulously. "There was *nothing* on his computer?"

Dorian watched Jess and Helen deflate before her eyes. Their shoulders sagged and they seemed to just...droop from where they sat close on the couch in the family room. Everyone had been hoping to receive good news when Celeste, Alisha and Luke returned from their latest pursuit of Craig Krueger.

Perched on a chair, Celeste said gently, "Nothing about you, Jess."

"Do we have the wrong man?" Helen asked.

"I don't think so. Celeste read him and believes we're on the right track." Luke's face was somber and he was pacing, which only made everyone else edgier.

Pointing to her handheld computeller, Helen asked, "Are you sure there's nothing on that thing about Krueger?"

"We told you before, Helen, no. I seek your forgiveness."

"I'm not ready to give up," Celeste put in.

"You're *not* going to be alone with that man again." Alisha surprised them all with the statement. "What I *did* find on his drive hard was enough to keep you away from him."

Jess angled his head. "What did you find?"

"Pornography. From what I understand, this type of thing is common in your time period. But his was of the sadistic-masochistic kind. I'm not letting Celeste near him."

"I can handle myself."

Dorian and Alisha, who'd been studying the notes she'd taken, said simultaneously, "No, you can't."

Celeste rolled her eyes. She was the best of all three of them at affecting some of the gestures of the time. "He's plotting to murder Jess. I feel it."

Turning her face into her husband's shoulder, Helen whimpered.

"I seek your forgiveness, Helen, but things have to be said aloud. Besides, now that we know Krueger's proclivities, we can use them against him if need be."

"Oh, yeah, like we're going to let you dress up as a dominatrix." Luke's voice was full of sarcasm, but it was easy to see his tone disguised worry.

Three blank faces. Then,

"What is that?"

"A what?"

"Oh, dear Nord."

While Helen explained the term, Luke shook his head. "Since we didn't get anywhere tonight, I'm going to arrange for the private security firm I've been in contact with to implement protection permanently. I asked Dick Anderson to stand by." He pulled out his phone. "Because we know that the…attempt will happen in a few weeks, a team will be in front and back of the house 24/7 until this is over."

Dorian felt heat rise inside her. "What do you think you're doing? I can protect Jess when I'm here. We can use Anderson when I'm not."

"We're all exhausted," Luke explained impatiently. "We need time to regroup. Plan. We'll be distracted with getting to Krueger, so I'm calling in reinforcements."

Dorian raised her chin. "Why is this your decision?"

"Because I know best."

"I object."

"You can object all you want, doll, but it's *a fait accompli.*"

"Whatever the hellor that means," she snapped. How could this man incense her so easily? She hated that.

Jess stood and crossed to her. "Dorian, I appreciate all you're doing, but Luke's right. We're tired, we're disappointed. It won't hurt to have the house staked out for a while. Especially since we know when…it's going to happen."

His plea soothed her some toward *him,* but she was still angry at Luke's autocracy.

A small voice in her head told her she was manufacturing the ire against him because the more they were together, the more they agreed, the closer she felt to him.

"One security man will accompany you and Dorian to work," Luke pronounced as he held up the phone. Someone else will watch over Helen, too, when I'm running down leads. Who knows what these people will do? So I'm getting coverage for all of you."

Dorian stopped protesting. And Luke punched in the buttons.

Anderson must have answered on the other end, because Luke said, "Hey, buddy. I'm gonna need you tonight…Oh, great. See you shortly."

Jess asked, "Are they coming?"

"Yeah, Dick's with one of them now. Both of them are coming. He'd freed up his schedule and was waiting to hear from me."

"Wasn't he a cop with you a while ago?" Jess asked.

"Yeah, we got in some tight spots. I bailed him out a couple of times."

The trouble probably had to do with women. And sex. The notion caused Dorian further pique.

"Megadamn you, Luke." With that, she turned and headed for the stairs that led to the lower floor. She rarely reacted with anger, but this man had been unsettling her, arousing her and brushing off her opinions for too long. She simply couldn't be in his company any longer tonight.

• • •

"WOMEN!" LUKE THOUGHT as he drove his SUV back to his place in lower Brooklyn instead of staying at Jess's. He was afraid what he'd do if he was there in the same house with Dorian.

"So, she's pissed. Who cares? At least they're all safe. *She's* safe." Though he'd kept it to himself, for a while now, he'd been obsessing about the danger all three women had put themselves in. Especially Dorian, who dove in front of a moving car to save Jess. Now, that thought was intolerable. Probably one of Luke's best traits was that he never kidded himself and he knew what he was feeling.

When he swerved into the other lane, he realized he was preoccupied, so he waited until he could pull into a rest area. Shutting off the engine, he slid down the windows, letting the cool night air soothe him. He lay his head back against the seat.

Fuck, this was a mess. The slicing fear that Jess's death was to occur sometime in the next few weeks combined with what he'd come to feel for Dorian was haunting him. He wasn't thinking clearly and he bet she wasn't, either. So he'd put in place Plan B. They needed help from Anderson, no matter how mad she got. He'd been right, damn it. *Mega*damn it.

A sudden fatigue swept over him and he wasn't surprised. His sleeping had been interrupted by fear for Jess and desire for Dorian. Raising the windows and locking the doors, he closed his eyes just for a few minutes…

Dorian approached him. She was wearing a short see-through nightgown. Beneath it were generous breasts, a nipped-in waist and curvy hips. When she came up to the bed, he got instantly hard. He reached for her…

The blast of a horn from the road had him bolting up in the car. His chest hit the steering wheel with a thump.

Luke looked around, trying to get his bearings. When he realized where he was and that he'd been dreaming about her, he started the engine and spat out, "Fuck this!"

• • •

THOUGH IT WAS late, and her neck was cramping, Dorian stared at the history chips on the computeller and sighed. Like Alisha, she could find nothing about the exact date of Jess's death.

She wished she could travel several weeks ahead in time and search this period's Internet to find out the method, date and time of it. Alisha would never allow that even if they could find a portal through the computeller to match the current date. Still, she might talk to her friend and see what they could determine.

Exhausted, she rose from the desk and turned on the video box. Though she'd never *vagued out* (their term) in front of it, she dropped down on the couch and searched the channels. Her eye caught on something that interested her. A *Star Trek* movie. She recognized it because Celeste had been remarking—maybe a little too much—how Alex Lansing resembled the captain of the ship.

Dorian watched their portrayal of the future with interest. Huh, they had something like a Multimed unit, which they used to fix inner organs, tendons and muscles. Then the plot turned to time travel. The spaceship jettisoned back in time by breaking the speed barrier—which had been proved to be impossible by her time period. What the hellor? They traveled in time to today to retrieve whales and bring them to the present so they could communicate with a threatening alien probe?

Dorian thought about the possibility of life on other planets. By 2200, communication with extraterrestrial species had been attempted, and then the pollution got so bad, any kind of space travel or interest in it became irrelevant.

As she watched the characters arrive and be weakened by the jump to the present, she said, "You got that right." Since she was talking to them, she added, "But you really shouldn't go back in time. You might meet a brown-eyed devil who throws your hormones into havoc."

When even a video reminded her of Luke, Dorian turned off the box and stood abruptly. She refused to dwell on Lucas Cromwell. Instead, she strode to the bathing room and decided on a hot shower. She and Celeste had used water for this purpose sparingly, still conscious of how these people squandered their natural resources. But tonight, she was lured into being showered in the precious commodity.

As soon as the spray hit her head, she immediately calmed. Taking a dollop of what Helen called shampoo, Dorian lathered her hair. For some reason, all of their hair had grown about a half inch per week. Alisha trimmed hers but Dorian and Celeste decided to let theirs grow longer to see what it looked like.

The soap felt luxurious. Its lavender scent filled the small space. Her scalp breathed. Suddenly she wondered what it would feel like to have her head massaged by someone. By Luke. His hands would be gentle, despite the hardening of them in spots. They would knead and press and bring forth sensations that would be paradoxically calming and arousing at the same time. Eventually, she rinsed.

Using the soap bar, which smelled like the shampoo, she began to wash her skin. She caressed her breasts. Suddenly, again, she was bombarded by the memory of having Luke's hands there, massaging her. It had felt so wonderful, so much more than she'd ever experienced in joining with another man. An awareness of that sensation bathed her as much as the water.

Without her conscious intent, her hands slipped lower over sensitized skin. She felt her ribs, her stomach—flat and taut—which would contract at Luke's touch. Her hands went lower. Luke would cover her here and press. Make small circles, first gently, then with increasing need. His breath would speed up like hers, and his body would tighten.

Megadamn, what was she doing? She'd made her need of release even greater. She could do it herself right here, of course, or use her vagino—each brought one with them—but tonight, that whole method of satisfaction was unappealing.

She shut off the water, left the shower space and picked up a towel. She missed the drying tube, and—oh, hellor—the abrasion of real cotton on her skin was stimulating. As if she needed more. Maybe she'd take care of this problem herself, after all. Wrapping the towel around her, she left the bathing room and entered the sleeping room to use the device.

And stopped short. "Oh!"

Slouched in the chair next to her sleeping conformer was Luke Cromwell, all masculine grace and arrogance, the latter proved true by his sensual perusal. He took his time; each area of her body he scanned reacted to his gaze...her mouth, her breasts, lower, and lower. After he finished, he said silkily, "Come here, Dorian." He arched a brow and megadamn, if that wasn't sexy. "And lose the towel."

CHAPTER 14

LUKE THOUGHT HE might swallow his tongue when she came out of the bathroom like some starlet in a grade B science-fiction movie, which wasn't a bad comparison, given their situation. The dim lamp from the corner of the room bathed her in an ethereal glow, outlined every supple curve he'd only imagined she had. Those thoughts—and a freaking erotic dream that would drive any healthy man crazy—had brought him here like some caveman, come to claim his woman.

She'd stilled at his command, and his gaze took her in. Could she be any more alluring, her skin still damp from the shower, her hair slicked back off her face, her features sharp and beautiful? For an eternity, she watched him, as if deciding… Ah, now she walked toward him, her head held high, her lips parted, her eyes glowing. She stopped in front of him, looked down, as he was still seated. He swallowed hard at the raw desire in her eyes that had him reaching for the towel. His big hand looked very male against her skin as he unknotted the white terrycloth. It slid down her body as it fell to the floor.

His intake of breath was instantaneous, and his hands went to her waist. He leaned forward and kissed her ribcage. Her fingers slid into his hair, threading though it, massaging his scalp. Moaning, he drew back, said, "Straddle my lap," and tugged her close. The chair was wide, thank God, and she maneuvered herself onto him. The sensation of having her in his lap, while she was naked and he was fully clothed, made his body buck.

Her eyes widened. "Oh!"

He growled. Nuzzled his nose between her breasts, licked her there. She smelled of soap, but Dorian had a scent of her own, too, all foreign and exotic, and his mind tripped with the fantasy of a king and a harem girl, who belonged to him.

She kissed his head and he moved his mouth to her breast. Most of the time, she kept these bound with cloth, except for that night in the dressy dress when she'd worn a bra. Now, unfettered, her breasts were plump and womanly. He took a nipple into his mouth, tugged on it with his teeth, and she jolted. "Oh, Nord. That feels so good."

He stopped. Looked up. "Don't you…in the future?"

"Yes, but sex then is more scripted, more clinical. Don't stop."

Grinning—he'd be damned if he wouldn't be special—he treated the other breast to the same attention. Then, he pushed her away again. "Here," he said. "Sit on my lap. Swivel around so both of your legs face one way." He helped her maneuver. "Now part them."

"What…? Luke, what are we doing?"

"Lie back on my arm. Spread your legs."

"Why?"

"Jesus Christ, you don't know what I'm going to do, do you?"

"No."

"You're in for a treat, baby."

He placed his hand between her thighs, found her clit and rubbed. She started to spiral quickly, so he plunged two fingers inside of her, and she went off like a shot. Her moans were the most beautiful thing he'd ever heard in his life.

• • •

DORIAN CAME BACK to consciousness and found herself nestling into Luke. She'd never sat on a male's lap, never burrowed into any man, but the reaction came naturally. Her mind was still spinning when he pressed his hand into her mound. Sensation slivered to every nerve ending.

"Now, how come you didn't know about this?"

"Men have never done this to me. I mean, I've felt orgasms with a device when I'm alone, but..."

"So all climaxes with men come during intercourse?"

"In joining, yes."

"Huh." He held her even closer; she was awash with so many emotions she couldn't identify all of them. "Huh," he added, "one down three to go." He glanced at his watch. "But we've already used up three minutes."

She chuckled. "Stop. We're not bound by the silly time frame."

"Hey, you insulted my virility. You said I couldn't satisfy you."

Putting her mouth next to his ear, she whispered, "I was wrong. Very wrong."

"Nope, you're not getting out of this one. Even if I have to take some little blue pills, I'm gonna do this."

Her whole body tensed. "No, don't even say you'd do such a thing." A thought assaulted her. "You haven't used those drugs before, have you?"

A smile. "Not yet. But I would."

"Oh, Luke, you have no idea what they can do."

He stilled. "Does this have something to do with your fertility issues?"

"I can't answer that. Just don't use it. Ever." She tugged at his shirt. "You need to undress."

"Women and men of our time undress each other."

"Earnestly?"

"Yeah. It's fun."

"I suppose I could try." She slipped off his lap and stood before him. "Okay, stand." When he did, she could feel an almost childish glee invade her. To be joking, teasing like this during the joining time was unthinkable in her society. She started with his white shirt. He'd already removed that awful neck thing he'd worn tonight, and she began to undo the fasteners. "We don't have buttons in our time. Material is made to adhere and pulls apart easily when necessary."

"I want to know all about how you make your clothes, but later. This is naughty-talk time."

"Naughty? I don't know that word."

"You will, sweetheart, before the night's over."

He sounded so smug she decided it was time to take the reins. She'd seen this done on the video box programs Celeste liked to watch, and so she slid the material off him and pressed her lips to his skin when it was bared. His chest was sprinkled with dark hair, dear Nord, unlike any man of her time. She ran her fingers through it and over his nipples. He jolted, just as she had. Hmm. Leaning in, she tongued the spot, scraped it with her teeth. Grasping on to her shoulders, he said hoarsely, "You're learning fast."

"Oh, good."

Her hands went to the crazy thing they called a belt. She unfastened that and the zipper, which she thought could do damage to his genital parts. Desire had returned, making her anxious, and she fumbled when she pushed his trousers down and was greeted with tight, black shorts. "Oh, my, those are...very appealing, very *cool,* I think you'd say." She gently snapped the elastic band.

He took her hand and placed it on his groin. "What's inside isn't cool, sweetheart; it's hot. Really hot. For you."

The sensuous female in her took over and she knelt in front of him, pulling off his shoes, trousers and then the under garment. He sprang to life in front of her face and she jumped back. Luke guffawed. He managed to say, "I'm sorry, but you should have seen your reaction."

"I've never had a genital part jump out at me like that."

"Genital part?" His laughter increased.

"What do you call it? I saw it on the history chips, but I forget."

"A penis."

"Hmm." She took his *penis* between her palms. "I know how to stimulate this penis of yours before joining."

He grasped her shoulders, tugged her up. "I'm sure you do, but I want to be inside you first time."

"That sounds so...intimate."

"It is." He brought her to the bed, pulled down the covers. "Slip inside," he told her coaxingly, and Dorian knew in that moment she'd do just about anything he asked right now.

• • •

HE STRETCHED OUT beside her and ran his hand over her neck. Her jaw. The hollows of her throat. He kissed her shoulders one at a time and licked her chest.

"Luke, please, touch me more. Deeper."

"Whatever you say." He'd only suckled her breasts for a few seconds, when she breathed out harshly, "I'm ready to join now. *Right* now."

"Nope. I'm not ready."

She slid her hand in between them. "I don't understand. You're like rock."

"I haven't gotten my emotional satisfaction yet."

She said again, "I don't understand."

"You will."

He moved his mouth over her stomach, tickled her behind her knees, kissed her ankles. She was squirming when he crawled back up her body and braced himself over her. "All right," he said. "I'm ready now."

"Thank the godheads."

He drew her up so she faced him. "What...what are you doing *now?*" Her tone was totally exasperated.

"This is one of my favorite ways."

"Ways for what?"

Oh, God. "How do you make love?"

"Make love?"

"Join."

"We join in two ways, either the man or woman on top."

"Shit. You don't do anything but the missionary position?"

"Luke, I don't know what that means. But I really don't care right now. Just—"

"I'll show you." He sat back on his haunches, then spread out each leg. "Now come and do what you did on the chair."

She looked wary but did as he asked. After she seated herself on him, he added, "Go up on your knees." She did. He took his cock in his hands. "Now settle down gently on me."

Grasping his shoulders, she slowly began to impale herself on him. So goddamned slowly, he thought he might explode before she even finished.

When she finally had him fully inside her, he murmured, "Look at me, love." His gaze captured hers. "There. Isn't that nice?"

"More than. But Luke..."

He placed his hands on her hips and moved her up and down.

Spontaneously, she participated. "Oh, dear, oh, Luke, I never, honestly. Oh, megadamn."

Then she stopped talking and, after a few thrusts, she spiraled out of control.

Watching her face as she came destroyed his control. Even before she was done, he began to push harder into her. The sensations came one on top of the other until they eclipsed everything else.

• • •

THEY STAYED PLASTERED to each other, which never happened during joining in her time. He smelled of sweat and sex, and the combination drove her crazy. Dorian whispered against his shoulder, "I can't believe I'm still alive."

She felt him grin against her skin. "I know. Me, too."

Moving back, she looked at him to see he was smiling. "Is sex always this intense in your time period?"

He brushed locks of her dark hair from her forehead. "No, not always. What happened between us was very special."

"It was totally different from anything I've ever done."

"Because of the position?"

"No, not just that. Luke, it was so intimate. I allowed you into me. And not just physically."

"I know, sweetheart. I did the same with you."

Shaking her head, she ran a hand through his chest hair. "No wonder you don't have multiple partners as a rule. You could never share so much of yourself with several others."

"I'm glad to hear you say that." He brushed a hand down her cheek, then eased her back to a lying position. Again, he stretched out beside her, slid his arm around her and pulled a sheet over them because of the chilled air coming through the open window.

"I like this, too," she whispered after a while.

"What, cuddling?"

"Cud-dul-ing?" She tried the word out.

"Yep."

"I feel very close to you."

He glanced down at her. "Then, why are you frowning?"

"I don't like you sometimes. I was very angry at you earlier tonight."

"And I was angry at you. We need to keep everybody safe, Dorian. It was necessary to call in more people."

She was quiet. "That concerns me, Luke. I've come here to protect Jess. At all costs."

"I know. But you getting hurt is just not acceptable anymore."

"Can we discuss this later? I don't want to fight with you. It's diminishing the closeness I feel to you. Let's sleep this way."

"Sleep?" he said, and she could hear the humor in his voice. "Not on your life. We got two more go-arounds left."

She giggled. "I have no desire for two more. I want to rest."

"Hmm," he said thoughtfully. "Maybe just once."

Leaning over her, he crawled his way down her body. She spread her legs and he knelt between them. And started to lower his head.

Dumbfounded she bolted up. "Are you going to do what I think you are?"

"Yep. Never done this either?"

"Never."

"Hallelujah. You're in for a treat."

She tugged on his hair. "All right, on one condition."

"What?"

"That you show me how to do it back to you."

Oh, God. Luke thought he'd probably died and gone to heaven. "You're on, babe."

CHAPTER 15

DORIAN AWOKE WRAPPED up in strong masculine arms. She was overcome by a sense of well-being so powerful it caused her to *cuddle* into the chest where her cheek lay. Slowly, though, anxiety set in.

By the godheads, what had she done? She'd never, ever spent the night in a bed with a man. And the early hours of the morning with Luke had been one of the best times of her life. She'd experienced pleasure like none other before. But there was a downside to the high of all that. Fear tinged it. She'd given so much of herself to a male. How did people walk away from their partners after doing what she and Luke had done together? All she wanted was to be with him again, experience the pleasure again. That was different enough, but it wasn't only the need for sex she felt; she needed to be in his company.

"Good morning."

She eased back. Nord, his beard had grown overnight and she longed to touch it. Taste it. Taste him all over as she'd done during the early hours of the day. "Hello."

Raising his arm—his scent was still of sweat and sex and not at all unpleasant, though he should clean his teeth soon—he rubbed his thumb between her brows. "Frowning again, sweetheart?"

"You alternated calling me *sweetheart* and *babe* last night." The frown deepened. "I like them both, though I find them extremely strange."

"Terms of endearment. You'll get used to them."

So he was planning to be with her again. Some of the tightness in her chest loosened. How did people react when the response from someone they'd just shared themselves with was negative?

"So, answer my question."

There was only one way to deal with this—to be honest. "My feelings this morning for you are compelling and something else. Needy, maybe."

He tipped up her chin. "That's how you're supposed to feel. We didn't have meaningless sex."

She hesitated, suddenly afraid to question him. But, no, she wouldn't be the shy, retiring female in this relationship. "Do you feel the same?"

The corners of his mouth lifted. Even that was endearing. "Ah, I can see there's not going to be any coyness here." She held his gaze steadily. "Yeah, I do. I want to be with you and not only for sex."

"I was thinking the same thing."

"Good." His hands snaked under the covers. "Because I want you again."

"And I—"

The door burst open and in rushed Alisha. She was fully dressed and appeared hassled. "Dorian, get up, quick—" Her mouth fell open.

"Jesus, Alisha, you have to stop interrupting us!" Luke was clearly irritated.

Alisha's eyes widened. "Oh, no, Dorian. What have you done?"

Feeling like a scolded youngling, Dorian wanted to sneak under the bed coverings but fought the urge.

"I think that's obvious," Luke said dryly.

"No, I mean, this is a terrible path to take. You can't trust men."

"Now, wait just a minute…"

Alisha stalked over to the bed. "I must insist you don't do this again."

"Good luck with that," Luke said, drawing Dorian close. "Now will you please leave? We're busy."

"No, I will not leave."

Luke stared hard at her, then shrugged. "Then, I might as well get up." Rolling out of bed, naked and beautiful, with a perfectly aroused genital part…penis, he stood in front of her friend.

Alisha's face reddened. Dorian had never seen her in such an awkward state. "The sight of that thing does not offend me." He didn't move. "Fine, I'll leave." She marched out, slamming the door.

"Busted," Luke said, turning to the bed with a big grin.

Dorian laughed. "I can figure out what that means."

"So, do you want to get up and get dressed?"

"Hellor, no." She reached out her hand.

"That's my girl." And Luke dove back into bed.

• • •

CELESTE'S STOMACH WAS churning and not because of anything she'd eaten or drunk. As she climbed the steps to the main part of the house, she was thinking about their unsuccessful attempt to find evidence of Craig Krueger's role in Jess's demise. *Botched,* Luke had called it.

She was also upset by the fact that such greed and longing for power existed in people today. She'd only told the others half the truth. Krueger wasn't an evil man, he just had pathological motivations, rooted in his childhood.

At the kitchen table, surrounded by the scent of coffee, she found a fuming Alisha and a more calm, but clearly unhappy, Jess and Helen.

"Hello." She went right to Helen. "Are you well this morning?"

"I'm trying to be strong," Helen answered honestly.

Celeste put her hand on Helen's shoulder.

"No, Celi, don't. You'll harm yourself."

Ignoring the plea, she drained some anxiety from Helen, making her own body weaker. "Stress is not good for the baby."

Helen smiled gratefully.

To get an energy boost, she crossed to the coffeepot.

"Caffeine is bad for the nervous system, especially yours." Alisha seemed more cranky than worried.

After pouring a cup and adding in some delicious cow product, Celeste took a place at the table. She sipped the still-tart brew, then asked, "What's wrong, Lisha?"

Before her friend answered, Celeste saw someone emerging from downstairs. Two people.

Unabashedly, Luke circled his arm around Dorian. "Good morning, everybody."

Jess smiled. "I guess it is for you two."

He kissed Dorian's head. "You got that right."

Grumpy Alisha's eyes narrowed. "Is this why you wanted additional support around the house? So you could join with Dorian?"

Now Luke's eyes burned. "No, it's not. I'll do anything to protect my brother." He faced Dorian. "Coffee, dear?"

"No, thank you. But I will have some of the juice of oranges. I like that."

Luke retrieved both juice for her and coffee for him, then he and Dorian dropped down in the remaining chairs.

When they were settled, Celeste began the conversation. "I have something to say."

"So do I." This from Alisha.

Dorian shook her head at Lisha. "We aren't discussing Luke and me. It's none of your busy."

"Business," Alisha corrected. "And yes, it is."

"I don't think so," Luke stated.

"We're here on a mission. We can't afford to be distracted by sex. Honestly, you all make so much of physical need. It's like craving water or sustenance."

Tired of bickering, Celeste slapped her hand on the table. "Stop, both of you!" They all thought she was mild mannered and weak. But she was stronger than they knew. And she was going to give them one chance to agree to her plan. "We have more important things to discuss. I'll start. I think I should contact Craig Krueger today. Make up a story about what happened last night. There's so much inside him that I'm bound to find a way to get proof. I simply need more time."

Helen, Jess and Luke said simultaneously,

"No."

"No."

"Hell, no."

Celeste exchanged looks with Alisha. She took in a deep breath—to calm herself?—and shook her head. "I agree with them."

Glancing around at the people she'd come to care about deeply, she sighed. "You all don't understand. Women don't need to be protected in our time. We're as capable as men in physical strength and stamina. I have all the tools necessary to continue this chase until we get what we need from Krueger."

Luke's face reddened, and Celeste knew his blood pressure had spiked. "I wouldn't want a *man* to walk back into the snake's pit."

Celeste frowned. "It's not your decision, Luke."

He stood abruptly. "The hell it isn't. I'm calling the FBI."

"And tell them what?" Alisha's voice rose. "We have no proof."

"They can talk to his wife."

"Do you really think she'll tell them what she told us?" Alisha asked. "We caught her at a weak moment."

"The bureau has ways to coerce her into talking. I'll bring her to them for questioning."

"I don't believe she will talk, Luke." This from Celeste. "When I stayed back after you two went to the auto vehicle, she indicated she wouldn't turn him in, I think you call it. And I sensed she won't."

Dorian touched Luke's arm in a gesture so natural it made Celeste almost jealous. "I agree with Celi. Our better choice is going with Celi's plan."

"No. Absolutely not." Luke again. "We'll figure something else out."

Jess and Helen looked frightened.

Alisha and Dorian seemed frustrated.

And Luke was mad.

Suddenly, this was no longer a good dawning.

• • •

FROM A MAP on the Internet, Celeste had memorized how to take the multi-rider vehicle called a bus to Lower Manhattan. She'd styled her hair, applied the makeup Helen had bought them and donned a peach sundress. They had no frivolous garments in her time, and she liked the feel of material on her skin and the breeze on her bare legs. She brought her small computeller on her mission so she could continue to study the history chips on the ride, but the smell of the fuel made her gag. The lurching and quick turns pitched her stomach. Reading was out of the question, so she turned her thoughts to something pleasant.

She called up a photo of the Lansing children on her device. They were beautiful, all with blond hair lighter than their father's. He was attractive, too. What had happened between Dorian and Luke came to mind. Celeste wondered if she would have to join with Lansing to do her job.

Would she have to join with Krueger today to get any additional information? Though the notion made her stomach even queasier, she could block her sensitivity when need be. She'd wall herself off from him. Because she'd do anything for Jess and his family, now. And for future generations.

Finally, the bus arrived. She exited at a place called Midtown Station. She bought nourishment at a stand, then took a paid auto vehicle to the correct building in Lower Manhattan, which held dwellings for multiple people. The streets looked different in the light of day with pedestrians walking about and less traffic, but she remembered the way.

Inside, she saw the building needed some repair: a new coat of paint, a correction of the chips in the tile. But basically, it was solid and clean.

Someone stood behind a front desk. She'd remembered that Krueger had told her a doorman was on duty during the days to accept packages and be available for tenants. She approached him with a smile. "Hello, there."

The man was young, with longish hair, wearing denim trousers and a yellow dress shirt. "Hello." He gave her a questioning look. And a very appreciative once-over.

"I was here last night with Mr. Krueger." She held up a bag. "I've brought him coffee and some pastries this morning." To confirm her statement, she opened the bag some, and the scents drifted out.

"I'll buzz him and tell him you're here."

She gave him a purposely sexual smile. Then she grasped his arm, and transmitted a powerfully positive feeling to the man. "I'd like to surprise him, if it's okay? I have a key." She produced the spare one she'd taken last night when they realized they weren't finding proof.

"I guess it would be all right, since you have a key."

"Thank you," she read his tag "Eddie."

As she walked to the primitive box that would take her up, she heard him mumble, "Krueger is one lucky bastard."

Really, how would Eddie know the circumstances of the man's birth?

Brushing off her question, she prepared herself for meeting Krueger again. She had a plan to follow. Still, her heartbeat escalated on the ride up. Making her way down the corridor, she arrived at 4467 and took a steadying breath, then slipped the key in the lock. The door swished open.

Inside, the place was still and silent. Unwashed wine glasses sat on the table in the main room, producing a stale scent. Where was he? Could she be so lucky that he'd still be sleeping? She fingered the vial in her pocket that she'd used on him last night. Today, it contained liquid not nearly as strong—she didn't dare disable him for as long as last night. Quietly, she ducked down the hallway and found his open door. By the godheads, he *was* still asleep. But would he stay that way? She couldn't take the chance.

Changing her mind about her strategy, she entered the bathing room off the hallway, removed and hid her clothing, and wrapped herself up in the terrycloth. Then she poured the sedative into the coffee she'd bought at Midtown. Making her way back to the bedroom, she took in a deep breath to gather

her strength and focus. Then she went to the bed and sat down on the edge of the mattress. "Craig, honey, wake up."

He moaned.

"Craig. Come on," she whined, hopefully in the way women did today. "I've been waiting all morning." She bent down to tickle his ear with her breath. The smell of sour liquor gagged her, so she tried to breathe only through her mouth.

Finally, he roused. "What the fuck?" he said after opening his eyes.

"Hi, sleepyhead."

"Celeste?" He took in her towel, her disheveled hair. Then looked down at his body. She wished she'd thought to remove his clothing last night, but who knew he'd sleep this long. "What happened?"

"I'm afraid you had too much to drink last night. You passed out in here."

He closed his eyes. "My head is killing me."

"Too much alcohol."

His eyes narrowed on the edge of the towel binding at her breasts. "You stayed?"

"I drank too much myself. I fell asleep on your couch."

"Did you take a shower?"

"Um, yes." She fingered the towel. "So, how about sipping some of this coffee?" She gave him a coy look. "And we'll try this again."

"You're on."

Four minutes later, he was out cold.

• • •

THIS IS YOUR dwelling?" Dorian asked when she and Luke entered his home on the side of Brooklyn that was closest to

Manhattan. Contrary to his brother's huge house, Luke's space was smaller (though large compared to her future dwelling). It consisted of one main area with leather furniture, tan walls and a video box with the largest screen she'd ever seen. A miniscule cooking room jutted off of it, and he showed her two sleeping areas down a hallway.

"Home sweet home."

She smiled. "That's a nice thought. I guess in my time, it would be dwelling, sweet dwelling."

He chuckled and kissed her on the mouth. They'd shared this easy affection since they'd left Jess's around noon. Celeste had gotten some pain in her head—a headache—and had gone to lie down, and Alisha went for a running out of inside. When Luke had suggested they go to his apartment so he could clean up (and be alone with her, she guessed) her first concern had been Jess…

"Look, the two security people are outside. One is my friend Dick. I'd trust him with my life. Like I said last night, we were cops together and he saved my hide more than once."

"Your hide? Like an animal's?"

He'd grabbed her around the waist and growled into her ear, "You do unleash that primal beast in me."

She'd felt herself warm…

"I'm going to get a beer. Want one?"

"I would like to try one sometime, but we'll be going back to Jess's in a bit and I have to be clearheaded." She gave a shy smile. "I very much liked how I felt after a glass of wine."

He grinned. "How about a soda?"

"Alisha strongly objects to those."

He kissed her nose. "Alisha isn't here, love."

Love. The word was never spoken between men and women of her time. Would he someday tell her his love was hers? Did she even want that? Her emotions were in a jumbled mass, so she wasn't sure of anything but the fact that she wanted to be with Luke.

They took seats on his couch made of animal skin, which was a preposterous waste, but the covering was soft and practically absorbed her. "We've only talked about life-and-death things, Luke. Tell me about your work."

Lounging on the cushions, he looked relaxed and happy. "I fight crime."

She frowned.

"Do you have crime in your time?"

"Some. Miscreants are rare because all needs are met communally, but there are some psychopaths who bring harm to others. We have a program to deal with them, which is very effective and has a low recidivism rate. And I cannot remember a time when a person's life was ended, though."

"Really? No murder? I think I'd like to live in your time."

"There's a ninety-eight point-six probability that I can never go back." The comment just slipped out.

"I know. I'm sorry." He cocked his head. "Or maybe I'm not. This way, you can't leave me."

"If I could return, maybe you could come with me. Though who knows what kind of society will exist if we are successful in saving Jess, and Celeste does her part."

"Which is? You can tell me."

"I'd better not. Alisha is already as mad as bees at me."

Again, he laughed.

"I thought I got that right."

Coming quickly forward from his slouch, he took the soda from her hand and set it next to his beer on the table made of real wood. "You got a lot right last night. You blew the top of my head off."

"I know you don't mean that literally, but I appreciate the sentiment, which I know means we had terrific sex." Cupping his jaw with her hand, she whispered, "It was so good, Luke."

"Wanna try it again?"

"You know I do."

He reached for the buttons on her blouse.

"Here? Not in the sleeping room?"

"Yeah, let's live dangerously."

He had her blouse off when her computeller buzzed.

"Let it go."

"I can't. Neither Celi nor Alisha would contact me if it wasn't important."

"Alisha would. Just to interrupt us."

She clicked into the machine. "Lisha?"

"I told you," Luke grumbled.

"We have a problem. Celeste is gone."

"Gone?"

"I went to check on her and she isn't in her sleeping space."

Dorian looked to Luke. "Celeste is gone."

"Goddamned, fucking son of a bitch." He stood and began to adjust his clothing.

"Where is she?" Dorian asked.

Luke came into view of the computeller. "She went after Krueger, right? Despite our objections."

Alisha's face was taut. "That's what I think."

"We're closest to town. We'll go down there."

"All right."

Dorian ended transmission. "She's in danger, isn't she?"

"Yes, she is. We have to hurry."

• • •

CELESTE WIPED SWEAT off her brow. Like Dorian, she hadn't had the sensation of sweat in her time, so the first time it had happened, she was fascinated. Now, she was simply frustrated. The small dwelling was hot and stuffy, but she was afraid to open windows or turn the conditioner of air on for fear of waking Krueger.

For an hour, she'd searched every space where he might have hidden proof of his intent to hurt Jess and found nothing: no second computer device, which they'd scoured the place for last night, no papers that were incriminating in the desk. Perhaps Craig Krueger was not guilty.

But she didn't believe in his innocence. The things of his she touched bore remnants of his resentments—the shirts in his clothing space, the dishes he'd used. Even his personal-hygiene equipment. She didn't always get vibrations from inanimate objects, but his *stuff* bore his ill will.

Discouraged, she pulled open a door that led to a little room that she'd learned earlier was called a closet. They searched it last night, but now she pulled back the heavy clothing and when she saw nothing, out of frustration she kicked the wall. A panel clicked open. Oh, Nord! Inside was a rectangular box. Picking it up, she tried to open the thing but it was locked. Hmm. Nothing else in the house had been secured. She took it out to the eating room and retrieved a utensil. The lock snapped the third time she jiggled it with the sharp object. She lifted the lid.

Inside was a key. Etched in it was *#456.* When she picked it up, she was overcome with sensation: ugly smells, loud noises and a sense of evil that knocked her back on her heels.

Think, Celi, think.

His computer? It had contained financial information. If he paid for the storage of something, there might be a record. She found the machine where they left it last night and called up his owed payments. After five minutes, she saw an item with the number 456: Midtown Bus Station. Something must be there that the key unlocked. Excited, Celeste left the room, then the dwelling. There wasn't a peeper out of Krueger.

In the reception area, Eddie smiled at her. "Leaving so soon?"

She pouted, another gesture of the time. "He's still asleep. I waited but..." She smiled shyly at him. Men of their time seemed to like that gesture. "He's still sleeping. He won't get up."

"Crazy fellow, then."

"I'll be back." She used the wink she'd practiced and headed for the door. She'd gotten a few feet down the walkway when a vehicle pulled up in front of the building. Dorian and Luke bolted out of each side, and Luke slammed his door. He circled the car and grabbed her by the shoulders. "What the fuck do you think you're doing? Are you crazy?" Fear poured out of him.

She touched his chest to calm him. "I seek your forgiveness. I didn't mean to worry you. But don't be angry."

"I'm angry, too," Dorian told her. "You could have been harmed."

"I wasn't. And I found something. You'll be glad I did this."

• • •

THE BIG STRUCTURE that held the busses swarmed with people. There were so many of them, with their scents so strong and conflicting, and the cacophony was so constant, Dorian had to steel herself from overreacting. She glanced at Celeste, who'd gone white from the sensory overload.

"All you all right, Celi?"

Celeste put her hand on her stomach. "This is the place the key is connected to. I recognize the sensations I got from holding it. The surroundings are hard for me to deal with."

"Yeah, well you're going to have a lot more to deal with after we get what we came for, doll. Like me! I'm furious with you."

By now, Dorian figured *doll* was an insult, but an affectionate one.

"Luke, please, not now."

He drew in a deep breath and put his hand on Dorian's shoulder. "You're right. Let's go. The lockers are this way."

They headed down an equally fetid hallway where small storage boxes were stacked one on top of the other. People banged open or flung shut several as they passed by, and the steel hitting steel reverberated loudly. Checking the numerals, Luke hurried ahead of them, his stride long, his steps determined. In a few minutes, they reached the four hundreds. Finding 456, Luke sent Dorian a hopeful look and held the key up to the lock. Stuck it inside. The small, metal door sprung loose.

Celi practically deflated and had to brace her arm on the wall. "Thank the godheads."

Luke peered into the locker. Dorian could see several large envelopes nestled on the bottom. He removed them and put them in a gym bag he'd always stored in his vehicle and brought inside with him. "Come on, let's hurry. We don't know when he'll wake up, figure out what you did and show up here."

"Oh!" Celeste's hand went to her mouth.

"You aren't going to vomit, are you?" Alisha asked.

"I…I'm unsure if I closed the door where I found this. I got so excited…"

Luke felt for the gun at the small of his back, and Dorian checked to see if her stunner was on. Megadamn, the weapon wasn't there. She hadn't expected to need it when they left Jess's to go to Luke's living space.

"All the more reason to hurry." He was trying to be calm for the women, but Dorian already knew him well enough to see that he was bluffing. As they rounded the corner of the hallway, they came face-to-face with Craig Krueger.

Before anyone could react, he grabbed Celeste, pulled her into another shorter—and deserted—hallway and jammed his hand into her back. He said, "I'll shoot her if you don't turn over what you took out of my locker."

• • •

LUKE SAW THAT Krueger's eyes were crazed. The drug Celeste had given him would still be coursing through his system, but he didn't seem sluggish.

"I mean it. I don't know who the hell you are or why you tricked me, but I've come too far to let you three bozos take it away from me." His shirt half open, his hair askew and face red, he was clearly unstable.

Flipping up his shirttail, Luke flashed his star, which was on his belt. "This bozo is a New York City cop, mister. And you know what happens when a cop is shot. The rest of the force will hunt you down like a rabid dog."

"Yeah, sure. Cops don't break into apartments."

Celeste raised her chin. "I did not break in. You gave me a key."

"You cunt!" He pulled his hand away; the gun in it waved in front of her face.

Luke knew the longer this went on, the more could go wrong. He had to end it soon. "Give me the gun, Krueger. You're caught. You can't silence all three of us."

Wildly, Krueger glanced around. There were no people in the small hallway, but someone would come in here soon enough. Then others would be in danger, and Luke couldn't let that happen.

Celeste yelped when Krueger jammed the gun into her neck again. Luke glanced at Dorian and saw her eyes narrow. She was figuring out how to help her friend. Luke had to do something before the crazy, brave woman did. Suddenly, shouts erupted behind Krueger. "Finally, reinforcements are here!" Luke yelled.

Krueger took his eyes off Celeste for only a split second. But that was all Luke needed. Gun in hand, he rushed Krueger. "Get out of the way, Celi," he yelled just before he tackled the guy.

Krueger hit his head on the concrete.

Shots rang out.

Everything went black.

• • •

DORIAN AND CELESTE were holding hands when Jess, Helen and Alisha, along with Dick Anderson, arrived at the hospital. Jess's face was taut. "How is he?"

"He's in surgery. The bullet lodged in his shoulder. They say it's not serious, but..." Dorian felt water mist in her eyes and let go of Celeste. Her friend wasn't taking on *this* pain.

Alisha sat down on the other side of Dorian. "Are you all right?"

"No, of course not. I'm gravely concerned." She stared beseechingly at Alisha. "Don't be mad at Celi or me."

"I'm not mad." Alisha squeezed her hand. "I'm worried about you." She nodded to the doors to the treatment rooms for emergencies. "And Luke."

Sometimes, Alisha could really pull through.

"Hi, everyone." They looked up to see David Ryan, wearing his collar, standing before them. "Helen, I got your message. I was already here visiting someone who had to come down to the city for treatment." His gaze scanned the room and landed on Alisha. "What's going on?"

"Luke got shot," she told him.

"How badly is he hurt?"

"Bad enough!" Dorian blurted out. "I can*not* believe you have instruments of destruction that wound people. And you're allowed to carry them at will. What is wrong with your society?"

"I agree, Dorian." David's tone was calm. "Unfortunately, groups of powerful people in the country don't."

"Dorian means no harm. She's upset." Alisha leaned in so Anderson didn't hear. "Don't forget, we have the mini-Multimed. We can use it when he comes home."

"The what?" David asked, his brows raised.

"I'll explain it to you..." Alisha's voice trailed off and Dorian tracked her gaze.

A man in blue clothing came out through the treatment space doors, and they all stilled. He consulted with a female hospital employee at the desk, then approached them. "You're the family of Lieutenant Cromwell?"

Jess, holding on to Helen, nodded. "I'm his brother."

"He's going to be fine. The bullet didn't knick anything vital. It lodged near a bone and we did a clean extraction. He'll be in pain for a while. But the news is good."

The sudden relief made Dorian weaker, and water leaked profusely from her eyes. David crossed to her, dragged her close and held on to her.

"I can't believe I'm weeping. I didn't even know I could. I'm just so glad..."

"It's all right to cry." Now David's tone was dry. "Jess is crying, and the rest of us are teary. We'll all feel better for it."

After a while, Dorian calmed. She looked up to find Jess had come to her. "We can go in one at a time as soon as he's out of recovery."

"M-may I go after you and Helen?"

"Honey, you can go first. I'm sure he'd rather see your beautiful face than my ugly mug."

She tried to smile.

The wait was interminable. Now that the mood among them had brightened, Dorian became aware of the acrid smells in the place, the sound of ringing archaic phones and occasional moans of grief.

Alisha and Celeste were in deep discussion at a table, a bit away from her. She finally found the energy to join them.

"Are you feeling better?" This from Celeste. "He'll be fine, especially after we get him home."

"I'll be better as soon as I see him."

Alisha said, "You have affection for him. I was right. Joining in this time made you close to him. What will you do about that?"

"What do you mean?"

"Surely, you don't intend to live your entire life engulfed in this kind of turmoil."

"Stop it, Alisha." Celeste grabbed Dorian's hand. "This isn't the time to criticize her."

"Of course you're right. I just worry so much about you two. But I seek your forgiveness, Dorian. You don't have to concern yourself with anything right now but Luke."

• • •

LUKE SURFACED BY degrees from the darkness. He could hear people talking. Smell things that stung his nostrils. Feel the covers heavy on him. Finally, he was able to open his eyes. "Hello, Lieutenant. How are you feeling?" A nurse. Dressed in white.

His voice was a croak on the first try. Finally, he got out, "Like a truck hit me. I'm sore all over. What happened?"

"I'll let your brother tell you. We told him he could come in as soon as you began to rouse."

"I'm thirsty."

She put a cup with a straw to his mouth. "Just baby sips."

Though it hurt going down, the water cooled his parched lips and throat. As soon as he finished, a vision appeared in the doorway to his room. Her clothes were mussed, as was her hair, but her face was shining. She just stood there and stared at him. Was she biting her lip?

He said hoarsely, "Come here, love."

The nurse snorted. "I take it that isn't your brother. But you're a cop, so we'll let the family requirement go."

After the woman left them alone, Dorian crossed the room and sat on the edge of the mattress. Up close, he could see her eyes were red and puffy. "Have you been crying? Because of me?"

"Um..." Her eyes misted again. "I was so worried. Perpetrators are stunned in our time and they recover quickly."

"That's good." He reached to take her hand and moaned. "I'm okay. What happened to Krueger?"

"Do you remember that you charged at him?" Her voice shook. Even in the throes of pain, he recognized he'd never seen Dorian this vulnerable.

"Yeah, then I got shot and now I don't remember anything."

"Your gun went off, too."

"Is Krueger dead?"

"No, but he probably wishes he was."

"Meaning?"

A small smile broached her lips. "You shot him in his genital parts."

His chest started to rumble, but it hurt, so he tried to stifle the laughter. "Yeah? Great. Has he made a statement?"

"I don't know. The police are in his medical room."

Suddenly something occurred to him. "Where's my duffle bag?"

"Alisha has it with her."

"We need to look at the envelopes, then decide what to do." His eyes narrowed. "The police will want a statement now."

Her face reddened. "You can't tell them the truth about us, Luke."

"'Course not. We'll have to explain as much as we can, though." He grabbed her hand and winced.

"What's wrong?"

"My shoulder hurts like a bitch."

"You need to rest." She swallowed hard. "We can decide all this later."

"Kiss me."

Her brows arched. "Earnestly? When you're in pain?"

"I need you to." Now his voice was even hoarser. "You could have been harmed. Or worse."

Leaning over, she pressed her lips to his. The contact was so totally different from any she'd shared with him, so sweet and precious, it brought those tears to her eyes again. And damned near his.

It was then Luke realized he was in love with her.

• • •

SUNSHINE FLOODED THE den in Jess's house through the wide windows. The room was spacious and the pullout sofa bed was the best money could buy. Two days after he'd been rushed to the hospital, Luke let Jess and Dorian help him to the bed. He was glad to be here for several reasons. "Get the girls and their magic wand. My shoulder's throbbing."

"We're here." Celeste and Alisha walked in right behind the others with their miracle medical device.

Frowning, Alisha was all business. "Let's do this now so we can all think clearly."

"Not a minute too soon for me."

Leaning over him, she turned on the remote thing she'd used on Jess's ankle and ran it over his shoulder. Immediately, he felt the pain relief.

"Better?" she asked.

"By about sixty percent."

"We can use it again tomorrow. Your injury is multi-layered and worse than Jess's injury. We have to heal it slowly so we don't overcorrect your muscles."

"That thing's amazing."

"Surgery is unknown in our time. I hope your archaic methods didn't do more damage than good when they cut into you."

He rolled his eyes. "Thanks for the encouragement."

"You should take some pain-relief medicine." This from Dorian, who was now hovering behind Alisha. She still looked pale.

"I will. I have to talk with the police first."

"When are they coming?" Dorian asked.

"Any minute now. Helen is waiting for them." Jess took a seat on a leather side chair adjacent to a small couch, where Alisha and Celeste dropped down on cushions. "I hope this part goes well."

"We have to stick with as much of the truth as possible." Though he was still in pain, Luke wanted control of the situation.

Alisha stiffened. "As long as no one reveals who we are."

Luke couldn't imagine telling that whopper to his captain. "We have to have our stories straight. Does everybody remember what they're supposed to say?" Nods all around. "Celeste, especially you?"

"I'll be fine." She arched a brow. "Remember, I was the one instrumental in trapping Krueger."

"Which I'm still angry at you for," Luke snapped.

The doorbell rang and Dorian said worriedly, "They're here."

He grasped her hand. "This will work out. I promise."

Alisha's frown turned into a scowl. Dorian left him to sit on one of the straight chairs that had been brought in for this meeting.

Helen, who'd taken a couple of days off from work, ushered his colleagues in. Both were dressed in the dark suits Dorian had worn when she and Luke met the first time. That felt like eons ago, so much had happened.

"Hi, Luke." This from Ann Thompson, a homicide detective. She'd come because of Luke's statement in the hospital that the confrontation had occurred because of Krueger's plans to kill Jess. He'd already given one brief statement to them and ended up turning over the evidence without getting a look at it. But that had been unavoidable.

"Hey, Annie."

From the corner of his eye, he saw Dorian scowl.

Luke nodded to his captain. "Hi, Al."

As they took seats, Al asked, "How are you feeling?" His captain studied him. "You look damn good for taking a bullet."

"I'm in a hell of a lot of pain. I'm just too macho to let on."

Ann rolled her eyes, and Dorian's frown deepened.

"We can't keep him up too long," Jess said, according to the script they'd rehearsed in order to shorten the interview as much as possible.

"We won't." Ann took out an iPad. She read from the notes on it. "In the hospital, you told us you were investigating death threats against Jess."

"This is the personal matter we discussed, right?" Now Al's tone was official. Luke knew why. He'd broken protocol by not turning the case over to the department from the beginning.

"Right."

Ann continued, "You tracked them to Craig Krueger. Then Celeste Hart *got close* to him to try to find evidence." She scanned the room. "Hello, again, Ms. Hart."

"Hello, Lieutenant Thompson."

"That covers it," Luke said easily.

"Before we talk about what we found in the envelopes," his captain put in, "I want to know why the hell you didn't go through channels when the matter first came up."

This part was going to be tricky.

"It's because of me." Helen was still by the door and knew her role, too. She placed her hand on her stomach. "I'm pregnant. Because we've been waiting years for this to happen, Jess didn't want me upset, so he asked Luke to look into the threats on the QT. It's why he hired a bodyguard." She nodded to Dorian.

Ann shook her head. "Luke, you know better than to try to pull off that shit alone."

"Yeah, I guess." He smiled at Helen. "But I'd also do anything to make my sister-in-law's dream come true."

"As a man," Al put in, "I can understand that. As your captain, I'm going to have to take some action."

"I know I broke rules. Whatever you decide, I'll accept without protest."

"Let's deal with that later. First, tell us how you got the envelopes. If the information was obtained illegally, we won't be able to use it against Krueger."

Here, they'd decided to doctor the truth. "When he got drunk, Craig Krueger told Celeste about his big plans that were going to make him a star at Petron. She said she didn't believe him, so he showed her where the key was to the bus locker."

"Did you take it without his consent, Ms. Hart?" Ann wanted to know.

"No. I pretended to be skeptical, though this was precisely what we were after. I played on his ego, which men have in great quantity, and he was drunk, so he gave me the key and boasted I could go check out the bus-station locker." She shrugged, totally looking as if she'd done nothing wrong. "So I went."

Al shook his head. "Something seems off about this."

"Remember, he'd had several manhattans." And chemicals Luke wasn't going to mention. "I think in his alcohol haze, he was trying to impress her to get her in the sack. Then he passed out. Since she was there to get evidence—and he'd told her to—she called me, and we all went together. Apparently, he woke up, found Celeste and the key gone and followed us."

Al didn't look convinced.

"She didn't commit a crime, Al."

Ann sat forward. "His lawyers will want to go down that path because the evidence in the folders was damning."

"What was in them?" They were all dying to know.

"Copies of emails from Krueger to and from someone at Petron. All were about your brother. We're having our techs trace the IP address at Petron. But there was more. There was a notebook with Jess's research documented."

Luke nodded. "That's damning enough."

"That isn't all of it, either," Al said gravely. "Do you happen to remember a problem a few years ago with the fire chief of Hidden Cove?"

"What is Hidden Cove?" Alisha asked.

"A town about an hour from here," Al explained. "Some people were trying to take the fire chief down. I know the chief of police up there, Will Rossettie. They're friends. The key to their discovery was a website where a person can go to find people to…eliminate others."

Dorian and Alisha stayed stone-faced. But Celeste gasped. "I've never heard of anything like that. It's so awful."

"You can get anything online," Luke explained. "We all know that. Even snuff sites."

"The FBI closed down the site discovered in Hidden Cove, but there were others, of course. Like this one."

"And Krueger kept evidence that he went to one? What an idiot."

"In some ways, yes. But he hired somebody to kill Jess."

The captain glanced at Helen, who was seated, with Jess behind her, gripping her shoulders. "I'm sorry, Mrs. Cromwell. This must be hard for you."

"At least we caught Krueger." As always, Helen was gracious.

"If Ms. Hart's story holds up. You can see now why it's important the evidence was obtained legally."

Luke tried to look innocent, though he made sure the story they told would indeed be acceptable. "We said it was, Al."

"And," Dorian spoke for the first time. "There was no one else there to observe anything different. So, what's the problem?"

"You're probably right," Al said. "Maybe I'm being overly cautious, but when somebody tries to hurt a cop's brother, I want to make sure he's put away."

"Have you found the guy he hired?" Luke asked.

"No. But from what we can tell, no money exchanged hands yet, either. So there shouldn't be anybody coming after your brother. We're not going to let up until we find the hired gun, though. And shut down the site."

"And Krueger will be charged with what?" Luke asked.

"Conspiracy to commit murder."

"So, is Jess safe?" Helen asked.

"We think so. Once we track the Petron connection, we should have even more information. Meanwhile, I think you—he nodded to Jess—should stay at home, keep your bodyguard with you and retain that private security outside. The police will also be checking your house."

"For how long?" Alisha asked.

Ann said, "It shouldn't be more than a few days."

"What's going to happen to Lieutenant Cromwell?" Dorian wanted to know. "For ignoring procedures?"

"You're off work for a while, anyway, Luke," Al said. "I'll determine, in conjunction with Internal Affairs, if I want to count that as your suspension."

"Whatever you say, Captain." And he meant it. Rules were rules. And he'd never broken any in the department before.

After the cops took official statements from Jess, Celeste, Alisha and Dorian, Al walked out with Helen. Ann stayed back.

"For what it's worth, buddy, I'd have done the same thing for my brother. This'll work out." She playfully socked him on his good shoulder and left.

Luke noticed Dorian's face was flushed and she spoke as soon as the police left. "What the hellor was that all about? *Buddy, Annie,* the playful touch on your arm? Have you joined with her?"

Luke rolled his eyes. "I'd like some time alone with Dorian."

Alisha sighed heavily. "I have something to pursue on the computeller. Celeste, you look depleted. You should rest."

"I'll rest, too," Jess said. "With my pregnant wife."

Luke grabbed Jess's arm as he turned to leave. "It's almost over, buddy."

"I hope so. And I can't thank you enough for what you did. Your career is going to be affected." His gaze encompassed all of them. "And you put your lives on the line for me."

"It was our task," Alisha said matter-of-factly.

When he and Dorian were alone, Luke patted the mattress. "Come here."

"I don't feel like being close to you." She folded her arms across the chest of that pretty, sleeveless, green top she wore. It made her eyes match the grass outside. "I don't like this thing called jealousy. Answer my question first."

God, she was cute when she was mad. "No, I haven't joined with Annie. We're good friends is all. Since you didn't have male friends in the future, you don't understand what you saw."

She raised her chin. "I still don't like it."

"Welcome to our world, babe. Now come kiss me."

CHAPTER 16

LATER THAT DAY, Alisha was in her individual space, working on her new laptop, checking the Internet, when Celeste walked in. "What are you doing?" Alisha asked her friend. "You're supposed to be resting."

"I couldn't sleep. I'm still worried about how Jess's situation will turn out, though I think the meeting went well with the law-enforcement officials."

"The best we could hope for. All right, sit down. We have to talk anyway. It's time to set up our trip to Virginia."

Celeste's face brightened. "Finally." She nodded to the computer. "I know Jess was our first priority. If it took time to find a way into Dr. Lansing's life, so be it."

Those were the exact words Alisha had said to Celeste at an earlier time.

"Still, I hope we can do this expeditiously."

"I recognize now after what's happened with Jess that we must accomplish our tasks." Celeste's tone was sober. Sad, almost.

But Alisha was glad to hear it. "I've got a program running that may tell us how we can orchestrate access to him."

"I'll wait to hear from you."

After Celi left, Alisha shook her head. She'd been worried from the beginning about her friend's ability to pull off her mission with Lansing, but after the turn Dorian took with

Luke—sensible, stalwart Dorian—Alisha feared Celeste was a hundred percent more susceptible than Dorian to the charms of men. Could she become close with Lansing in the same way? He was attractive enough, though Alisha preferred the lean build and the arrangement of David Ryan's face. Hellor, where did that come from? He was a minister, for the godheads sake!

The computeller pinged, ready to recite its findings, and she swiveled her chair to face it. "The woman who gives care to Dr. Lansing's children is Patricia Mason, seventeen, offspring of Sam and Joe Mason, five siblings, all younger. She's been at the apex of her class and applied to Johns Hopkins University, where she was accepted to study environmental science."

An irony, Alisha thought.

She addressed the computeller. "How can she attend an educational institution in a different town and be the Lansing's caregiver?"

"She is not attending college. She did not receive a scholarship to the educational institution and her parental units do not have enough money to send her."

It was still unbelievable that people of this society couldn't get the kind of education they wanted. In Alisha's time, the system was highly efficient and accessible: those in certain jobs willingly transmitted their areas of expertise to the younger generation and then trained them. She thought of their dwindled population: there weren't the number of people in the future as there were here, so that fact might have made education easier.

After she turned off the computeller, Alisha clicked into Johns Hopkins University. Their cost was fifty thousand dollars per year, and Alisha knew from her experience of exchanging their diamonds that this was a significant amount.

Sitting back, she stared at the ceiling fan whirring around. Being a caregiver for younglings would be perfect for Celeste.

If she was in the Lansing home daily and had access to Dr. Lansing's computer, the task might not even take very long.

Maybe, just maybe, there was something they could do to Patricia Mason to free up the job. Hmm, maybe she could engineer a minor accident for the girl. A broken leg would prevent her from caring for the children. Alisha would have to travel to Virginia to accomplish this. Though she hated to harm someone, the future of the planet was at stake.

• • •

SHOUTS CAME FROM the lower level of the house where the Sisters of Doom were staying. It had been two days, and no word had come from the police about the state of the investigation. Luke had told Jess this silence was common, that the department wouldn't release anything until they had their facts confirmed, but everyone in Jess's household was on edge. Still, he'd never heard the women have a knock-down-drag-out. He crossed to the top of the steps to listen in.

"Under no circumstances will I be a part of this." Celeste's voice was full of emotion. The only other time he'd heard her be so forceful was when they didn't want her to take the lead with Krueger.

"I agree with Celi." This from Dorian. Her comment was also heartfelt.

A pause. "Maybe you don't have a choice." He could picture Alisha's insistent stance. "If I just do something—"

"Then I won't go to Virginia. I pledge that to you, Lisha. I won't."

"The girl is only seventeen," Alisha added. "She'll heal fine. And our work here is only half done. We must get on to our next task."

"We'll have to look for another avenue to pursue," Dorian said. "Surely there are other ways we can infiltrate his life."

Jess didn't know what their next task was, or who it concerned, but he didn't like the sound of this, so he shuffled down the steps.

They were around a table in the common area of the lower floor, Dorian and Celeste seated. Alisha stood over the others, her hands on the wood surface, just as he'd envisioned. Dressed today in his time period's clothing, their hair in contemporary styles, he could almost imagine they belonged here in his time.

He asked, "What's going on?"

Alisha straightened. She shot a fulminating look at Jess. "This is none of your concern."

"It is if you're yelling loud enough to wake the dead."

"You can't do that," Celeste said. "Can you?"

"It's an idiom, Celeste." Alisha's tone was more than impatient.

"We're sorry we bothered you," Dorian put in. "We'll be quieter."

"Too late for that. I overheard you saying you were planning to hurt someone."

A gasp came from behind him. He turned to find Helen had also come down to the lower level. She seemed stronger today. "Hurt someone? Why?"

"To save the Earth." Alisha's voice rose a notch. "And I don't have to explain this to you or get your permission. As soon as we're done here, we'll go on to the next task and never see you again."

Dorian gasped.

"We can't allow you to knowingly hurt someone." Helen approached Alisha and touched her arm. "There has to be another way."

Footsteps on the stairs. David Ryan appeared in the room, wearing his collar. "Hi, I let myself in through the open screen and heard the commotion. Can I help?"

Sighing heavily, Alisha nodded to the table, which sat six. "All right. Sit down. I'll tell you some of it. But don't ask specifics about what we have to do."

Once they were seated, and people calmed somewhat, Alisha related the story about Celeste needing to take the place of a caregiver in someone's home. "I won't tell you why, but it's imperative that Celeste become a part of the lives of a certain family. A position in child care would help us immensely. It's an expeditious solution."

"Hurting someone is out of the question," David said softly. "Isn't there any other way to get this girl out of her job? Something good we can do for her to make her leave?"

Celeste asked, "You haven't really considered another way, have you Lisha?"

"All right, I haven't. This is so simple and immediate. We could be done with everything in a few weeks."

"Let's look at it from another angle." David again. "She's a bright, socially conscious individual, who didn't have money to go to Johns Hopkins." His face lit from within. "Maybe we can arrange for a scholarship. I'll contribute."

"We have the currency to do that, Alisha." Celeste again.

"We can't very well send her a diamond!"

Jess or Luke had been traveling to different stores in the city to exchange them for cash when needed.

"No, but we could offer an anonymous scholarship." Jess liked the idea that David had brought up. "I know some people at Hopkins. Some scientists. They could engineer the acceptance of a bright young student."

"More people cannot know about us!" Alisha was getting agitated again. "I must insist."

"I could do it without explaining why," Jess went on. "Call down there to tell them I want to be the benefactor of a student I'm a distant relative of. It will be viewed as a philanthropic endeavor."

David smiled. "It *will be* a philanthropic endeavor."

"Would the college arrange it anonymously?" Dorian asked.

"Why not?" Jess said. "This is a perfect solution. And you should like it. She's studying environmental science. Maybe she's the one to keep my research going when I retire, to discover more ways to get clean energy. Maybe *she'll* save the world this time around."

Dorian and Celeste grinned. Alisha rolled her eyes. "That is so far-fetched."

Celeste shook her head vehemently. "It's not, Lisha. We know in some theories of time travel, we were meant to change events in history."

Helen leaned in. "Please, let us try the gentler way."

Alisha glared at all of them.

But eventually, she agreed.

• • •

LUKE'S SHOULDER WAS still sore when he awoke, despite the use of the Multimed earlier that day. At least the wound had healed enough so he didn't need a sling. He lay back on his pillows and watched the ceiling fan whir, listened to the birds chirping outside. He couldn't believe the turn his life had taken. If he dared to confide in anybody, they'd think he was nuts. It was lucky that—soon, he hoped—this whole thing with Jess would be over. They were waiting for information from the police, and worst-case scenario, for the date of the article Alisha found on their fancy computer to arrive. If they got the magazine, and it showed Jess's article was published when he was alive instead of posthumously as it originally ran, they'd succeeded.

His cell phone buzzed. Snatching it up, he said, "Cromwell."

"Luke, it's Al. I have some news. Our guys traced the IP address at Petron. It's a big fish. I'm heading over there now to talk to him."

"I'm coming with you." He started to get up, and pain shot from his shoulder to his hand. Fuck!

"Under no circumstances are you to interfere with my investigation. Internal Affairs and I decided your suspension will be for the time you're taking off."

"Thanks, Cap."

"Don't thank me too much. I'm putting a letter in your folder that you played cowboy. And worse, I'm still pissed as hell at you for not trusting me with this."

"I hear ya."

As soon as he clicked off, the door to the den opened. Dorian stood in the entryway, dressed in white shorts, a soft green slip of a top called a camisole, and she was barefoot. She looked every inch of a modern woman, and he felt his body respond. Jesus. Even now, when he was in pain. "Hey there, sweetheart? Did you come to comfort me?"

She walked into the room and sat on the edge of the bed. Brushed a lock of hair off his face. The tender gesture made his heart lurch. "You're incorrigible. You're sick and in pain, and you still flirt."

When he grabbed her hand, he felt her pulse leap. "I'm not the only one interested."

She grinned. "You're not. But it's mid-revolution, and there are a houseful of people around us."

"I guess we'll have to wait until tonight. You can sneak into my room."

"We'll see." He noted now that there was conflict in her green eyes. "What's wrong?"

"We've been arguing about our next task."

"You and the Sisters of Doom?"

"And Helen, David and Jess. Everybody got in on the discussion."

Luke didn't like being left out. "Tell me."

She related the story. He could see she was upset, but he had to give his honest opinion. "Huh. I agree with Alisha. One broken leg is a small price to pay for saving the future. And if it will solve the problem quickly…"

"The other path will get her there soon, too. And no one will be harmed."

"Who's the guy?"

"What guy?"

"That Celeste needs to get an in with."

"I can't tell you, Luke. You know that, yet you keep asking."

"I hate that you don't trust me with this." He was parroting Al, but his objection was nonetheless heartfelt.

"The people who sent us here made us swear we wouldn't reveal our next mission to anyone." She bit her lip. "*They* don't trust you."

"You told Jess who you were and what you were doing here. Why can't you follow the same pattern next time?"

"Because we needed to convince Jess quickly, for obvious reasons."

"Which still pisses me off."

She shook her head. "I'll never understand that saying."

"Really? It makes perfect sense to me."

"Because you're a man. In any case, as soon as the date passes for that megadamned article, we'll be leaving."

What the hell? "What do you mean, *we?*"

Now she cocked her head. The fact that she was surprised by his reaction made him even madder. "I don't understand."

"Celeste has to do this, right?"

"Of course. But Alisha and I need to help her."

"After what's happened between us, you can't go, Dorian."

"I don't understand," she reiterated.

"We just...got together. I want you to stay here with me. Let Alisha go with Celeste."

Dorian's expression turned dark, and suddenly he saw the other side of her again. The professional, competent woman from another world. "I can't do that. This is my job. My life's mission."

Sinking back into the pillows, he wondered how to get his way. Hmm, she wasn't used to seduction. He grasped her hand. "Baby, I just found you. I don't want you to go."

Her eyes widened and she moved farther down the mattress. "Don't do that to me! Don't use this closeness you forced on me to your advantage."

That got his hackles up. "Forced on you? You were a willing participant."

"No, I wasn't." Visibly, she tried to shake off her anger. "Look, Luke, I like what's happened between us, though it frightens me. But when you try to manipulate me, like you just did, it makes me angry. I'm still not comfortable with what's between us."

He wasn't used to women telling the stark truth. And it shamed him. He squeezed her hand. "You're right; I'm sorry. I just don't want you to go, but I shouldn't have used my masculine wiles on you."

She calmed, missing the joke. Did men even have wiles?

"Okay, here's the deal. Tell me what you're going to do so I'll feel better about you helping out Celeste."

Her face blanked.

"Look, if it's dangerous like your assignment for Jess, I have a right to know."

She held up her hand. "I won't tell you anything."

"I can't let you go without knowing what you'll be doing."

"*Let* me go?"

"Um, yeah." He made his voice nonchalant because he knew he was on shaky ground. Still, he *was* pissed.

"You have no say over me in that regard. In any regard."

"I guess that puts me in my place."

"I don't understand, Luke." She kept saying that.

"No, doll, you sure as hell don't. Now get off the bed, so I can take a shower."

"I'll help you."

"I'd rather to be left alone."

"Luke, why are you doing this?"

"Just get the hell out of here, Dorian." When she didn't move, he barked, "Now!"

The look on her face sliced him to the core. She was an innocent in the ways of men and women, and he was manipulating her. But, hell, she might be a woman of the future, but he was definitely a man of the present. And, goddamn it, couples compromised.

As much as he could, he stalked to the bathroom. Maybe a shower would help.

But he kept seeing the confused and hurt look on Dorian's face, even as he let the hot spray pummel him.

• • •

DORIAN STOOD BY the window in the lower level of the Cromwell house, dressed only in a white islet gown she'd bought on a shopping trip with Helen. Who knew Dorian would be susceptible to such feminine lingerie? A few months ago, she didn't even know what lingerie was, let alone wear it to bed. People of the future slept nude because making clothing for sleep time was a waste of resources.

"What's wrong, Dorian?"

She turned to find Celeste behind her, dressed similarly only her gown was pink.

"I can't sleep."

"Go to Luke." She gave her friend a knowing smile. "He won't mind."

"Luke and I are having a fight. You know, the kind the three of us have sometimes."

Celeste cocked her head. Her hair swirled with the motion, not that it was well below her chin. "What's it like to fight with a man?"

"It's very hurtful. I don't know what to do with all these emotions."

Celeste touched her, drained some of the anxiety.

"I wish you wouldn't do that. Take my negative energy."

"I took only a little. Now you can think more clearly."

"You're a nice person, Celeste."

"Thank you. Now go see Luke." She winked. "Helen told me make-up sex is the best."

Chucking, Dorian hugged her friend then climbed the stairs and walked through the dark house to the space Luke occupied. His door was ajar. He faced the window, silhouetted in the moonlight. The beams kissed his dark hair and illuminated his shoulders. He wore only those incredibly appealing tight briefs.

She pushed open the door.

He didn't turn.

"Luke? It's me, Dorian."

Still facing away from her, he said in a low voice, "I didn't know if you'd come."

"I didn't know if you wanted me to."

He pivoted. "I wanted you to." She wondered why he hadn't come to her. This must be another convention of their time, another one she didn't like. He said, "Lock the door."

She did.

"Come here."

Her steps were faulty. She was almost afraid, not knowing this enigmatic side of Luke. But there was a dark spark of excitement from it kindling inside her, too.

When she reached him, he towered over her, making her feel even more intimidated. Instead of cowering, she lifted her chin. Then she placed a hand on his chest. His heart thrummed.

Roughly, he grabbed her wrist. "I don't like what you do to me."

"What do I do to you, Luke?"

"Scramble my brain. Make me crazy. Turn me on so much I can't think straight."

She smiled.

He moved in closer. "You pleased by that?"

"Definitely."

He kissed her nose. "Witch."

Then he lowered his mouth to hers. The contact was rough, possessive. Since the same emotions swirled inside Dorian, she cupped her hand around his neck and asked for more. Opening his lips with her tongue—godheads, this kissing was wonderful—she explored him, nipped his mouth, pressed some more. His arms banded around her and he lifted her up so they were flush with each other, so their hearts beat the same tattoo.

When he dragged his mouth away, it was to set her back and draw the sleeping gown over her head. She stood before him, bathed in moonlight herself. After a few seconds, he scooped a hand under her legs and one around her back and lifted her. "What…? Luke what are you doing?"

He stopped at the bed and asked, "You've never been carried?"

"Not since I was a youngling." She nuzzled into him. "I like it."

"Damn you, I was going to dump you on the bed and ravish you. But you bring out a brutal tenderness in me."

She understood the oxymoron.

Gently, he set her on the bed. Shed his briefs. And covered her body with his. Threading her fingers through his hair, she kissed him with some of that brutal tenderness, too.

Then he explored her. Every single part of her. He found erogenous zones she didn't know she had—her ear for the godheads' sake. By the time he finished she was writhing. "Now, Luke, please."

He parted her thighs and thrust himself into her. Another thrust, then one more, and they both spiraled out of control. His groans met her moans until they became one long chorus of pleasure. When he collapsed on her, Dorian had never felt so connected to him or anyone else.

Helen had been right. Make-up sex was the best!

• • •

A FEW MINUTES after sex, the likes of which he'd never experienced, Luke lay beside Dorian on the mattress, holding her hand. He'd never felt this way before, never felt so close, so much a part of somebody. Wasn't it his luck that he chose a woman from the future? Angry about that, and at her, still, about her choice to leave soon, he rolled over on his side and peered down at her. "I love you, damn it."

He saw her eyes widen in the moonlight. Then glisten. "Oh, Luke, my love is yours, too."

The combination of anger and pure joy that mixed up in his heart made him speechless. Finally, he said, "We're in a hell of a fix."

"I know. I'm sorry I anger you." Some of her idioms were slipping from the future sayings to how they were phrased now. In a lot of ways she was becoming a modern woman, and in other fucking ways not. But still…

"I'm sorry, too." He kissed her breastbone.

She smiled. "I've never said my love was his once to a man."

"I'm glad."

"You had a spousal unit. I suppose you told her."

"I did. But it was different." He shook his head. "I can't believe how much I mean the words with you."

Again, she smiled.

He asked, "What are we going to do about all this Dorian? You going off on this *mission*. Me staying behind. Will we be together again? Will you come back here? Are you sure you can never go home, and if you could, would you leave me?"

"I don't have any of those answers, Luke. We need time to figure things out."

"Including your secrecy about what you do next."

"I'm sorry, yes."

"You—"

She put her hand on his mouth. "Luke, please. Don't spoil what just happened. We aren't even finished with our task concerning Jess. We have time to make this work for both of us."

Because she was right, he shut up. The problem was *his*. He'd been having this niggling feeling that she was indeed going to go away for good. And, now, that thought was untenable. Yet he couldn't box her in with promises.

"Luke…" she whispered hoarsely. "Make love to me again."

Make love. Not join. At least they'd made some progress. So he gave up his anger for tonight and kissed her.

Kissed the woman he loved.

CHAPTER 17

FOUR REVOLUTIONS LATER, on what was called a weekday, Alisha found Dorian and Celeste in front of the television watching yet another science fiction film. They all were fascinated with the genre, so she sat down and viewed it with them for a moment. This one was not in color, and there was a big robot named Klatu speaking to a tall, thin man.

"The video is almost over, Lisha." This from Celeste who was, of course, enthralled.

While Alisha waited, she got the gist that aliens had come to save earth—which was totally unrealistic. Finally, it ended.

"Come with me, you two." Alisha stood. "We need to learn some basic things Helen has been doing for us in order to take care of ourselves in Virginia. When we leave here, for example, we have to know how to clean our clothes, run the dishwasher and other household appliances, pay our bills."

"Can we hire a cleaner of the home, like Helen does?" Celeste asked.

"No, the fewer people we come in contact with, the better our chances of accomplishing our goal in secret. So today, while Helen's at work and Luke is out on errands, Jess in his study, and the security people right outside, we're going to learn some of these things."

"Who's going to teach us?"

"I've been studying up on it. And I've watched the cleaners."

Dorian snorted. "Of course you have."

First, she showed them how to vacuum. Celeste sneezed, so she assigned Dorian the task of cleaning the rugs on the bottom floor of the house, where they stayed.

"I'll take care of the bathrooms," Alisha remarked, "since the cleaning products will probably affect Celi too much."

"I can do the laundry," Celeste said. "I watched someone use the machine on the video box."

"I'll show you what I've learned, too." They headed to the small, square room that held machines that washed and dried garments. In their time, everything went through the Repurification Chamber. Alisha explained the rudiments of cleaning clothes, then left.

First, Celeste mentally went over what she should do. Separate their clothing colors. She took a moment to admire all the different choices they had; though Alisha tolerated the need for so many things, and Dorian was partial only to nightwear, Celeste loved the feel and smell of everything—the rougher denim jeans, the lacey panties, the soft silk of a blouse.

Then she went to the...washer. She had to start using the terms of the time more, and she'd learned most of them. Once she was established in Alex Lansing's house, nothing could go awry. Her mission would be hard enough. As she poured liquid, which smelled sweet, into the cup, she thought about his... children. Would they like her? Would she enjoy child care as much as she thought she would? His face appeared before her. He was so handsome...

Megadamn! Alisha was right. She had to stop thinking about him. Quickly, she added the water and clothing and set the cycle.

Not liking this cleaning stuff very much, she took out the computeller she'd put in her pocket and sat down on a chair to wait for the clothes to wash. She was interested in Madison Lansing, the teenager. She'd never met an adolescent before, and all the shows on the video box portrayed them as intractable. But the girl had a lovely face…

She got lost in the study of teenagers and younglings, of what they liked to eat, what activities they preferred, how they talked, but when she heard a loud, booming noise, she looked up. Oh, no! She bolted off the chair. The machine itself was moving out inches and making an awful sound. Soapsuds spewed from the top at a volume that stunned her. She rushed to the machine and opened the lid, hoping to stop the mess; instead, soap and water tumbled over the edges.

Celeste panicked. What should she do? She went to get the directions for the machine on the shelf across the room and slipped. She fell on her derriere into about an inch of water covered by a foot of suds.

And started laughing. This was a predicament, but an amusing one.

"What the hellor is going on…" Dorian came to the door, and her words trailed off. The look of concern on her face changed to one of levity. "Swimming in the soapsuds, Celi?"

"I don't know what's happening." She shrugged. "I must have put in the wrong amount of soap." Which could very well have happened because she'd been dreaming day of Alex Lansing. She raised her hand. "Come help me."

Gingerly, Dorian stepped into the water and walked to Celeste. "It smells nice…godheads, Celeste what are you doing?"

"Painting your legs with suds."

Dorian giggled. Bending down, she scooped some up and covered Alisha's hair. "Since you like those bubble baths so much..."

Without warning, Celeste tugged on Dorian's hand, causing her to fall to her rear, too, with a big splash that wet her clothing. Instead of getting angry, as Alisha would have, Dorian cupped up more suds in her hands, and before Celeste knew what was happening, they were covering each other with bubbles.

"Megadamn!" They heard from the doorway.

This from Alisha. Her stern face and rigid stance made Celeste whisper in Dorian's ear, "Let's get her."

The two crawled over to an unsuspecting Alisha. Before she realized their intent, they wrestled her down into the suds.

After only a few minutes, Alisha was bathed, too. For once, she grinned and participated in the fun by soaping them up, too.

Later, they heard, again from the doorway, "What do we have here?" This from Luke. "The Sisters of Doom know how to have fun?"

Jess circled around him and managed to make his way to the washer to turn it off.

The three women exchanged glances.

Then they went after the men.

May 20

The levity of the day before had broken some of the tension that had settled over the household. Luke and Jess had been congenial with the laundry fiasco and responded to the play by getting water from the faucet and drowning the three of them. Then they'd all spent an hour cheerfully cleaning up the mess. The good clean fun (no play on words intended) had been helpful to all of them. By the time Helen got home, the laundry room was spotless and she enjoyed their story.

Each day brought them closer to the publication of Jess's magazine article, originally put out posthumously. Though they didn't talk much about it, Jess and Helen barely left each other's side when the two were home together; Luke and Dorian stayed near them, even with the additional security outside. Celeste and Alisha were busy mapping out the next mission.

This morning, Dorian stood at the kitchen counter making breakfast—she actually liked to cook—with a wonderful-smelling, animal product, called bacon, and the eggs from real chickas. No, chickens. She was developing a tolerance for their sustenance and was glad. If she was going to stay in this time period, which no longer made her incredibly sad, she needed to adjust to their ways.

The doorbell rang, interrupting her rumination. She had a clear view of Helen, Jess and Luke in the family room. She saw Luke stand and feel for his gun at his back—Dorian wore her stunner, though concealed—and he left the family area. She imagined him going to the door in that long stride of his and looking out the little peephole.

"It's my captain," he called back to them. Soon, the two men appeared in the kitchen.

Al Patchet seemed less worried today. He wasn't as tall as Luke, and his hair was receding to eventually become like Jess's, but he had a kind face when he was smiling. When Luke told him to sit, Helen and Jess joined the men at the table. Dorian turned the cooking devices to warm and sat, too.

"You look better, Luke." The expression in Al's brown eyes was pleased. He held affection for Luke.

Faking pain, Luke rubbed his shoulder. Dorian knew he was fully recovered but couldn't reveal that to his captain. "Shoulder's still sore, but I'm good."

"I got something that will make you all feel even better."

"Hold on a second." Dorian ducked downstairs and summoned Alisha and Celeste.

The three women hustled up to the first floor behind her. "Good morning, Captain," Celeste said.

Alisha greeted him, too.

When they took places at the table, Luke announced, "The captain has some good news."

All gazes focused on Al Patchet.

"We traced the emails from Petron to Krueger back to a Jared Cummings, the CEO of the company. So we paid him a visit yesterday. Seems as if Krueger and he met regularly to talk about the developments in the areas of clean energy Krueger was monitoring. As corporate-oil people, they want to stop the twenty-first century leap into alternative sources of fuel. Eventually, Cummings let his hair down with Krueger."

None of the women knew the meaning of that term, and exchanged glances. Luke caught it and he shook his head—for them to stay quiet, she guessed, in front of the captain.

"Cummings said he might have remarked how he'd like to stop the damn fracking and wind research. He and Krueger laughed about it. Krueger mentioned getting rid of all scientists. Cummings jokingly agreed."

"This is nuts." Luke gripped the coffee mug and Dorian could tell he was appalled.

"Cummings had no idea he was dealing with someone sick. It looks like the offhanded remark was enough to spark Krueger's crazy thinking. He maintains that he actually believed he had a directive from Petron and decided to start with Jess. We think because Jess was a close target to New York."

Jess's eyes widened. "So the Petron brass wasn't involved?"

"As far as we can tell, no. But Kara Krueger was right about her husband's obsession."

"One man caused all of humanity—" Jess began.

"Would you like some coffee, Captain?" Celeste asked, loudly scraping back her chair to interrupt Jess's rumination.

"Sure."

She squeezed Jess's shoulder when she went by him in silent warning to watch what he said.

"What's going to happen to Krueger?" Helen asked, her features tense. "You're not letting him go, are you?"

"His lawyers have a judge looking into the case and are asking them to dismiss it on grounds that he didn't actually *do* anything. And they contend that the information was gained during entrapment." He looked up at Celeste as she set a cup in front of him. Its scent was strong. "You're going to have to go before the judge, but it will be in his chambers and my guess is you'll convince him."

"Of course," she said easily. Knowing her, Dorian thought, she'd probably manage to touch the judge and read his or her emotions to say the right things.

Celeste asked, "When do I do this?"

"Tomorrow morning."

"I'll bring her down to the courthouse," Luke said. "She's um, become like a sister to me."

Although Dorian knew the remark was made to convince the captain that this very unusual connection among them was normal, it warmed her.

Al faced Jess. "I'm thinking this whole ordeal is nearly over, Dr. Cromwell. Hang in there just a while longer."

"I will. Thank you for all you've done."

When the captain left, they all stayed at the table and Alisha asked, "What will happen to Krueger if he's found to be mentally ill?"

"He'll get treatment for his condition and probably go to jail afterward." This from Luke in his cop voice.

"In our time, all miscreants are considered mentally ill," Alisha said. "They go through extensive rehabilitation, mostly of a virtual nature."

Dorian had explained that to Luke, but the others might not know it.

"That sounds as if it would cost a lot of money," Helen commented. "How many crimes are committed a day in your city?"

Dorian's eyes widened. "In one revolution? Hardly any. There are about ten a year."

Jess choked on his coffee. "You only have ten arrests a year?"

"Yes, and most of those are reformed quickly."

"It sounds wonderful," Helen said.

"As I mentioned before, we're a peaceful society. We have to be to continue to exist."

As they discussed the penal system of both time periods, Dorian rose to serve their breakfast, which she'd kept warm. The captain had indeed brought them good news, but no one would rest until confirmation came in the magazine. It was—what did they call it—nerve-wracking.

When they finished eating, Alisha cleared her throat. "I have some news."

"I hope it's good." Helen said. "I feel partly relieved by the captain's visit but could use something pleasant."

"It is. Jess's plan worked. I discovered early this morning that Johns Hopkins has offered Patricia Mason a scholarship. She accepted and will leave at the end of the school year for orientation and a special summer session for freshmen."

"How do you know this?" Celeste asked. Dorian could tell she was excited.

"I hacked into the Mason girl's email."

"Good," Jess responded. "At least that's done." He smiled. "And we helped a kid go to college."

Luke grabbed Dorian's hand. "What does that mean for you three?"

Alisha answered. "We hope to leave right after we get the final news that we've succeeded with Jess."

Luke's face turned dark. Suddenly, Dorian didn't feel so good anymore.

CHAPTER 18

FOR THE FIRST time in thirty-nine revolutions—she must learn to say days—Alisha was feeling optimistic about their ability to complete both tasks. She knew in her heart that they'd succeeded with Jess, believed the article would show he was alive and well.

And she'd made progress with Alex Lansing.

When Celeste returned from the courthouse, where she'd told her story to the judge—which he'd accepted—Alisha asked Dorian and Celeste to come downstairs. They took seats on the couches in the main area. Over here, the windows were bigger, the light brighter and the scent of green grass and dirt filtered in through the open glass. Alisha took a moment to enjoy the out of inside she loved so much. Then she turned to her friends, who were also staring out the windows. "Patricia Mason must have resigned from her job with the Lansings for the summer, because Dr. Lansing's advertisement for child care went up last night."

With her legs curled under her, Celeste smiled broadly. "We should follow up right away on my behalf."

"I already answered the advertisement, posing as you, using your email address. I gave you exceptional credentials and superlative recommendations. He's asked to Skype with you tonight and also said he would check a few references before that. Dorian and I will pose as your previous employers, using the identities I've already created for us on what Luke terms the burner phones, so nothing can be traced back to us."

"Skype means…?" This from Dorian.

"A primitive video communication that was the forerunner of our computeller."

She nodded.

"Everything should be completed in the next few days, so we can leave right after the *Science Today* article confirms Jess is alive and well."

Dorian looked away. "That would be next week."

Alisha frowned. "Don't forget our mission, Dorian. We don't know whose research is the cause of the blank wall in 2589."

"I know I have to come with you." She spoke matter-of-factly, but there was a regretful nuance in her voice.

Though she didn't have Celeste's powers of insights into others, Alisha read her friend's reaction just fine. "You don't want to leave Luke. I wish you hadn't joined with him." Though her words were harsh, she'd modified her tone because she cared about Dorian.

"Maybe you were right. But I can't change how I feel now."

"Distance *will* change it."

"What do you mean?"

"Being out of contact with him will alter your feelings. If necessary, we can find someone else for you to join with, and get you back to your old self."

"Oh, great. That's just fucking great."

They turned in unison to see Luke Cromwell standing about ten feet away, loaded for beara.

• • •

"JOIN WITH SOMEONE else, my foot!" Luke said aloud as he took to the pavement. What was with these women? Over his dead body would she make love with another man!

An inner voice told him, *You better be more understanding. She's not like modern women.*

But he wasn't thinking clearly because he didn't want to let her go—so much, the emotion floored him. Damn it, though, he was right about some things. First and foremost, he had no idea what danger she would be placing herself in—hell they all would—in Virginia. Second, she didn't trust him enough to tell him what she would be doing. Last, and of course, not least, he wanted to be with her.

Sweat poured down his face as he ran hard for two miles. When his shoulder started to ache, he stopped and bent over to catch his breath. Jesus Christ, he'd gotten himself in a fix. He'd never planned to start a serious relationship with a woman again. Truth be told, he felt he'd blown his first marriage by working too hard for the department and not listening enough to his wife's concerns. She'd turned to another guy, and he hated being a failure at anything. He'd never wanted to put the time and effort into another relationship. Until now.

He'd fucking fallen in love. And he was damn pissed about it.

Are you, really? he asked himself honestly.

Running again but slowly this time, he headed toward Jess's. When he thought of how her eyes sparkled and her face shone when she said *my love is yours,* tenderness welled in his heart.

Join with someone else? Like hell.

As he took the last street to his brother's home, he tried to blank his mind as he slowed to a walk when he got close to

Jess's. Where he saw something that made his heart beat like a drum.

Under the big tree that shaded Jess's front lawn, the mailman had slipped something into the mailbox.

Luke's cop sense prickled. He had an intuition about certain things, which had saved his ass more than once in his police work. Right now, it kicked into high gear. With a big intake of breath, he approached the house, nodded at the guy, who said, "Good morning," as he walked away, leaving Luke to open the little white box.

A big manila envelope was stuffed inside. The advance copies of the *Science Today* had finally arrived.

• • •

ENSCONCED IN THE family room, alone for once, Jess knelt before Helen with his hand on her belly. And waited. "Oh, my God, I felt it."

"I'm so glad. It's really too soon for movement, but that little nudge is more like butterfly wings, flapping gently." Tears clouded her eyes. "I never thought I'd feel this, Jess. It's wonderful."

Jess's eyes welled, too. "I know. Everything's going to work out."

Grasping his hand, she sighed. "I wish we knew for certain."

"You're going to get your wish, Helen, in about three seconds." Luke stood in the wide opening to the kitchen, holding a large envelope. Large enough to contain a couple of copies of *Science Today*.

"Oh!" Helen raised her hand to her mouth.

Then the three women who'd come to save Jess entered the room. "Why did you call us in here, Luke?" Alisha asked.

He held up the envelope. They stilled, and utter silence descended. Luke handed the package to Jess. "Here, you open it."

Standing, he pulled Helen up and close to him. "I can't."

Luke looked to Helen.

"I can't either. You open it, Luke."

His brother ripped off the top. Drew out the glossy green magazine. And stared at it.

"If I recall correctly," Alisha put in, "the article is on page twenty-seven."

Luke felt his own eyes well and he bit the inside of his cheek to keep back the emotion. "We don't have to look on page twenty-seven." He turned the magazine around so everyone could see the cover. Jess's smiling face captured their gazes.

"That doesn't mean anything," Helen began. "It could—"

Jess interrupted. "Read the caption, honey."

They all stared at the big black letters that read, *Can he save the world? Dr. Jess Cromwell's research summary inside.*

• • •

CELESTE SAT DOWN in front of the small, seventeen-inch screen of the primitive computer and waited for Alex Lansing to come on to Skype with her. Her insides were jittery and she had to struggle to keep her hands from shaking. She'd gone to see the judge today with Luke, and good news had come out of it. The evidence they stole would be accepted and Krueger would go to trial for it unless he bargained a plea for mental problems. Cruelly, he'd be held behind bars until then, instead of injecting him with a locator chip, dosing him with a medicine to quell his violent tendencies and confining him to his dwelling until his treatment could be completed.

A strange popping noise came from the screen, startling Celeste. From off to the side, Alisha said, "It's the Skype's way of calling. Click on *answer*. And try to remember your idioms." She held up a pad made of yellow paper. "I'll scribble the meaning of any you don't know."

An image appeared before her. Alex Lansing! "Hello there, Ms. Hart."

Celeste's pulse skyrocketed at the sight and sound of him. He did indeed resemble Captain Kirk of the show *Star Trek*, but his shoulders were wider, he was bigger in general and that voice was low and husky. She knew his eyes were blue, but not this beautiful shade of it.

She had to clear her throat before she could answer. "Hello, Dr. Lansing. Thank you for considering me for the job of caring for your children this summer."

"Thank you for applying. As I told you in email, I had someone lined up, but it recently fell through."

She knew that meaning. "I'm sorry your plans did not work out." She smiled and watched his face react. Even from afar, her powers of sensitivity seemed to lure people to her. "But I can help, if you'll give me a chance."

"That's why we're Skyping. I was drawn to your résumé, and then this afternoon, I checked your references."

Alisha and Dorian had assured her that went well.

"I'd like to interview you in person." He patted his computer. "Much as I depend on this for my work, I insist something as essential as good quality care for my kids be judged in person."

"I understand."

"Your résumé says you haven't moved to Virginia yet."

She glanced at Alisha, who wrote, "The end of the week."

"My sisters and I are coming in this week to find a home. You and I could meet anytime."

Obviously pleased, he smiled and Celeste felt a blast of… heat so strong it silenced her. "That would work." He leafed through something on his desk. Now the light sparkled off the top of his dark blond hair. "How about next Friday, around noon? I have meetings before and after that." He rolled his eyes. "For fundraising. Which I deplore."

She pretended to understand. "Noon would be good. Dr. Lansing, if my interview goes well, what would be the next step?"

"For you to meet the children, of course."

The notion delighted her. "I can't wait."

He didn't answer but stared at her strangely.

"Is, um, something wrong?"

"No, not at all. It's just that the expression on your face when I mentioned meeting my kids was…stunning."

His compliment warmed her. "I love young…people."

"I can tell. Then I have much to look forward to."

"As do I."

"I'll email you the particulars."

She glanced at Alisha who scribbled "details" on a paper.

"Oh, yes, do that."

When they disconnected, she turned to Alisha. "I did well, don't you think?"

"All except for the flirting."

Flirting—a social and sometimes sexual activity involving written or verbal communication involving one's body language? "I was *not* flirting."

Ignoring her protestation, Alisha sighed. "I know I've been harsh with you before about this, Celi. But consider Dorian's predicament. She's miserable at leaving Luke. And I don't think he's going to give her the room she needs to help us."

"She can come back to him."

"Maybe. But he's a man..." Alisha shook her head. "Anyway, you can't afford to get emotionally, or physically, involved with Dr. Lansing. Especially given what you're going to do to him."

"The thought of what I must do saddens me."

"All the more reason to hold back. Don't open yourself like you just did on Skype. You're fully capable of blocking people and you'll have to implement that technique with him."

"I will, Lisha. I promise."

Again, Lisha showed her softer side. That was happening more and more. "Dorian and I will be there to help. Just try to set your mind in that direction before we go, all right?"

"I'll try." She stood. "I'm going to go ask Helen to take me shopping tomorrow for suitable clothes. Would you like to come?"

"No. I'm want to stay here and see if I can find more out about the Lansings. Knowledge is power."

Celeste nodded. Her heart was heavy as she climbed the steps.

• • •

DORIAN WAITED IN bed for Luke to come to her. He'd left the house after the discovery about Jess, and the reiteration that her days with him would end soon, and hadn't returned when she'd gone to bed for the night.

A soft knock.

"Come in."

In the dim light from the lamp in the corner, she could only see the outline of his shoulders as he stepped inside and closed, then locked, the door. Quietly, he approached the bed.

For a moment, he simply stared down at her, then he sat on the edge of the mattress. Gently, he took her into his arms and held her against his chest. His heart beat a slow, strong rhythm. His woodsy male scent encompassed her. "We'll talk. Later." He cupped her cheek, kissed her nose. The underside of her jaw and her neck were his next target, where he spent time kissing her, giving her small love bites. His tender ministrations made her moan. Her hands went to her gown.

"No, let me." His voice was rough.

For some reason, the unfastening of her long silk nightshirt by his big masculine hands, the gentle slide of the cloth off her shoulders was almost as sensual as his touch. He kissed every inch of the skin he bared. Dorian was overcome with the gentleness and his actions. Lying down on the mattress, he pressed his mouth to hers and Dorian stopped thinking altogether.

• • •

THEY *CUDDLED* TOGETHER in bed, with the sheet pulled up, after spectacular sex. She'd learned a lot in a few months, and so had he. Now, as Luke held her close to him, he wondered how to begin. How to convince her she belonged with him. He could think of only one way.

She whispered, "I don't want to leave you."

He hadn't expected an opening. "Then don't."

"Oh, Luke, you know I have to go tomorrow."

"I didn't know it would be that soon." His throat got tight at the thought, and his eyes burned.

"Please understand. My love is yours, so much, but I have responsibilities."

He waited a bit. "Marry me, Dorian. Be my wife."

Moisture leaked from her eyes and he felt the wetness on his chest. "I will. But not now. After we're done in Virginia, I'll come back."

He couldn't believe she'd still go after saying she'd marry him. Anger pushed him to say, "That's not good enough."

Raising herself up on her elbow, she looked at him in the dim light. Her hair was messy from his hands, and her lips swollen from his mouth. "Why can't you be more reasonable?" she asked, sounding irritated. That in itself didn't sit well.

"Why can't you? You don't seem to understand how rare what we have is."

Her laugh was sardonic. "Much more than you do, I'm sure. You don't know how to compromise."

"Maybe. Okay, fuck it, Dorian, there's more. I'm can't stop worrying about you. And the other two. You have to tell me what you'll be doing."

"As I said, many times, we promised the Guardians that we would not trust anyone, even if we thought we could. The nature of our mission is too important."

"That shouldn't include me. You made a commitment to me when you said you loved me. Would marry me."

"I seek your forgiveness, Luke, but I can't waver in this. When we're finished with our task, I'll come back."

Her calm incensed him, when he was feeling so much turmoil. He drew away, slid out of bed, donned his clothes and walked to the door. When he reached it, he stopped and turned around. "Don't bother," he said as he stormed out of the room.

Dorian cried.

CHAPTER 19

ONCE AGAIN, ALISHA approached the church. She'd never get used to these huge buildings that were houses of prayer. She climbed the steps and opened the heavy, ornate door with the big brass handle. When she stepped inside, she marveled at the details in the open space—the beautiful stained-glass windows, the real metal called brass everywhere, the precious wood that was made into what they called pews.

She knew David Ryan's office was in the back, so she hurried through the house of a god who'd forsaken the future.

I sent you here, didn't I?

Hellor, now she was hearing the voice of this godhead. She knew believers experienced the same thing, but she accepted none of this. Instead, she believed people simply talked to themselves and called it god. She moved quickly in the opposite direction of where they held services.

David's office door was ajar, but the space was empty. Glancing around, she saw him through the window, bouncing a ball on a paved section of the lawn. Above him, a hoop with a net hung off of a space to house cars. A garage. She let herself out the door to the back and crossed to the pavement.

He didn't sense her presence, so she watched him. He'd removed his shirt, and the play of his muscles along his back when he propelled the ball through the air mesmerized her. Lowering her gaze, she watched his buttocks in the short pants he wore. They were toned, too. Clearing her throat, she called out, "David?"

He turned. His soft brown, curly hair was damp, and his hazel eyes sparkling. "Alisha, how nice to see you. Helen already called me. I'm so relieved about Jess."

"Yes, we are, also. Our task in New York is completed."

When he came closer, she was pleasantly assaulted by the scent of his sweat. All kinds of emotions swirled inside her. Picking up his shirt off the ground, he wiped his face with it, then poked his head through the neck and arms through the other holes. It fell to his waist but not before she got a glimpse of gleaming, dark blond hair all over that chest. Something she'd never seen on a man up close and in real life. Nice pectorals. A flat abdomen. Men of her time did *not* look like this.

"Let's sit." He led her to a wooden table, constructed oddly. She had to climb over on the bench to sit on it, opposite him. "You know, I'm already used to these seats that are not conformers."

"It seems like you've all adapted."

"Celeste the most. I'm worried about her."

"Why?"

"We leave tomorrow for Virginia to complete our second task."

Clasping his long, and now a bit dirty, fingers in front of him, he held her gaze. "You can talk about that to me, Alisha. I'm bound by my ministry to keep it private. Your feelings… your next task…anything."

"No, thank you. But I do feel bad about forcing Dorian to leave Luke. I'm not sure I can identify the emotion."

"Explain it to me."

When she did, he said, "You feel guilty about taking her away from Luke. It's human."

"There isn't much guilt in our time."

"Lucky you. But then you don't have religion." For some reason, he chuckled at his own statement.

"No, we don't."

"What will you do when you've finished in Virginia?"

"Come back here, probably, if Dorian makes a life with Luke. I hope she does."

"True love will find a way."

She chuckled. "That sounds more like the *LifeLine Television* Celeste watches than a minister's perspective."

"I can be a romantic and a man of God."

"I suppose." She watched him. She'd never noticed how his eyes seemed to change color depending on the surroundings. The bark of the trees made them darker.

"Is that the only reason you came here, Alisha?"

"That, and to say good-bye."

"Ah."

"And maybe to get some comfort."

His even, white teeth showed when he smiled. "Did I give it to you?"

"Talking with you helps calm me. Clear my head."

"What a wonderful compliment."

"Except when we argue about religion. Then you muddle my mind."

He laughed heartily. "I'm convincing you of its value."

"I doubt that." Though she wasn't much of a toucher, she reached out and squeezed his hand. "I must leave. Good-bye, David."

They both stood and started toward the front. But before they got far, David grasped her shoulder, turned her around, and gave her a full body hug. No one, not Luke or Jess, had ever hugged her like this. Huh! Alisha liked it.

• • •

HELEN AND JESS were sitting on the porch when all three women walked out of the house. Dorian's heart was in horrible pain at the loss of Luke, and now she had to leave these two people she'd come to care about deeply.

"All set?" Jess asked, standing.

"Yes." Dorian frowned. "I am sad to leave you."

Helen came to his side. "It's only for a little while, right?"

"If we complete our task and return here."

"Oh, I just assumed…"

Celeste crossed to Helen. "What, Helen?"

"You can't go back to your time, right?"

"With the probability at ninety-eight-point-six that it won't happen, we're operating on the belief that, no, we can't."

"Then we're the only family you have in this time period. I assumed you'd come back to Brooklyn and settle near us."

Dorian averted her gaze. Jess said, "He'll come around, Dorian. He's pigheaded, but my guess is he'll come to his senses and wait for you."

"I was hoping to say good-bye to him, too."

"I'll say it for you." He took her in his arms and hugged her. She remembered how she'd thought the male and female contact between people who weren't joining was odd when she first came here. Though they'd only been in this time period for nearly six weeks, it seemed as natural now as using their language and terminology.

They embraced Celeste warmly and even hugged Alisha.

Helen said, "I'm not coming to the train station with you. Car rides make me sick."

Celeste put her hand on Helen's stomach. "I hope we're back when the baby is produced."

Jess laughed. "Born, honey."

Helen gave Celeste one last hug. Dorian knew, of all of them, those two had gotten the closest.

After they climbed into the automobile, Dorian stared through the window and her throat closed up. She'd had no idea what would happen to her in this time period when she arrived.

And she felt so bad, so angry and sad all at once, she almost wished none of it had transpired.

• • •

"YOU'RE AN IDIOT."

"Thanks," Luke said sulkily. He was sitting on the front porch with his brother, who'd just returned home from the train station. Helen was inside resting. "Next time you need your life saved, go find somebody else."

Jess took a seat on the swing, which overlooked the yard. Luke had been out here for the hour Jess had been gone. He'd come back, maybe to see Dorian, maybe not. When he arrived and they'd already left, he considered that a sign.

His brother shook his head. "All three of them are furious at you. Even Helen's mad."

"Women." The reply was curt. He didn't have much to defend himself on.

"The Sisters of Doom have to go, Luke. And keep their task a secret. It's not like you to behave so childishly."

Ignoring the slur, Luke said, "I could find out what they're doing on the Internet."

"We're not supposed to know."

"And look for who their next victim is." His fist curled on his knee. "Police databases can trace the women."

"They use cash."

"Everybody leaves some kind of trail."

A long silence stretched out. Those things used to be common and comfortable between them. Finally, Jess touched his arm. "Why did you come here this morning?"

"To check on you."

"That's bullshit. You know what I think? That Dorian scared the hell out of you and you're using her refusal to confide in you to split with her."

Because Luke was feeling bad, because he was frustrated and because he'd begun to understand that exact thing last night, he answered, "Maybe."

"Luke, there hasn't been anybody serious in your life since your divorce five years ago. It's time to move on."

"Jesus, did I have to pick somebody from the fucking future?"

"So, I am right."

Restless, Luke stood and moved to the railing. He stared at the lawn where he'd found Dorian the night she'd gone out with Carson. It reminded him of all they'd been through in these past weeks. "Yeah, you're right. She turns me inside out, Jess. I never know what's going on in her mind."

"Celeste could tell you," his brother joked.

"Which is another thing that burns me up. How do we know *she'll* be safe? It's *her* task. Or even if Dorian and Lisha will be when they assist her? It drives me crazy to think they're going to complete whatever task it is alone."

"We have to trust them. They succeeded with me."

"It's not like we'd tell anybody."

"No, but one night when you get pissed all over again that she's gone, you'd charge down to Virginia and find them. You could spoil everything. Besides, they swore to their Guardians they wouldn't reveal their task. They take their vows seriously."

Because he'd accused her of breaking a vow to him and felt bad about the harsh words between them, he said, again, "Yeah, maybe."

"Of course, it's too late to do anything about it now," Jess said evenly. "She's probably on the train."

"What time does it leave?"

He glanced at his watch. "At two. They wanted to get there early to acclimate themselves."

"I could have helped her with all that."

"Luke, stop being such a baby. Forget your pride. Go after her."

He remained mute.

Jess stood. "Your call, big brother. Just don't come crying to me later when she's long gone and you realize how pigheaded you were." He squeezed Luke's shoulder, said, "I'm going to check on Helen," and walked into the house.

Luke sat alone on the porch, staring into the beautiful day, with gloom in his heart.

• • •

"ALL RIGHT, NOW that we're alone, tell us what happened with Luke." Celeste had been brimming with curiosity, but they tabled any discussion this morning in an attempt to prepare to leave and say good-bye to the Cromwells.

Except for one.

Dorian glanced around the train platform. The air was tinged with a metallic scent, but the day shone with a bright sun that warmed them. The area had been cordoned off for people with tickets, and only a few were sitting on benches; they were far away. "He gave me an ultimatum. I hated that. I hate these emotions gnawing at the inside of me."

"I guess I was right." Alisha sounded sad, not gloating. "Emotions and joining do not mix well."

Celeste studied Alisha. "It seemed like you were getting cozy with David Ryan before we left."

"No." Alisha adjusted her sunglasses. "He's just a nice guy. I didn't mind spending time with him."

"That's the first step," Dorian warned.

"Don't tell Celi that. She's already looking forward to seeing Alex Lansing too much. She'll be spending a lot of time with *him.* And getting emotionally involved with the man could have terrible consequences."

"I'm here, you know. And frankly, seeing Dorian so upset makes me wary of having feelings for any man."

Conversation lapsed and Dorian thought of Luke, how tender he was during joining the night before and then how he told her not to bother coming back to him.

"Are you crying again?" Celi asked. "I heard you last night."

She wiped her eyes. "No."

Thoughtful, Celeste grabbed her hand. "You're devastated. Maybe you should go back and settle this with him and meet us later."

"No!" Alisha sounded horror-struck.

It didn't matter. Dorian had no intention of crawling back to Luke Cromwell, as the women did on the damned video shows.

"Nobody needs to tell me that, Lisha. I'm going to help complete our next task."

A whoosh of noise preceded the large train coming down the tracks. Celeste coughed and Dorian's eyes stung. Alisha shook her head. "More carbon emissions. Worse ones. They seep from every means of transport here."

That silenced the three of them. Their purpose in this time period had never been clearer.

When the large steel cars stopped, the machinery grated against the tracks making a god-awful noise. All three covered their ears. Dorian stood. "The train is a full thirty minutes early."

"This is common practice," Alisha told them also rising. "They have to board everyone, check tickets, let them get settled and the baggage stowed."

Celeste stood, but Dorian remained seated.

Alisha started forward. "Let's get on. The smell is terrible out here. Inside the train cars can't possibly be this bad."

She led the way, and Celi tried to grab Dorian's arm. But Dorian shook her off. "You've got to stop taking on emotion for your own good. It's your turn now to be strong. We can't forget our mission." She shook herself. "Besides, I want to stay as mad as hellor at him. Leaving will be easier that way."

Her two friends—they would be sisters in Virginia, which seemed appropriate—reached the train first and climbed the steps. Dorian had followed up one, when she heard behind her, "Dorian, wait!"

Her heart practically leapt out of her chest. Turning, she saw Luke running toward her. His hair was messy, and as he got closer, she noted his beard had not been removed and his eyes were bloodshot.

She'd never seen a more beautiful sight.

When he reached her, Dorian jumped off the step and into his arms. He grasped her tightly. "Oh, God, sweetheart. I'm sorry. I know you have to go. I know you can't tell me the details. I was being a real bastard."

Having his arms around her was the best thing in this world. "I understand. I seek your forgiveness for hurting you."

He set her back from him and saw the two women on the steps of the train. Alisha drawled, "So much for wanting to stay mad at him."

But Celi smiled sweetly. She said, "It's about time, Lucas Cromwell."

"How did you get on the platform?" Dorian asked, standing close, holding on to his shoulders.

"I bought a ticket."

"You can't come, Luke." This from Lisha.

"I know. It's the only way I could get out on the platform. I don't even know where it's for."

A man in uniform approached them. "Ladies, sir, it's time to board."

Alisha and Celeste walked into the train car, and Luke pulled Dorian out of the way of other passengers. He cupped her face with his hands. "Call me as soon as you can. I won't ask any questions about your whereabouts or what you're doing."

"We can video phone—Skype—so I can see your face."

He nodded and smiled. "My love is yours, Dorian. Always."

She smiled back. "I love you, too, Luke."

• • •

FOR NOTIFICATION OF Kathryn's new work and information about her books, be sure to sign up for her newsletter at http://on.fb.me/12dhOtc.

If you liked JUST IN TIME, you might want to post a review of it at http://bit.ly/1bc9biT

Visit or Contact Kathryn at

www.kathrynshay.com
www.facebook.com/kathrynshay
www.twitter.com/KShayAuthor
http://pinterest.com/kathrynshay/

AUTHOR'S NOTE

WELCOME TO BOOK one of my new series, Portals of Time. This trilogy has been a labor of love for me as I've always been a science fiction/time travel aficionado. But since my first love is romance, there never seemed to be an opportunity to combine the two genres until now. I came up with the original concept for the trilogy years ago, and at last it's come to fruition. Since all the stories take place in the present, I think I was able to keep the books classic Kathryn Shay with a twist. I thoroughly enjoyed creating the new world of the future, playing around with language, and at the same time building a great romance and saying something important about society.

As for JUST IN TIME, I relished setting up the dynamic between Luke and Dorian. Truthfully, I didn't know how they'd react to each other in the beginning. I'm partial to reluctant lovers and, boy, are these two determined not to fall for each other. Fate, though, has something to say about that, as usually happens in my books. Didn't you laugh their sparing? And swoon over those kissing scenes?

Finally, Jess and Helen became so special to me throughout the books and I hope they were to you, too.

Don't miss the next two novels, PERFECT TIMING, with Celeste and Alex, and ANOTHER TIME, Alisha and David's story. I can guarantee each presents something different.

Chapter Excerpt from

BOOK 2 PERFECT TIMING

Chapter 1

THE WOMAN ALEX Lansing had arranged to interview today to care for his children was late, and if he could reach her—he tried the one phone number she'd given him, but there was no answer—he'd tell her he wasn't going to consider her for the job. Punctuality was an important quality he required in a sitter and she apparently didn't have it. His life was too busy to have unreliable people surrounding him.

You're life's too busy, anyway, darling.

Damn it to hell. Sometimes he could hear Lila's voice as if she was in the room with him. And she often chided him like this, especially about working too hard. The voice had started not long after her death three years ago from uterine cancer and came to him periodically. He was half tempted to go see a shrink.

He waited for the caregiver in his home office in a separate wing of his house. Though he had a lab and private work space at Global Pharmaceuticals, the organization that sponsored his research, he preferred to work here as it was more private.

Finally, his phone buzzed and his housekeeper, Ann Kramer's voice came over the line. "Dr. Lansing, Celeste Hart is here to see you."

"I'll be right out." As he locked up the room and made his way to the foyer, he pictured the woman he'd spoken with on Skype. Her voice had been soft and coaxing, and he'd felt… reassured by it. She'd said everything he wanted to hear. And her face, when she'd talked about his kids, mesmerized him. But she was going to need to impress the hell out of him now for him to change his mind about finding someone else who dealt better with time.

When he came face-to-face with her, that magnetic draw returned, only more intensely. He took in her dark auburn hair and clear blue eyes and felt as if he was drifting closer to her, almost touching her, though he was rooted to the spot where he stood. Instead of squirming, she studied him with interest.

When he realized he was staring, he coughed nervously. "Good morning, Ms. Hart, let's sit in there." He pointed to the living room off to the left.

"Hello, Dr. Lansing," she said then preceded him into the room. She was a tall woman, but there was a delicacy about her. Dressed in white pants and matching jacket with a pink shirt beneath the suit, she took a chair across from him in the room they didn't use much anymore. They used to spend a fair amount of time in here when Lila was alive.

Before he could comment on Ms. Hart's lateness, she spoke. "It's unconscionable to be eight minutes past our arranged meeting time." She shrugged a shoulder. On closer examination, she was well toned and feminine at the same time. "I'm not familiar with your mass transit, and I'm afraid I became lost."

Something about her dignified apology calmed him. Hell, something about *her* erased his irritation and gave him a settled feeling inside. "You don't drive?"

"Ah, no. I took a bus here."

That could be a problem. Maddy had her license and drove Lila's car, but the boys sometimes needed to be taken places after school. They often carpooled, so maybe he could work something out with his neighbors.

She added, "I can assure you, I'm usually punctual."

"You're from out of town, then?"

"Yes, a small city in upstate New York. We didn't have mass transit and we walked everywhere." She reached into a bag. "You've seen my references and résumé, but these are harder copies."

Harder copies? He took the papers. Their fingers brushed, and he settled even more, amazed at the sense of well-being enveloping him. "Thanks for these. But I'd prefer you tell me about your life." Alex knew people revealed more when they talked about themselves.

"I grew up in South America, where my do...parents were missionaries. We moved to the United States when I went to a study course at college. I attended a small, private educational institution in Rochester. I married my college sweetheart when I was twenty-one. He died in a car accident when I was thirty." She gave him a sad smile. "That's when I stopped driving vehicles. I've worked in day care or done private child sitting all my life. I...cannot bear children of my own."

He was surprised at the personal remark, so oddly phrased. "What brought you to Virginia?"

"One of my sisters recently obtained a job in Washington, D.C. We wanted to be together."

"You live with your sisters?"

"Yes." She cocked her head. "That isn't a problem, is it? I understood this job was for daytime and occasional evenings."

"That's not an issue. I work from home. My office is on the other side of the house. I have a housekeeper during the day, too, because you'll focus on the children."

She studied him oddly. Then she asked, "Do you work at home to be close to the young…ones?"

"No."

In actuality, he conducted the analysis of his research from the privacy of his home office because early in his career, when he was employed by City University, his work had been hacked, changing the entire course of his professional life. He'd left the academic setting because of the theft, though for a year now, he went to City U to teach an Ethics in Science course.

Once Global had hired him, providing state-of-the-art security, he did his hands-on research at their facilities, but old habits died hard, and he still formulated his analysis at home. The only ones allowed in his office were the kids—when he was with them, of course—and his housekeeper.

"I'd like to spend more time with my children, though."

"Sometimes," Celeste began, "when we're in the midst of our life's work, we ignore those closest to us. People adjust, so long as it's not forever."

"Tell me about your views on child care. My children's welfare is paramount to me."

"I believe children need adults to like and respect them, yet not be considered a friend. A sense of humor is important. An understanding of human needs, no matter what age."

Hmm. Again, almost his exact thinking.

"What about spanking? TV? Junk food?"

For a minute she seemed confused, then her eyes widened and she drew back. "I think spanking is barbaric, and if you hit your children, I couldn't work for you. What's more I'd advise you not to—"

He held up his hand, palm out. "I don't spank. And wouldn't hire you if you believed in corporal punishment."

"Oh, well then." She composed herself but that spark of fire intrigued him. "As far as junk food is concerned, a few indulgences seem harmless. And I confess I like the video box, but again, if you're spending quality time with the children, that wouldn't be an issue."

Leaning back in his chair, he watched her. She was one of the calmest people he'd ever met. And she came across as totally sincere. "I like your answers, Ms. Hart."

She didn't seem surprised. "I'm glad."

"I'm a bit worried you don't drive."

"I…I didn't know that was a requirement."

"It's not," he decided suddenly. "We'll compensate if we choose you. Would this job be enough for you? I pay well, but a high school student did it before and didn't need to support herself."

"I have adequate funds."

"Money isn't important to you?"

She looked at him blankly for a minute. Her eyes were pure blue, with no hint of other colors. They were quite unusual. "Of course money is important. But I have a family fund of trust—trust fund—and I don't need to work. I enjoy children. I would like to have a chance to know yours."

Again, something about her pulled him in. He knew in his gut she'd be good with his kids.

"All right," he said, despite his earlier misgivings about her punctuality. "Let's give it a shot. I need someone tomorrow at four and the young woman I have until the end of May is busy. I was going to cancel my meeting, but now I won't have to."

She smiled mysteriously. For some reason, he felt as if she knew he'd do exactly what she wanted him to.

• • •

THE DAY AFTER the interview, Celeste braced herself when she rang the doorbell to the Lansing dwelling. The wonderful sun had been beating down on her as she walked from the transit stop, and the air surrounding her was blissfully warm. She'd been in this time period for six weeks, and thinking about the constant gray air out of inside in the 26th century, she knew she'd never stop relishing the light of day. She still didn't take for granted the sun, the trees, which blew in gentle breezes, or even the wood this house was made of.

The door opened. The small, silver-haired woman from yesterday stood before her. Ann Kramer, the keeper of the house. "Hello, Ms. Hart."

"Mrs. Kramer. Nice to see you again."

"You, too. Come in. Dr. Lansing's waiting for you in the office with the children."

Celeste stepped into the small space called a foyer. Today she'd dressed in a yellow, cotton blouse that bared her arms and a skirt that did not cover her legs. She loved the feel of the material on her skin. In her hand, she held what the women of today carried...a purse...and followed Ann Kramer from the large entryway, across a real stone floor down a wide corridor. This house was even larger than Jess Cromwell's dwelling. They passed rooms on either side of a hallway, one where she'd been interviewed. Each was filled with beautiful colors and textures and different-shaped couches and chairs. Her terminology was improving though she occasionally misspoke and labeled them conformers. She entered the last room and was amazed by the deep, rich red of the walls, the burnished wood on the high ceilings and tall shelves stuffed with real books.

Alex Lansing sat at his desk. A male youngling played a game on a small handheld machine. Another worked from books and papers at a nearby table. The female youngling wasn't present.

"Dr. Lansing?"

Turning, he glanced up and covered the speaker of the phone he held. "Hold on a sec, Dad. Hello. I didn't hear the bell."

In front of him sat his computer. His research notes would be in the system. It was Celeste's task to find a way to access that work.

"Come on in. I'll be done in a minute." Back into the device, he added, "Have fun, Dad. Just don't let Mom go parasailing again. See you in a month." After he clicked off, he said, "That was my father."

"Are they enjoying their Mediterranean cruise?" Mrs. Kramer asked.

"Very much so." He turned his attention to Celeste. "Good afternoon, Ms. Hart."

"Dr. Lansing." Coming fully into the room, she transferred her gaze back to the younglings—she *must* call them children. Dr. Lansing said, "Kids, this is Ms. Hart."

"Hi." The littlest stood. She glanced at his donor...father. As the computeller had shown, they shared the same light complexion and blue eyes and dark blond hair. The tilt of their mouths was identical when they almost smiled. "I'm Cody."

"Hello, Cody."

The boy seemed content. Kind. Something else, too, but she wouldn't be able to intuit what it was until she touched him.

The other male stepped forward. Fascinated by his hair—it was lighter than any she'd seen so far—she moved closer and took a good look at his face. His visage was too sober for a child, and complicated vibes shimmered off him. "I'm Jonathan."

"Hello." She scanned the room. "Where's Madison?"

"She had a meeting at school today that I didn't know about," Dr. Lansing explained. "She's very active. She'll be home later, but I'll be gone. Ann can show you around before she leaves."

"Would it be possible for the children to acquaint me with the house?"

Dr. Lansing gave her a full smile. "Sure." He said to the younglings, "All right, guys?"

Jonathan stared over at his father. "Do you have to go, Dad? It's Saturday."

"Sorry son. But you'll have fun getting to know Ms. Hart. And I'll be back before you go to bed."

The resignation on Jonathan's face tugged at Celeste.

Mrs. Kramer cleared her throat. Celeste had forgotten she was there. "I'll be in the kitchen, finishing supper, while the boys take you on your tour. I hope you like chicken, Ms. Hart."

Animal product of the poultry family. Helen had cooked some, and Celeste liked it.

"I'm not fussy about food." *Because we never had any.*

"Well, good." Dr. Lansing stood.

Today he wore nicely fitting tan trousers and a shirt of brown that accented his coloring. He took a coat off the back of his chair—it was lightweight and tailored—and shrugged into it. "I'm off." Bending down, he kissed Cody's cheek. "Don't give Ms. Hart a hard time on the first day, kiddo."

"Me?" Cody's smile was devious.

Dr. Lansing ruffled Jonathan's hair, then stood back. "I'll escort you out." He waited until they were in the hallway, locked the door, then walked away carrying a chip-like thing called a flashdrive.

"So," Celeste said, "I'm all yours."

Cody grinned and took her hand. Ah, that was it, he liked to play pranks, to have fun at the expense of others. She, Dorian and Celeste engaged in some of those when they were young. This little one was…what was the word…oh, yes, mischievous.

She glanced at the older boy. He was shorter than her five foot, eight inches but getting some good form on him for being eleven yearlings. "Is it Jon or Jonathan?"

"Um, Jon."

"Jon. I know you wish your dad was here and not me. But he has work to do. And I'd like to get to know you. Would you show me your room first?"

"Okay." He brushed Celeste's arm as he headed down the hall. She was hit with a sense of sadness so strong it momentarily immobilized her. This was one unhappy child.

They climbed an open staircase made of richly grained wood, and the ceiling had glass apertures in it. Sun streamed through them and she sighed.

"I like the sun, too," Cody said, catching her reaction. She'd have to be careful around this one.

"Good. Maybe we can go for a walk out of inside."

Jon frowned. "Out of inside?"

"You mean outdoors?" Cody suggested.

"Um, of course." Megadamn, she kept making that mistake.

Jon gave her a skeptical look, one she'd seen on Alex Lansing's face, too. When he reached the entrance of a room, he stopped.

"Is something wrong?"

"Dad says a lady should always enter first."

"How sweet." She hadn't known about this particular etiquette.

She and Cody went through the doorway.

The room was similar to those she'd seen on the chips for young boys. There was a poster of a male in short leggings and a shirt that was too small for his torso, with number thirty-three on it. She remembered similar men on the video box at Jess's. They threw balls and tackled whoever caught them. She thought the game exceptionally violent and often winced when she watched a play or two.

One side of the room held shelves of books, as in Dr. Lansing's office. And pictures. She crossed to them. They weren't 3D, and they didn't move like the holograms of her time, but they were similarly used as reminders of people. She scanned them, and her heart tightened in her chest at the beautiful woman inside the frame. Her hair was as blond as Jon's, and her eyes smiled. In one, she was laughing with Cody. In another, holding Jon close against her. A final one, kissing Dr. Lansing. For a moment Celeste stared at their embrace and found her hand touching her lips. When Celeste turned, she saw Jon staring at her. "Is this your mother, Jon?"

He nodded, and the knob at his neck bobbed. The bleak expression on his face made it difficult to look at him.

"She's very beautiful."

He didn't say anything. Neither did Cody.

"Will you tell me about her sometime?"

Averting his gaze, Jon stared down at his shoes. She put a hand on his shoulder. Her skin felt scorched. So much was emanating from every pore in his body. It was a kind of pain Celeste had never experienced. She couldn't help but drain some of the negative emotion from him. She felt weakened by it, but he brightened a bit.

"It's all right, Jon, if you don't want to talk about her."

"I do." This from Cody. "I wanna talk about her, but I don't remember much 'cause I was two when she died."

"Does your father or sister speak of her?"

Finally, Jon said, "Nobody talks much about her anymore. We did at first."

"If you want to tell me about her, I'd love to know what she was like."

He nodded. To change the subject, Celeste wandered over to the bed. The covering was decorated with hats of some kind. A protective helmet with glossy decals on it. A cap. A big, wide-brimmed one; she had no idea what it was. Glancing off to the side, she saw the real things on a high shelf.

"I have a hat collection." Jon's tone was shy.

Because of the Domes, Celeste's society had no need for head coverings. "Will you tell me where they come from sometime?"

"Yeah, sure. If you stay around. Patty's leaving." Ah, the boy felt her loss, too.

Cody tugged on Celeste's hand. "Come on, my turn."

His room was more cluttered. On a big table sat a large, square box with water and...oh, my, he had flish in it. Real live flish. She'd only seen some replicas in Zoolawn. Crossing to the glass box, she stared at the little creatures moving and darting and coming up to the exterior. Her hand went to the glass. All those colors—orange, yellow, black and white.

"You like fish, Ms. Hart?" Cody asked.

"Indeed, I do."

"Cody snuck some frogs from outside to put in there, but one escaped." Jon giggled.

"What makes you laugh?"

"It ended up in Dad's bed."

Again Cody grinned. "Boy, was he mad."

Celeste laughed with them. The thought of Dr. Lansing pulling back sleeping covers and finding a slimy, jumping stoad in it did seem funny.

They examined more of Cody's space, then walked out into an open area on this floor with a video box, a second computer and books. The children called it a playroom though it wasn't self-contained. "Do you like to read?" she asked them.

"Yeah, sure." This from Jon.

"I don't know all the words yet." Cody grinned.

"Maybe we can read together before sleep time."

They bypassed Madison's room because Celeste preferred the girl to show it herself, then ended up in front of Dr. Lansing's private space.

"Maybe we shouldn't go in—" Before she could finish, Cody burst open the double doors and raced in. Again, Jon waited for her to enter before him.

Once inside, Celeste noted a huge bed, which appeared soft, even if it wasn't a conformer. On it was a cover with subtle greens all mixed together. It matched the color of a stripe around the middle of the walls. The floor was covered with wood.

She breathed in the scent of the room, and her skin tingled. Sometimes, the very space she occupied sent a wave of images through her, as they had at Craig Krueger's small dwelling. Briefly, she closed her eyes and could practically see Alex Lansing in here. Feel the texture of his clothes, see the contours of his body. Hear him breathe. A vision of naked shoulders swam before her eyes. Forcefully, she shook off the myriad feelings. Uncomfortably stirred by all the sensations, she eased them all out of Alex Lansing's masculine domain as quickly as she could.

When they reached the first floor, Mrs. Kramer was in the foyer, shrugging into an outer garment of knitted material.

"I'm leaving. Dinner's on the counter in the kitchen. You don't have to wait for Maddy. She called to say she won't be home till seven."

"Thank you for all this, Mrs. Kramer." At least Celeste knew the mechanics of serving and cleaning up a meal. Alisha was right to make them learn this keeping of the house.

"Let's eat," Cody said as he ran into the kitchen. Jon followed more sedately. The sustenance was set out on the counter, and the boys served themselves. Celeste took small portions.

Sitting down at the table, she picked up the knife and fork. Cut the meat. Put it in her mouth. "Hmm." The cheesy chicken was tasty, the potatoes fluffy. She tried the round green things, and her nose wrinkled at their taste.

"We don't like brussel sprouts, either," Cody said, catching her reaction to them.

"But Dad says we have to eat them," the boy continued. "We could give them to a dog if we had one. I want a puppy for my birthday next month."

Her mind raced to keep up with him. Birthdays were an odd custom to her, because in her time, children came out of produceries and were never actually born. And what would it be like to have a drog in the home? How could she encourage Dr. Lansing to obtain one?

When they'd finished their meal, each boy brought his eating plate, utensils and drinking cup to the sink. Jon rinsed them in real water again—here she wouldn't be able to conserve it as they had at the Cromwell's. Then he put the plates in the washer of dishes. Celeste copied their actions, made the table clean and stored the rest of the food in the oven for Maddy, as Mrs. Kramer had instructed.

"What shall we do now?"

"Read to me?" Cody asked.

They went upstairs and she smiled as she watched Cody jump each step with two feet. He made a game of everything.

"I'm gonna go to my room," Jon said. "I have to study for exams."

She and Cody settled in the playroom, and he went to the book shelving—they were all over the home—and picked out a tome. *Harry Potter and the Chamber of Secrets.* She was unacquainted with the story.

"Dad keeps saying he's gonna read this with me but never gets around to it. Maddy read Jon and me the first Harry Potter book."

She began the strange tale and was fascinated by the wizards and all sorts of odd creatures that she didn't think even existed. On the soft couch, as she read, Cody inched over by degrees and cuddled into her.

Celeste's heart brimmed with emotion. There was nothing in her past that compared to the feeling of having a little boy sitting so close to her. *Motherhood* must be wonderful during these times.

They'd read four sections, called chapters, when she heard from below, "Hel-lo."

"We're up here, Mad," Cody called out.

In minutes, Madison Lansing appeared in the doorway. The girl was seventeen, but she looked older. She was tall and graceful, wore long hair with light-colored streaks in it, around a heart-shaped face. Her eyes were a dark blue.

"Hi, I'm Madison. Dad said the boys had somebody new tonight."

Standing, Celeste crossed to her. "I'm Celeste Hart." Purposefully, she held out her hand so she could read the girl.

Madison hesitated, then shook it.

Bombarded by Madison's feelings, Celeste had to grab the end of the desk to keep herself from stumbling backwards. Her own shoulders slumped, and her neck ached. Along with anxiety and sadness in this child was an overwhelming sense of weariness. Maddy Lansing was exhausted.

After Maddy excused herself, Celeste helped Cody into bed, checked on Jon, then went to the first floor and out of inside to sit on the porch. Seating herself on what she'd learned at Jess's was called a swing, she looked up at the stars. Their beauty usually calmed her, but her heart was full of conflicting emotions. The connection she felt with these children was strong already. And a yearning to ease their life—as well as their overworked father's—was stunning.

Alisha would be angry if she knew Celeste's line of thinking. Celeste wasn't here to do any of those things. Instead, she'd been assigned a task to complete, and her actions wouldn't ease the burdens of this already troubled family. Instead, what she had to do would increase them exponentially.

Closing her eyes, she forced herself to recall Rhea's announcement of what Celeste's work here would entail: *Whereas Dorian is to save the life of Jess Cromwell and insure his research continues, Celeste, you must destroy the life's work of Alex Lansing.*

www.ingramcontent.com/pod-product-compliance
Lightning Source LLC
Chambersburg PA
CBHW031302170626
46807CB00001B/273

* 9 7 8 1 9 3 9 5 0 1 2 4 0 *